Travels with Truelove
Confessions of a Celebrity Chef

David Pickering

Copyright © 2016 David Pickering

All rights reserved.

Most of the characters in this book are fictitious, and any resemblance to actual persons, living or dead, is purely coincidental, though occasionally deliberate.

ISBN-10: 1539013650
ISBN-13: 978-1539013655

Dedicated to my mother, my agent, my editor, my colleagues in the biz and my fans everywhere.

Foreword

As a trainee chef I learned my craft alongside Tremayne Truelove and great chefs of the current generation and I am now proud to be on first names with the likes of Jamie, Gordon, Heston and so many more. All of them are far more accomplished than me, so I consider it a privilege as well as a surprise to be selected above them by the publishers to contribute a foreword for this, Tremayne's latest book – particularly as I had no idea he was writing it, having rather lost touch with him after his latest series 'ended'.

I haven't read the book myself yet, having been terribly busy with my own new series, but I gather Tremayne will be relating his recent travels around the Mediterranean and his exploration of the region's culinary traditions, while bringing to vivid life the places he has visited and the people he has met. Well, he is certainly the man for the job and I doubt if it will be quite like any other cook or travel book anyone else has ever written.

There are two overriding passions in Tremayne Truelove's life: cookery and travel. As a TV chef and occasional travel presenter, his face will be instantly familiar to millions of television viewers on both sides of the Atlantic (*Cooking with Truelove*, *Truelove goes Transatlantic* and *A Taste of Truelove*) as well as to readers of the popular press for his many celebrity connections. Sometimes a controversial character, he has always excited strong reactions, not least among other chefs, with his flamboyant and imaginative approach to cuisine and life in general. He's gifted in other ways too. His is a disarming, overwhelming, sometimes irresistible presence. Like a tsunami, a tsetse fly or the need to eat, he is truly impossible to ignore.

Tremayne is a much-travelled man and it is greatly to be hoped that he will get to continue his peregrinations abroad. I understand from the publisher that his text is to be accompanied by his own sketches, so that will be an added ingredient to spice up the dish in Tremayne's own inimitable fashion.

I expect Tremayne hopes this slim volume will find a place in kitchens around the world alongside well-thumbed classics by other dear friends in the cooking biz.

I wish him luck.

Bettina Dawson
Host of ITV's *Bettina Bites* and BBC TV's *Better Baking with Bettina*; *People's Monthly* TV Chef of the Year 2016

Horse d'oeuvres

It is a truth universally acknowledged that a single man in possession of a trout will also need a decent-sized frying pan or wok, some clarified butter (French, sheep's not cow's), a few capers, just a pinch of tarragon and a bestselling travel and cookbook by a leading international TV chef to tell him how to cook it.

Or, to put it another way, if you give a man a trout he will probably just coat it in batter, serve it up with chips, mushy peas and ketchup and feed himself, probably feeling vaguely disappointed and wishing he had gone out instead – but *inspire* him in the cooking of it and he has taken an important first step towards opening a swanky fish restaurant of his own in a bijou resort on the south coast where he stands to do very-nicely-thank-you by overcharging his wealthy clientele. Even better if he manages to palm the tips before the waiters get their unwashed paws on them.

Hence, humbly, this book.

So. A few years ago I got into a public spat with a member of the royal family concerning the eating of horse, as a result of which I doubt I will get a knighthood any time soon. It wasn't that we disagreed on the said royal's notion that eating horse was a good idea. Far from it, it's an excellent meat that should be transferred without further hesitation from stables and riding schools to kitchens up and down the land. No, it was rather upon the way in which horse should be prepared for the table. I must say, by the by, that after her initial pronouncement I was surprised that the said royal (no names here, you'll note, your highness!) should be so squeamish about eating what I consider to be the choicest parts of the creature, but far be it from me to pass judgement upon the morality of waste in other people's kitchens. I shall say no more. Though many's the time I've remarked upon the fact that we eat every part of a pig but the squeak – and I don't see why we shouldn't apply that admirable approach to all our food.

But enough of politics. The truth is that when presented with something new or unexpected to eat, such as horsemeat or the flesh of some other animal not normally encountered on a menu (snake, for instance), our standard response is either to avoid it completely or to try it reluctantly and then ignore its subtleties and, as often as not, observe that it *tastes like chicken*. I've probably said it myself a thousand times, though to be fair I have also eaten chicken that tasted like snake.

Such a description could fairly be given to many foods I have consumed in faraway places, but prepared in the manner that I prepare horse no one is ever likely to confuse it with chicken (or snake). I picked up my favourite horse recipe, incidentally, on a little island off east Africa where horses are a delicacy. This is probably because it's a small island where horses are themselves a rarity and no one seems to have the slightest idea what else to do with them. I'm not going to give full details of how the dish is prepared by the natives for special occasions on the island – you can buy my forthcoming cookbook for that as soon as the publisher gets his arse into gear, in time for Christmas hopefully. Suffice it to say that bananas, sour lemon, Tia Maria (homemade, not the insipid version you'll be used to) and fermented seaweed are vital ingredients. If you're really stuck, Marmite will do as a replacement for the last-mentioned.

The point is, why should we dismiss so many exciting new foods by comparing them with something as dull as plain old chicken? Why should that be our automatic comparison? Why are we so hidebound by convention that we draw up short at accepting new foods or startling new combinations of tastes and textures on their own merits? If we stopped being so governed by habit and prejudice, wouldn't we greatly expand the range and variety of our diet?

Fans of my TV series on both sides of the Atlantic will know that bland is my enemy. If some of my recipes, like that for neck of horse à l'orange, seem outlandish (this is especially true for my US fans) then you may at least rest assured that they won't taste like chicken. My dishes will take your taste buds to places they have never been. You may never want to come back.

Finally, as I put forefinger to keyboard at the start of this project, this isn't to be a book about food alone. Not at all. My intention is also to put before my public a fascinating account of some of the truly amazing places and extraordinary people I expect to encounter in this new chapter of my life after the premature close of my latest TV series. I hope readers will find it as succulent and delicious in every way as the recipes themselves.

Bon appétit!
Tremayne Truelove

For Starters

It will explain a lot about the narrative that follows if I freely admit here and now that I have absolutely no sense of direction, either geographically or in life generally. I'm very like a woman in this respect.

Many of my culinary and other adventures have been triggered when I took a wrong turn, misread a map or misinterpreted directions someone has given me. I don't know what it is, but as soon as a person reels off a series of instructions about where to go or what to do I go into a kind of daze and start wondering what colour you would say their eyebrows are or, if they're at all attractive, if they'd like to go to bed with me. I expect many readers will recognise the impulse.

None of what follows would have happened if my quick-tempered brute of a BBC producer hadn't taken issue with me over my preparation of poached pear brioche with vanilla crème anglaise during recording for my current hit cookery series. It's not a complicated dish by any means, but it was to lead to complications I could well have done without.

'You can't do it like that!' he erupted as I added the double cream to the mixture in the bowl.

I wasn't having a good day, to be honest, and my patience was already wearing thin. Being midsummer, London was wearyingly muggy and the studio kitchen I was in was stifling, what with the addition of the heat from the ovens and the lighting equipment. Now, on top of everything else, here was a jumped-up television nobody who apparently felt he could start lecturing me on how to do my business. Like any cook worth his or her salt, I like to feel I am in command in my own kitchen and I don't take kindly to having my authority questioned.

'I'll do it any way I choose, if you don't mind,' I retorted firmly as I kept on pouring. 'I'm the chef here, not you.'

Even as I spoke I realised I'd picked up the wrong jug, thinking it was the cream, but to go back now would be humiliating so I stuck to my guns. God knew what it was that I was enriching my creation with in such generous amounts.

'You bloody idiot!' my accuser went on. 'You're ruining it!'

When I cross swords in this manner in a television studio, I usually adopt an air of distant disdain and get my revenge later on by wearing clothing with lots of tiny spots and stripes so that an interference pattern results when I'm next in front of the cameras. That gets you noticed, I can tell you. On this occasion, however, such refinements of civilised behaviour were beyond me. My critic got the whole pot of half-prepared crème anglaise over his head. We then embarked upon a frantic and very noisy chase sequence through Television Centre that would have done the Keystone Cops credit. My producer, it should be noted, was a large and physically-minded individual who did not take kindly to having things upended over him and I didn't relish being cornered by him and having my errors explained to me in blow by blow fashion.

I hurtled up the stairs, shouldering assorted BBC executives out of the way and trying my best to keep just beyond my pursuer's creamy grasp. I'm not sure why I opted to go upwards instead of down where logic might have told me I stood a better chance of finding a door at ground level through which I might escape the building but that's my lack of a sense of direction for you. Perhaps I thought I would find shelter hiding behind the skirts of the Director-General or something. Alternatively it may have occurred to me that by leading my producer up several flights of stairs he would have time to reconsider his actions and come to a better understanding of the offence he had caused me. Perhaps he would even feel an apology was in order.

No such luck. I finally ran out of stairs and I could hear my nemesis still hot on my heels, swearing viciously between gasps for breath. He sounded like he was ready to tear me limb from limb. I could only suppose the heat of the London summer had got to him too. Where were the security men when you really needed them?

There was a metal door in front of me so I wrenched it open and dashed through it, only to find myself outside, on a rooftop overlooking west London. I rushed from one parapet to another, desperately seeking a fire escape or some other route that might offer me a way out of danger, but there was nothing. I wheeled to face my seemingly inevitable fate.

My producer lurched through the metal doorway, his face purple with anger and exhaustion. He spotted me not a dozen yards away and emitted a strangled growl of pained triumph, then started towards me, eyes staring and arms outstretched before him, looking for all the world like some paunchy Frankenstein's monster, but for the custard dripping down his face. I backed away but my retreat was cut off by the parapet behind me, so I hastily sought for something to say that might soothe his clearly far from tranquil brow.

'Now, listen,' I began, 'I understand you're upset, but I think if we both just sit down and talk things through–'

He uttered another menacing growl and I could tell that he wasn't in a mood to be reasonable. I gave a whimper and raised my hands to fend off the coming assault.

And then he gave a small sigh and just crumpled to the ground at my feet, groaning softly and frothing at the mouth.

I stared in bewilderment. What the hell just happened?

It wasn't until other BBC staff appeared on the rooftop and belatedly took matters into their hands that all became clear. My would-be assailant had suffered a minor heart attack brought on by sudden physical exercise. Paramedics appeared on the scene within a few minutes and they carted my stricken foe off on a stretcher, leaving me to reflect that he only had himself to blame really, being always first in the queue to polish off the dishes I prepared for the show. I hoped it would be a lesson to him.

Those then were the circumstances in which my Mediterranean adventure began. But there was more to it than the incident at the BBC, of course.

To complete the picture, there I was, an internationally renowned TV chef and traveller in his early forties, or thereabouts, yearning for something to get the senses tingling and the *jus* flowing again. Apart from anything else, my ratings were down while everyone else's were (people kept telling me with tiresome enthusiasm) up, especially Stateside.

I felt I needed to find a new direction in my cuisine. In any case, I was tired of the cookery I had grown up with and hungry, literally, for new flavours and taste sensations. Coupled with that, I had spent too much time in television studios in London and LA and needed to get away from it all, away from the tawdry hero-worship and the cocaine-fuelled parties with Kate and Liam and the rest, to get back in touch with the real cookery, the *paysan* styles of old Europe with all their historical redolence and authenticity.

So it was in a mood of exhilaration and not a little creative desperation that I decided to walk (temporarily) out of my career and onto a plane for – where else? – the homeland of European culinary excellence, France.

Naturally, there were those who did not want to see me go.

'Where are you off to, Tremayne?' Barry Cullis, my red-nosed, gnome-like agent, quizzed me anxiously as I gathered up my bags in the expectation of my taxi waiting for me outside my place later that day. He had called at my flat in a flap after hearing that I'd last been seen storming out of Television Centre and telling anyone who cared to listen that I'd had just about enough of their crap and was off into the blue yonder in search of something new. 'What are the bags for?' he asked, like an idiot.

'They contain my clothes, a couple of books and my favourite wok, if you must know,' I told him. 'I'm off to France.'

'*France?* But what about the show? You've got three episodes still to film for the BBC. I'm sure I can smooth things over if you'll just apol –'

'No. Sod the show. Sod the BBC. Sod you. Sod everything. I'm flying to Bordeaux.'

'You don't mean it. Of course you don't.' His eyes narrowed as he struggled to get his walnut-sized brain around the idea of my going on my travels. 'Is this about the papers going on about your alleged fling with the talent show woman? You know I can handle that.

There'll be some temporary unpleasantness, I suppose, references to May and September romances and "at his age too", but it'll die down. Look at how we got through the horsemeat thing a few years ago. Everyone's forgotten about that.'

I bristled. 'Everyone except you, it seems. No, Barry, I won't say the thing with Amanda isn't yet another bloody nuisance I'll be glad to leave behind, but it's not that.'

'But why then? Why? What'll you do?'

'As a matter of fact, I've decided to get on with that book deal you arranged a while back. The Mediterranean cookery thing. I've had enough of telly for now, possibly for ever. Can you move, please? I can't get my suitcase past you.'

He was so surprised he stepped aside to let me past, then hurried after me in a panic as I clambered down the steps to the cab that had just drawn up at my front gate.

'But – but – you can't!' he stammered. 'What do I tell the BBC? And the papers – ah!' His face, if you can call it that, lit up in the usual fatuous way. 'It's Bettina's award, isn't it? That's what this is all about.'

'It's nothing to do with Bettina's award. I couldn't care less about Bettina's award. As if anyone reads *People's Monthly* anyway. I don't. For the last time, I couldn't care less about bloody awards.'

'So it is about Bettina's award.'

'No, it *isn't*! Help me with these bags.'

I got Barry to hold the taxi door open while I heaved the bags inside, then I paused and looked him squarely in the eye, though I had to bend the knee to do it.

'The book deal is still on, isn't it?'

'Yes, of course. Though if you walk out on the TV show…'

'They signed the contract, didn't they?'

'Well, yes, but–'

15

'There you are then. I'm off to write the bloody thing, satisfied? Get that editor I had before – what's the interfering bastard's name?'

'David Pickering.'

'Yes, him. Get the chinless wonder out of the pub and tell him he'll have a manuscript off me by the end of the summer, okay?'

'But–'

'Where to, guv?' asked the taxi driver.

'Heathrow. Please don't call me guv. Goodbye, Barry.'

'But–'

'I'll phone if I need anything.'

'But–'

And that's how I left Barry, butting like a stunned haddock on a London pavement in bright summer sunshine as I hurtled off towards my future, which as far as I was concerned was to comprise a straightforward, healing sojourn in La Belle France. The very thought of it soothed the soul and lifted the wearied esprit de corps. Alors!

You'll appreciate then that it was quite a surprise when I woke up after a sleepy flight and found myself in Venice, Italy.

Now, I'm not sure exactly how I ended up on the wrong plane, flying to the wrong country. Why don't people at airports get you on the right flight and do their jobs properly? What else do airport staff have to do, for heaven's sake? You have to do nearly everything else yourself these days as it is, from finding someone to wheel your bags off towards the check-in to finding your own way to the VIP lounge. I ask you. I don't pretend to be an expert when it comes to international travel – that's *their* speciality. I wouldn't necessarily expect a passport officer to know how to prepare foie gras au torchon with apple ginger, chutney and cacao nibs tuile at the drop of a hat, unless they were a serious fan of mine, so why do they expect little me to comprehend the intricacies of modern air travel?

Anyhow, if those dim-witted trolley-dollies had had the vaguest idea of the hell they were consigning me to they might at least have double-checked what it said on my boarding pass when I staggered on board straight out of the VIP lounge two hours after parting with Barry Cullis.

International air travel is further complicated, I could add, by the fact that you can't walk fifty yards in any direction through a terminal these days without passing a bar or a fake pub, and when you've got hours to fill before the airborne omnibus pulls up at the stop, well, you can't blame me for taking advantage of the opportunity to wet the proverbial whistle. I don't wish to go on about it, but it's hardly surprising so many regular travellers lose track of things, or their marbles completely, in the face of such challenges and temptations. You've only got to look at the royal family, bless them.

But, feeling charitable, I will put it all down as just another illustration from my turbulent history of my chronic inability to find my way through life, a victim yet again of that lack of direction I was telling you about.

Mind you, it would be dishonest of me to say I complained that much when they woke me from my gin-induced slumber to let me know we had arrived. As I stepped out of the plane at the Marco Polo Airport the early summer breeze caressed me like a hundred soft hands that had just been kneading warm dough and every part of me sighed like an Eskimo drinking his first hot chocolate (made with one hundred per cent cacao, naturally).

My insistence upon speaking in French to the Italian

customs people, all the while brandishing a British passport, caused some confusion, it's true, but we got it sorted out in the end and, after they had finally convinced me I was in north-eastern Italy rather than on the western seaboard of France, I settled into my seat in the vaporetto and condescended to let it churn its way through the water towards the finest city on God's earth. Falling under the charm of that extraordinary place for the umpteenth time, I felt incapable of harbouring a grudge against those who had conspired to misdirect me. Like the trouper I am, I recognised the hand of fate when it laid its sweaty palm upon me and I determined to make the best of it.

After all – France? Italy? *Quelle difference?*

My Favourite Plaice

The one place in the world I feel truly at home is a kitchen. But where did this lifelong love affair with food begin? It's a question I've been asked in television interviews countless times – Melvyn Bragg, Jenni Murray, Graham Norton, that chap off Look East, they've all asked me. But for those who haven't heard it before, I'll fill you in, as briefly as I can.

Like so many internationally acclaimed chefs, I trace the start of it back to my mother. Dear mama, with her smudged lipstick and pursed lips and her fondness for ruffling my hair and telling me I looked like someone she had a fling with before my father, wherever he is now. It was my turbulent relationship with my mother and her demented style in the kitchen that shaped my own unique approach to food and taste, for which I've never been sure whether to bless or curse her. How well I remember the packed lunch she provided for me for a school outing at the age of six – a single Weetabix coated with sandwich spread and three wedges of a chocolate orange.

My mother had been brought up in a well-heeled

London suburb in one of those houses where there were still funds available to get someone in to do most of the cooking, as well as the cleaning, ironing, gardening and general maintenance – just about everything really bar claiming credit for it all. Consequently her style of cookery, if one can call it a style, was based on a bewildering fusion of ignorance, playfulness and desperation. Most of the eccentric meals she threw together when the domestics were no longer on hand were inspired by whatever luckless ingredients chanced to remain uneaten in the cupboard.

My mother did things to poultry, fish and other staples that I imagine had never been done before. She has to be the only chef in world history to have envisaged a happy marriage, for instance, between minced meat and strawberry jelly. To be fair, I suppose I should really call it a threesome because she added, as an afterthought, some tinned sardines in tomato sauce. Either way, the relationship ended in divorce between the unwilling partners. Threesomes of another kind were, incidentally, something I gather she had quite an interest in, and in this too I must credit or blame her for an inheritance she has, the gutter press will have you know, seemingly passed to me.

At any event, my mother's chaotic cookery made me wary of food from a young age. As I grew older it helped me to discern and deplore the routine blandness of the cooking at my boarding school, where the liveliest taste in a plate of curry was the rice. It then drove me to notice that most cookery being committed in kitchens up and down the land in the latter half of the twentieth century was similarly lacking in the adventurousness that was my mother's unconscious trademark.

So I must, albeit reluctantly, credit my mother for her unprincipled and imaginative approach to food, which I am bound to admit has been a formative influence upon my own culinary development. I should add, however, that my celebrated taste for travel did not come from her. She has always considered anywhere beyond the reach of the underground suspiciously remote from civilisation, and the continent of Europe and other further flung territories entirely abandoned to barbarism. No, my taste for travel must surely have come from my father – again, wherever he is.

Because my mother found kitchens tiresome we regularly ate out as soon as I could hold a knife and fork. As she hadn't yet succeeded in frittering away quite all of the inheritance that had been passed down to her through the generations, we were familiar faces at decent eateries like the Savoy Grill and the Dorchester. During my teenage years, I took delight in scandalising my mother by complaining that the fare produced by the chefs at such places was boring and old-fashioned, to which she would typically respond by going very red in the face and challenging me to do better if I knew so much about it. Ah, how were we to know where such rash challenges might lead!

I won't test your patience with a full record of my training as a chef, the many accolades I received and the prizes I won. Likewise, I won't bore you with my rapid rise through the ranks and my installation as head chef at an unheard-of young age at one of the finest restaurants in the country. Or with my years spent extending my range and technical knowledge of my craft abroad – the lost years I sometimes call them, due to my unfettered indulgence in the good things in life and the consequent periods of tedious rehab I was obliged to endure. No, all this is a matter of public record thanks to the unstinting efforts of the world's press, or vermin as I prefer to call them.

But, to return to the matter in hand, my favourite place in the world outside the kitchen would have to be, as I have already intimated, la bella Venezia. There's something about the place that never fails to grab me by the vitals, enchanting and infuriating me with its changing moods and startling contrasts of new and old. People rant on about the grandeur of London, New York and other modern metropolises, and they have their attractions it's true, but compared to Venice they are little more than heaps of characterless, oversized Lego. Sorry, all you denizens of such places, but there it is.

Anyway, having found myself so unexpectedly thrown into the old dame's arms once more, I registered at my usual hotel overlooking the upper bend in the Grand Canal and, to my gratification, was given one of the best rooms, with a splendid view of the Rialto, which was swarming as ever with hordes of bewildered-looking tourists. After banging off a text to Barry to let him know my whereabouts, I set myself up on the balcony in the warm early evening with an ice-cold prosecco and a few olives to contemplate the pleasing prospect before me and my immediate future.

It hadn't been my intention to start work on my Mediterranean cookery-cum-travel book quite so abruptly, but there was plainly no prospect of mending fences with the BBC until everyone had had a chance to cool down, so I'd just have to bend the mind to it, whether I was ready to or not. Venice wasn't a bad place to begin, of course, with its superb seafood, supplied by the waters of the lagoon, its ice-cream and its wonderful market, to mention but a few of its gastronomic attractions.

I mused as I watched a couple of gondoliers below me sharing a cheerful exchange, probably about the gullibility of the tourists who agree to their exorbitant charges. You'd think they'd cotton on how we're ripping them off, wouldn't you, says one. Yes, but here we still are after all these centuries, says the other. It can't last, replies the first one. No, agrees his friend, so let's sting them for everything they've got until it all goes belly up. Right-ho, says the other.

It might be an idea, I thought, to start in Venice and then make a leisurely progress through the regions of Italy before heading off to Greece, or alternatively going westwards to France and Spain. Or maybe it would be better policy to devote a separate volume to each country? That would mean three or even more separate trips to different regions to explore local cuisines, all at the expense of the publishers, if they would wear it. I'd have to sound Barry out about it, though perhaps I'd give him a few days to grow more fond of me than he had evidently been when I left him in London.

I'd have to brush up on the old writing style, of course. It was quite a while since I'd put finger to keyboard in a serious manner and it might take a while before I got back into the flow of it. I rather pride myself on my rhetorical powers, I confess. Why use one adjective when you can use two or three, I often ask when that bully of an editor of mine tries to curtail my exuberance. I began to string some sentences together in my head, to see how they sounded (I know that sounds unlikely, but some of us are simply gifted that way).

The sun, I mentally observed, had begun its glorious golden descent towards the glittering, indigo waters of the lazy, languorous lagoon where swarthy, grinning gondoliers guided their sleek black craft with dexterous, subtle movements, belying an expertise that had been passed down without words through countless generations of canal folk. Hello, that was the first paragraph down already. Sapristi! This was going to be a doddle.

I was interrupted by a demonic row from my mobile phone, demanding that I pay it attention. I regarded it with a jaundiced eye, reminding myself that of late it had seemed to bring me exclusively bad news. I picked it up and saw that I had received a text from Barry. He had heard that the producer was on the mend but the BBC were going mad and he doubted I'd ever get another contract with them. What the hell was I thinking etcetera etcetera.

I put the phone down. Barry would have to sort it out. That was his job, after all, not mine. If he wanted his cut of all my earnings, then he'd have to dab a spot of grease on the elbow and do whatever was necessary. I had new and better salmon to sauté. Some allowance has to be given to the artistic temperament – surely people understood that, even the BBC?

I polished off the rest of the prosecco, stretched out my arms in a big yawn, then patted the belly with satisfaction at the immediate prospects. All right, the contretemps with the BBC was a setback, but it had served to open up new vistas of opportunity. Things could be worse.

I was in Venice. And it was time for dinner.

Having my Gâteau à la Banane Léger et Moelleux and Eating It

Ah, Venice, crowning jewel of the Adriatic! It is celebrated far and wide as the capital of romance and intrigue, of carnival and character, of licence and licentiousness, where literally every stone beneath your feet has been trodden a thousand times by Casanova himself, where no night is too long and no day too bright – ah, Venice, Venice, Venice!

That would make a stirring enough start to the next chapter in the book I was supposed to be working on. But, to put it more succinctly and to keep you up to date with events, the sun was shining and I was in the most beautiful city in the world. However, after a week or so in the place I came to the gradual realisation that something just wasn't right with me. Things just weren't clicking like they are supposed to.

It wasn't that the book wasn't coming along, as I've already indicated. I'd tapped an opening chapter into the laptop and it was looking very presentable – well, it would after my editor had bestowed a quick wash and brush up. Good enough for Barry anyway. The BBC had given up bothering me with threatening texts and Barry himself had similarly decided to leave me to sort myself out without the benefit of his helpful advice. So it wasn't that. It wasn't even the lack of communication from

Bettina in the wake of our last bust-up several months before.

No, worse than all that. It was food itself.

I had treated myself with trips to several of my favourite eating places in the city and nothing, but nothing, had thrilled me like I would have expected it to, like it always had done in the past. I just couldn't figure out what I was doing wrong. I had made all the right choices, chosen my restaurants carefully, and selected only the most promising items on the menu. I had eaten cod baked in a crust of salt on the waterfront; polenta e osei (made with spit-roasted songbirds) overlooking St Mark's; and fegato alla Veneziana (made with veal liver) on an excursion to Murano. Nothing. Even the charming and knowledgeable Walter at the Bistrot de Venise, for my money the best maître d' in the city, hadn't managed to produce the magic I yearned for. It had all been undeniably delicious, but somehow only routinely so.

'Did Signore Truelove not enjoy his pumpkin gnocchi in lamb ragu?'

'It was magnificent, as always, Walter,' I assured him. 'But no, I'm afraid he didn't. I'm sorry, Walter – it's my fault, not yours. I don't know what it is but I don't seem able to enjoy anything at the moment. Not even your soft shell crabs or your goose pasta. They all just seemed to pass me by somehow.'

Walter stared at me with tears in his eyes, appalled and deeply moved by my plight.

'The tiramisu?' he inquired, his voice shaking a little.

I shook my head sadly. 'Not even the tiramisu.'

He gave a tiny groan and turned away from my table.

The simple truth, I gradually realised, must be that that I was jaded, literally fed up. And not just with the food either, with life in general. I found myself contemplating the realities of my existence in the past few years and they made me squirm with dissatisfaction.

The bust-ups with the BBC, with Bettina, with countless others in recent months were all, I began to suspect, symptoms of an underlying malaise that was blighting my life and hurting me where it caused me the most pain – in the tastebuds.

I stared dismally at my shimmering reflection in the water of the Grand Canal below my balcony. What was I to do? How was I to break out of this cycle of ennui and despair? I simply couldn't see a way. If not through food, then through what?

It was beginning to get me down. I perked up a bit when I saw that I'd got a text from Jamie. I presumed he might be asking me to help with whatever mega-lucrative project he was doubtlessly cooking up, but it only turned out to be an ad for his new book, damn his mercenary hide, so in a fit of pique I swore and tossed my mobile into the Grand Canal.

Usually when the chargrilled canine of depression bites at my heels I shake him off, when all else fails, with a little dalliance avec les dames. Accordingly, I spruced myself up, donning blazer, tight white trousers and shiniest evening shoes and practising my most dazzling smile in the mirror until I knew myself to be utterly irresistible. Then I strode to the door with a spring in my immaculately shod step. I would put my troubles aside for a few hours and find solace in the arms of a beautiful woman, with which Venice is historically well supplied. It helped a bit to know that without my mobile no one, not even Barry, could intervene to ruin things.

What followed was one of the most dispiriting evenings of my entire life. It was to have consequences too.

It began well enough. I had selected a swanky rooftop bar-cum-restaurant as a likely venue for amorous opportunities and soon found myself attracted to a tempting Texan copperhead with a vivacious mouth, plump bosom and frequent, if deafening, laugh. She struck me as mature, relaxed and open to engagement with the world in general. Tonight, I resolved, I would be that world.

My plan was to start off with some flirtatious small talk, followed by a couple of drinks and a fine dinner under the stars, then at the end of the evening a boat ride up the Grand Canal to my hotel for a sleepless night of champagne-assisted conviviality and passion. What redblooded female could possibly resist?

This one apparently.

My initial overtures were met with interest and some lookings up and down but after that promising beginning everything I said to her just triggered hoots of laughter. Now, sometimes a bit of humour is a good sign and an invitation to greater intimacies, but the increasing scale and frequency of this girl's roars of amusement was frankly rather frightening, as well as embarrassing. Several other guests turned to see what could possibly be causing such a disturbance. Perhaps they feared that some creature was being put to a painful death. I'm not easily dissuaded, however, when a good-looking female offers such a ripe corsage for general appraisal so I opted, unwisely as it turned out, to soldier on. I plied her with cocktails, whose arrival made her shriek with laughter, and then offered to help her choose from the menu that was brought to us after she consented to have dinner with me. She pulled a face at most of the choice dishes that I ordered for her and called them 'funny', which made me frown. She noticed my expression, of course, and that made her laugh even more.

She positively howled with merriment at my suggestion, after two hours of her alarming company, that we take a moonlit boat ride up the Grand Canal to my hotel and I finally decided it was time to give the whole thing up for a bad job. I forked out the necessary to cover the astronomical bill and made a quick getaway while she thought I was in the gents. I could still hear her laughing three storeys below as I melted into the shadows of the ancient canalside walkways.

I was mystified by my lack of success. I didn't usually meet with such incomprehensible jollity when out on the prowl. It was both unsettling and confusing. To calm my shaken nerves I stepped into a modest little bar and ordered a strong nip of something to top up the already substantial amount of champagne swilling round the system, and in the process came face to face with the second unmitigated disaster of the evening.

Mariana was a pretty but sullen-looking Italian girl somewhere in her early twenties I guessed. She had lips that she had painted a deep purple and glowing, resentful eyes, lined with thick black mascara, that dared you to approach her. There was a distinct touch of Lucretia Borgia in there somewhere, in amongst the punk-goth chic and pouting lips. I really should have known better, but I was in no mood to discriminate. Anyway, she had beautiful silky long black hair and, beneath her short leather jacket, a trim, youthful figure that deserved appreciative attention.

'Ciao, bella,' I greeted her with more confidence than I truly felt right then; I was gambling that she even spoke English. 'After the evening I've just had, I'm ready for this drink. Can I buy you one?'

After a brief hesitation, a curt nod of the head indicated that she understood and I could, though she clearly wasn't going to get gushy about it. In a trice we were ensconsed in a shady corner where we could size each other up over our glasses without fear of interruption.

'I'm having a hell of an evening,' I told her mournfully. 'I'm hoping you will cheer me up.'

She shrugged and sipped at her drink. Well, at least she didn't laugh.

'What's your name?' I inquired.

She pointed to her black necklace that, when I looked closely at it, had been shaped into a single word. I also saw that it was studded with what were unmistakably real diamonds, so this little miss was evidently not your average bar girl – more likely a rich young heiress having a night off from the tourist hotspots and slumming it with the locals for kicks.

'Ah. Mariana,' I read, admiring the pale softness of the skin against which the black necklace rested. 'What a pretty name. There's a Mariana of the moated grange in Shakespeare, if I remember correctly.'

Mariana didn't respond. Not a Shakespeare buff then. Or maybe they chose Dante over Shakespeare in Italian schools.

Thrusting aside alcohol-induced weariness, I launched into a series of scintillating observations in a mixture of English and cod-Italian designed to impress, amuse, provoke and titillate at the same time. I expect most of my readers have a similar store of witticisms and insightful comments for use on just such occasions. They were reasonably well received by my correspondent, if the odd grunt or nod of the head counted as a positive response. Her black eyes contemplated me throughout with unblinking frankness.

I began to feel like things were going my way at last. We had a second round, then a third, and I was really getting into my stride, fixing my adoring attention upon her while sharing my thoughts on a range of fascinating topics that I was sure she would find both illuminating and intriguing.

After about forty minutes of these preliminaries I gave a big, significant sigh, then leaned forward so our faces were just a couple of inches apart. I treated her to my most ardent smile.

'I've really enjoyed talking to you,' I told her. 'It's unusual for me, but I feel we have a real connection somehow. Forgive the boldness, but do you feel the same at all?'

I laid a paw gently over her small left hand. The effect was somewhat marred by the fact that she was wearing a couple of heavy gold rings mounted with big black stones that jutted uncomfortably into my palm but I resolved to continue regardless.

'Would you like to go on somewhere perhaps?' I queried.

Mariana kept her left hand where it was and then downed what was left in her glass with her right.

'Okay,' she muttered.

I took that to mean she acquiesced in whatever plans I might have in mind for the rest of the evening and I felt my pulse quicken. Things were definitely looking up. Memories of the frightful Texan with the terrifying laugh dissolved completely.

As she seemed so compliant, I took Mariana's hand and guided her (with scholarly commentary about the locale, of course) swiftly through the darkened alleyways that led, as it happened, more or less directly back to my hotel.

'Would you like to come up for another drink?' I suggested, after I had explained to her, with a look of surprise on my face, that somehow we had ended up where I was staying.

She nodded and, still holding my hand, led the way into the hotel, the precocious madam.

The promised drink didn't get poured till quite a bit later. The moment the bedroom door had closed behind us she was all over me. Off came my blazer and her leather jacket and in seconds they were joined in an untidy heap on the floor by the rest of our clothes.

Now, I don't like to brag about my looks, which will be familiar to most readers, I dare say, from my many telly appearances and from photos in magazines and so on. More than one person has ventured to suggest I look a bit like actor Rupert Everett. I don't have a particular view on that one way or another, though I do think it a bit of a cheek for them to liken me to him when it should be the other way round, surely.

Whatever the truth of it, most women I set my sights on find the prospect agreeable enough to spend some quality time with me, and you won't hear me complaining about it. Mariana proved herself thoroughly taken with the idea, despite her superficial air of reticence (I doubt if she said more than three words to me the whole night long). When it came to making love, she had all the enthusiasm and energy you might expect from someone her age and a good amount of gymnastics formed a central part of the amorous itinerary that we pursued over the next few hours. She didn't seem to want to settle in one position for more than a few seconds at a time and she clearly preferred matters to proceed at a frenzied pace so I found myself getting a proper workout, until the sweat was pouring off both of us. Fortunately she was light as a feather, with not a superfluous ounce of fat on her, so we achieved a number of things that would have worn me ragged with a more substantial partner.

There weren't many breaks between the repeated bouts of passion, but neither of us was ready to call it a day until the light of dawn was seeping past the heavy curtains and the first watercraft could be heard on the canal beyond. I lay, panting, on the bed as we slowly got our breath back. I felt utterly drained, too spent even to amuse myself deciphering the various words and symbols that were tattooed in strategic and not readily discovered locations around Mariana's supple and delightful body.

Then she surprised me by abruptly sliding out of bed altogether and starting to pull on her clothes.

'Aren't you going to stay for breakfast?' I asked her, bewildered. 'They do a good spread here.'

She shook her head.

I propped myself wearily up on one elbow, admiring her lithe form as she pulled up her tight black jeans. 'Come on. We could spend the day together. How would you like a boat trip to the Lido?'

She shook her head again.

'Well, just tell me what you fancy and I am sure it can be arranged.'

'No. I must go.'

It was the longest sentence she had spoken since I had picked her up in the bar the previous evening.

'Why?' I pressed her. 'Stay a little longer.'

'I can't.'

'Why not?'

She slipped her arms into her jacket, without looking in my direction. 'You are too old for me.'

With that, taking advantage of the fact that her reply had rendered me speechless and gaping like a stunned haddock in the way Barry Cullis does so well, she slipped her shoes on and with nary a glance in my direction let herself out of the room.

The door closed softly behind her.

'M-Mariana?' I stuttered, finally getting my voice back in order. But of course she was halfway down to the square outside by then.

I sank back on the pillows, mind reeling.

What the hell did she mean, too old? Too old?

The little trollop!

Stewing in my own Jus

I stayed in bed till lunchtime, morosely turning over in my head what had happened and trying to ignore the horrendous hangover, the residue of too much champagne and too little sleep, that had replaced the euphoria of the early hours.

Eventually I forced myself to get up and get dressed, feeling moody and ill done by. Not only had I this almighty hangover to cope with, but the little baggage had also considerably hurt my feelings. And I had to admit to myself that I was disappointed not to have the chance to enjoy some more of her company too. I couldn't think why she had abandoned me like that. It really was most inconsiderate.

Still feeling disconsolate I stalked through the alleyways towards St Mark's Square, hoping the fresh air would clear my head. It was a baking hot day, however, and the stench coming off the water under one or two of the bridges did nothing to aid my recovery.

The open space in front of the doge's palace was teeming with the usual horde of tourists, consulting maps and posing for selfies with looks of concentration on their faces. The Japanese girls always seemed to pose with their fingers raised in V for Victory fashion – something I've never quite understood. The historical irony of it appeared to be lost on them. Pretty though many of them were, I wasn't in the mood for lingering in their vicinity and instead directed my steps along the waterfront towards Harry's Bar, Ernest Hemingway's favourite drinking haunt in the city many moons ago and still a popular place to relax. I hoped a bit of the hair of the dog might do the trick and get the brain back into something like fully functioning trim.

The bar was busy, as it usually is, but the white-jacketed waiters were full of bonhomie and eager to serve. I found myself a seat on its own in a corner and slumped there after ordering myself a suitable pick-me-up. While I waited for the drink to arrive my eyes fell upon a discarded magazine on a seat beside me. People's Monthly. With a start I realised I was looking at my own face.

'Here is your drink, signore,' breezed the waiter as he transferred a tall glass from a silver tray to my table. Then he caught sight of what I was reading. 'Ah! The signore is on the front page of the magazine!'

Normally, of course, I'd be only too pleased to be recognised as the celebrity I am in this public manner, but right now I wanted none of it and waved him away impatiently. I needed to know what my face was doing there. What bit of publicity-seeking chicanery had Barry perpetrated on my behalf this time?

It wasn't a flattering photograph. It showed me in the studio, looking very cross and clearly shouting something at the top of my voice. Judging by the fact that I was in the act of picking up the bowl of crème anglaise, it appeared to have been taken at the very moment tempers had flared during the making of my late lamented television series for the BBC, the one that had ended so prematurely with me storming out of Television Centre, much to Barry's consternation. Some swine had snapped me at the height of my fury and now here I was, undignified rage exposed for all the world to see and wonder at. The headline alongside the picture read 'What's cooking?' and the subtitle underneath ran 'What on earth's wrong with our celebrity chefs?' Well, I could have waxed lyrical on that subject as regards most of my colleagues in the biz, but it seemed grossly unfair that I of all people should have been singled out as the prime example of their failings.

I'd half a mind to telephone Barry right there and then and tell him exactly what I thought about him letting this kind of thing loose in the media, but then I remembered that my mobile had joined the detritus of the centuries at the bottom of the Grand Canal, so I took a big swallow from my glass instead.

When I felt a little stronger, I flicked the magazine open to find the relevant article. It turned out that there wasn't really very much about me personally, beyond a few snide remarks and a couple more equally unflattering photographs taken on the same day. Honestly, the rubbish that gets printed these days! The writer clearly had it in for the lot of us – Jamie, Bettina, Heston and yes, little me.

The gist of the thing was that we were all prima donnas who were far more interested in our public image than in the recipes we cooked up, just as likely to take a swipe at a journalist as flip a crêpe suzette. It was harsh, unforgiving stuff, and the accompanying photos only made it worse, with me throwing my tantrum, Bettina snarling at a photographer as she left a nightclub rather the worse for wear, and Jamie looking equally out of sorts as if he'd just got up after three weeks in bed. The insinuation clearly was that we would fly off the handle at the slightest provocation. If the originator of this trash had been present I'd have floored him without a moment's hesitation.

I closed the magazine with a groan. It was typical of my recent run of luck for this to come out just when things had gone pear-shaped with the BBC and I needed more than ever to look like the sort of sterling chap that they just couldn't do without in their schedule. Barry would be having fits.

The more I thought about it, the worse the situation appeared. It was all right for the others. For one thing, it wasn't their picture on the front cover. They all had their own series to pursue and the public would forget any bad publicity within twenty-four hours as their agents trotted out more positive news stories about them. But it was different for me. Until I managed to get a more sympathetic image before the public gaze, which seemed improbable right now with no series with which to beguile the common herd, this image of me ranting and raving in a studio would be the world's latest and probably lasting mental impression of me. God, it could be terminal for my career!

I placed the magazine face down on the seat beside me and ordered another drink. The reality of the crisis I found myself in began to dawn on me. I had felt bad before coming into Harry's Bar; now I was feeling positively suicidal. How on earth was I to get back into public favour with no series to help me on my way? It was no use relying on Jamie and the rest to rally round and defend my reputation. Celebrity chefs don't work that way – we're far too busy cutting each other's throats. I doubted that as my agent Barry would rush to help me out either. 'I did everything I could for Tremayne,' I could almost hear him saying, 'but he's too volatile. He just can't help himself, so I've had to wash my hands of him.' Apart from the book deal, there were no prospects of further work from any quarter. At this rate I could end up back doing time in some ghastly sweat-hole of a hotel kitchen somewhere.

God, what a mess.

I stayed in Harry's Bar for a couple of hours before staggering out, the magazine stuffed in my jacket pocket to stop anyone else seeing it, but with absolutely no idea where to go next. Even for a person with no sense of direction, I was more lost now than I could ever remember being before. I tried to jam the magazine into a bin outside the bar but the thing was already overflowing with discarded Macdonald's cartons, so I stuffed it clumsily back into my pocket and followed the waterfront aimlessly back to the doge's palace, where the jostling of the crowds nearly dropped me in the waters of the lagoon itself.

How could all these people be so carefree? Couldn't they see the agonies a fellow human being was going through? Didn't they care? They acted as if they didn't even know who I was, for Christ's sake!

It was appalling. I don't often drink to excess, but right now it seemed like the best solution, the only solution, to my current woes. I looked for another waterfront bar, sparing barely a glance for the Bridge of Sighs as I crossed over the water some fifty yards downstream of the thing. Sighing was nothing compared to the misery that had settled upon my soul. Bridge of Howling Despair would have been nearer the mark.

I won't depress you with a precise account of my inebriated progress through the bars of central Venice that long afternoon. Suffice it to say that by early evening I was in full flow – loud, clumsy and dishevelled – but still, I am sorry to report, less than joyous in frame of mind. Let's just say it was a damned good thing there weren't any press swine around to record the scene for posterity.

It occurred to me, as the shadows on the lagoon began

to lengthen, that I hadn't eaten a thing all day. No wonder, I told myself with the certainty of one who knows these things – no wonder I was feeling so woozy. So boozy-woozy-woozy. As I had fetched up somewhere off the tourist trail in an area that I didn't know especially well I aimed my path towards the first likely-looking door and stumbled over the threshold.

I blinked in the dim light beyond. My first impression was that I had landed in a relatively upmarket pizzeria, complete with festoons of artificial grapes and gaudy paintings of Italian seaside villages, but when I managed to focus on the menu I saw that possibly I was doing the place an injustice for the listings included several of the region's more adventurous and less often encountered dishes. It would do, I decided, and I slumped behind a round table, while roaring for the wine list.

As the waiter poured me a generous glass of red, I surveyed my neighbours, of which there weren't many. There were some timid Japanese tourists at a table beside me, tucking into spaghetti by the look of it, and, across the way from me, a diminutive middle-aged Italian in an expensive-looking business suit. He appeared to have almost finished his meal and was rounding things off with a small coffee.

I ordered a couple of potentially interesting items from the menu and transferred my dissatisfied gaze to the view beyond the window. I watched as two young men pushed a large handcart-cum-display stall loaded with souvenir postcards and carnival masks past the restaurant, doubtless heading back towards wherever they stored it at night. Overseeing the operation was a substantial Venetian grandmother with a limp and a sour look on her face.

I don't know why exactly but the sight of that woman got me thinking about my mother. It was some time since I had paid mama a visit and I fell to scolding myself for my negligence. Giddy, temperamental and trivial though she could be, that silly female was the only person in the world right now who could be relied upon to be sympathetic towards my plight, utterly wretched as I was. I didn't deserve her, I told myself, I really didn't. I didn't deserve to have anyone in my corner, fighting for me, what with the mess I was making of my life. If I'd had my mobile on me I'd have called her up there and then to tell her so. Instead I sniffed and raised my glass in a toast.

'Mother!' I intoned in a shaking, tearful and somewhat over-loud voice that made the other diners turn in my direction.

The Japanese party cast startled glances at me, though one woman among them had a certain softness in her regard. She probably thought I was in mourning or something, sorrowfully lamenting my lost progenitor. I didn't venture to correct the misapprehension or to explain that in all likelihood my ageing parent was almost certainly on her third gin of the evening by now, and probably in the company of her latest beau, whoever he might be. Better on the whole that they picture her dead, but just looking like she was asleep, in a grand, silk-lined coffin.

I downed the wine and refilled the glass, spilling some of it on the tablecloth. I felt horribly alone in the world. Was there anyone anywhere who really cared whether I lived or died? I couldn't bring myself to provide the answer to my own question. It was just too upsetting to contemplate.

A minute or so later the waiter arrived with my first course, which he deposited in front of me with an ostentatious flourish. Cheeky sod, I breathed – it was hardly as if he had made it himself.

Then I looked down at what he had brought me and forgot all about the waiter. I couldn't believe what I was seeing. It couldn't be! Could it? It was the prosciutto-based dish I had ordered from the menu, sure enough, but more than that, there was something weirdly familiar about it, something so completely *known* to me that it quite took my breath away. In the name of all that was holy, I was looking at one of my own recipes!

Befuddled though I was, I had absolutely no doubt about it. I had given a traditional favourite a new twist by adding a few innovative embellishments, such as shredded olive and crispy fried capers and asparagus, all presented in a very particular manner. And that was exactly what was laid out on my plate.

I looked suspiciously up at the waiter, but he merely nodded and wished me bon appétit before walking off, apparently unaware of any connection there might be between diner and that to be dined upon. It was, then, an unconscious act of homage that had been unwittingly offered to me.

Numbed, I picked up my knife and fork. It was one of my signature dishes and one that always went down well. I had devised it way back during my cookery student days with Bettina, if I remembered rightly. In fact, I believe she was the first to try it, which made it especially poignant. Since then I had prepared it on a couple of television shows of mine and it had also been published in one or two books. If it was well done on this occasion, it might go some way to restoring my faith in my fellow-chefs. I popped a forkful into my mouth and chewed expectantly. Then I stopped chewing.

What the hell?

There was something radically wrong here, a flavour that was completely out of place, so acutely at odds with everything else on the plate that it made my taste buds shrivel and my throat tighten. It was impossible to tell exactly what it was – cheese? Grappa? Socks? Not chilli surely?

I cast my knife and fork down with a clatter and reached for the wine glass, which I drained in a single gulp. Then I was up on my feet and shouting. My table upended itself and the bottle and glasses went flying to destruction on the floor, sending shards of broken glass in all directions with a huge crash.

'What's the meaning of this? Is this a joke of some kind?' I yelled at the waiter, who threw up his hands in self-defence and started retreating towards the kitchen door. 'What the hell have you done to it? It isn't meant to taste like this!'

The waiter mumbled something unintelligible as he grappled for the door handle.

'That's right,' I roared at him, ignoring the squeals of fright coming from the Japanese party, 'fetch the chef – if you can call him that! Bring him out here and we'll see what he has to say for himself!'

The waiter disappeared into the kitchen like a rabbit up a drainpipe and a moment later a bulky chap in white aprons emerged, looking red-faced and indignant.

'You!' I shouted, indicating my plate of food, which I still had in my hand. 'Are you responsible for this, this, outrage!'

The chef glanced at the plate, then at me, his eyes narrowing and his fists clenching.

Normally I find the idea of engaging in fisticuffs appalling and it's not something I consider part of my repertoire. But right now, after the day I had had, I really did feel like kicking or punching something, and here clearly was my opportunity. Unfortunately, however, most cooks aren't good at kicking or punching. They just aren't designed for it. Shouting like a foul-mouthed lunatic and pinching and jabbing maybe, but not kicking and punching. You'd never see Delia or Mary B. lash out at a fellow-presenter, for instance, if their scones weren't quite up to par. In any case, I still had my plate in my hand.

'This recipe isn't meant to look or taste like this! You have turned a work of art into a – a travesty! A pile of horse manure!' With extravagant theatricality, I let the plate drop to the floor where it shattered and added to the general mess at my feet.

The cook growled and took a step towards me. Rather out of character, I stood my ground.

'And if you want to know how I know that your cooking is horse manure, I'll tell you,' I told him in a marvellously calm, steadfast voice. 'This happens to be my recipe you've spat all over, you grubby little plagiarist – mine!'

A look of uncertainty crossed the man's face, though his fists remained clenched.

'Yes, that's right!' I pressed on. 'It was me who invented it! But I don't suppose you even know who I am! You don't, do you?'

The cook shook his head and looked belligerent. Behind me I was aware of the Japanese party throwing money on the table and hastening out of the restaurant before things got even more violent.

'Well, I'll have you know exactly who I am!' I bellowed. 'I am an untinational – international chef with a – a reputation – yes! Famous! I'll have you know I've cooked for – for – politicians, royalty, footballers, people whose names appear in the paper every bloody day! And my work deserves better than you messing about with it till it looks and tastes like nothing on earth, you fat talentless little sh–'

At this point the chef interrupted me with a huge shout and launched himself at me. It must have been something I said. Alarmingly, he had acquired a cleaver from somewhere and had raised it high above his head, preparatory no doubt to bringing it down on my skull. The weird thing is, I remember recognising the cleaver as something familiar – I had one exactly like it in my own kitchen at home, and horribly effective it was too. I stood stock still in terror and surprise and waited for the lethal blow to fall.

Suffice to say, it didn't.

The little Italian businessman, as soon as he saw the cleaver, stood up and stuck out a beautifully shod Italian foot so that the cook tripped and collapsed in a disorganised moaning heap on the floor between us. The cleaver went skittering harmlessly under a nearby table.

'Ha!' I yelled in triumph. 'That'll teach you!'

As if obeying a signal, the rest of the restaurant staff sprang into action, hauling the stricken cook up off the floor and pushing him back into the kitchen, out of harm's way. I, meanwhile, was brushed down and reassured that I was all right by the neat little businessman.

'If anything has been broken and needs paying for,' the man told the manager in English, presumably for my benefit. 'Just send the bill to me, Luigi Vanni, and I will cover it.'

The mention of the man's name seemed to have a miraculous calming effect on all present. The manager looked cowed and mumbled apologies, dismissing the very idea that there was anything to pay for and studiously ignoring his underlings as they set about tidying up the appalling mess I had created. All this I noticed only vaguely, however, being too far gone to take in much detail. All I knew was that thanks to the dapper little businessman I had been saved a good thrashing by that lunk of a cook, and for that I was extremely grateful.

I attempted to communicate my gratitude to my saviour, but my mouth wasn't working like it should and all I could do was lean on his shoulder and grin stupidly at him as he steered me towards the door.

Once outside my new friend leant me gently up against the wall until I had taken a few breaths of fresh air. He looked at me quizzically, as though considering something.

'I think you are all in one piece,' he observed at last. 'Do you feel all right?'

'Never better,' I lied.

He nodded. 'Tell me, are you really what you say you are, a famous international chef?'

'I most certainly ham – am.' I tried to draw myself up to my full height, but the knees didn't want to cooperate, so I started grappling at my pocket instead. 'Look!'

I fished out the crumpled magazine from Harry's Bar and held it in front of the man's face. 'There! That's me. You see? Right there. Tremayne Truelove, in black and white. Right – there!'

I was getting angry and tearful again, so I let the man take the magazine from me and sagged against the wall, lamenting my life and everything that had ever happened to me, good and bad.

The stranger looked at me with concern and curiosity in his face.

'What are you doing in Venice, Signore Truelove?

'Being threatened and – and – disrespected. By everyone.'

My new friend sighed. 'I apologise, signore, for the unforgivable rudeness of my fellow countryman. This is not the way a great artiste like you should be treated.' He helped me away from the wall and steadied me. 'Let me make it up to you, I beg of you. Let me invite you to my house. You could come tomorrow, if you are free. I am sure you would find it interesting. Or do you have plans for tomorrow?'

I shook my head despondently. 'No. I have no plans for tomorrow. No plans at all.'

'Good. That is very good.' He shot me a big smile. 'I

shall send a boat to pick you up at noon, if you would be kind enough to tell me where you are staying.'

I told him and then let him support me the few yards to where a water taxi was waiting and see me into it. My friend pressed some money into the driver's hand and waved me off as the taxi started on its way.

'Don't forget, signor Trueloво,' he called after us. 'Noon tomorrow!'

I waved farewell in his vague direction. 'Noon tomorrow. Fine. I'll remember. Muchas gracias – I mean, grazie, signore.'

The boat bucketed up the Grand Canal and I raised my head to the stars, still feeling drunk as a skunk.

The Oyster is My World

If I thought the hangover after the night with Mariana was bad enough, the one I woke with on the morning after my calamitous meal out was much worse. I spent most of the morning in bed as isolated scenes from my day-long debauche came back to me, hammered into my brain like so many rusty nails.

My inclination, when I finally remembered about it, was to ignore the invitation extended by my rescuer at the restaurant, whatever his name was. He may have been well-heeled and I was grateful to him, of course, for his timely intervention, but businessmen of any nationality do not generally make the best company and the idea of being bored to death by discussions of stocks and shares and Italian office politics while struggling with a crushing hangover was far from appealing.

However, I scolded myself, I was without a friend in the whole city – the whole world even – and I could hardly afford to be offhand with the one person who had gone out of his way to help me out. I would just have to steel myself to the task and make the best of a bad job, if only because that's what an Englishman does.

So, when a speedboat arrived at the jetty outside my hotel at the appointed hour of noon and the driver asked for Signore Truelove I was there, be-blazered and presentable, if a little unsteady on the feet.

The driver was a swarthy, dark-haired Italian in black rig who looked like he did a lot of weight-training. He helped me onboard and sat me down but proved singularly uncommunicative when I tried to find out from him where my new friend, whose name I now belatedly remembered was Luigi Vanni, lived. I soon gave it up, realising that the man spoke little or no English.

My Italian, I should explain, is far from perfect. Functional maybe, but not fluent. In fact, I sometimes joke that I speak it like a native – a native of any country but Italy. The same is true of all the rest of the world's languages, but as ninety-nine per cent of foreigners speak English almost as well as I do I generally get by. Most of what little I do know of foreign languages is of a culinary nature, I might add. Thus, when one adorable little senorita in Portugal once asked me if I was the famous cook who did such marvellous things with his sausage I got hold of entirely the wrong end of the stick and spent an uncomfortable two hours in a police station before my misapprehension became apparent. If things get desperate I also have a tendency to panic and throw in words from other languages, which only adds to the confusion – so silence is my preferred policy when the language barrier is raised too high.

The boat, I saw, was taking me back down the Grand Canal where grand and ancient palazzos, many of them hotels or art galleries, line the waterfront. I presumed we'd turn off the main drag at some point and fetch up at one of the more modest addresses down one of the smaller canals, but not a bit of it. The engine slowed and I saw that we going to moor outside one of the more magnificent buildings at the lower end of the canal, complete with arches, balconies and traces of golden decoration on the pink plaster. I looked in admiration up at the fluted columns and tall windows that rose some four storeys above the waterway, which opened up into the lagoon a few hundred yards further on.

When my unspeaking driver offered his hand to help me out of the boat and onto the private jetty I tried to ask him in Italian 'Are you sure?' but he just waved me towards the big front door so this was presumably the right place. When I checked it, I saw the name Vanni was there on the brass nameplate. The fact that it was the only name led me to deduce that my new friend occupied the whole building as a private residence. I whistled quietly to myself. It took some money to obtain an entire palazzo like this for private occupation. Tedious businessman or not, I might have to reassess Signore Vanni's standing in the world.

The door from the jetty was slightly ajar so I pushed it and went on in. Many buildings in Venice have relatively modest ground floors because of the risk of the water coming in and wrecking them, but this palazzo had been properly defended from any chance of flooding and was richly and immaculately decorated from the ground floor up. Huge paintings depicting Venice in its heyday in the seventeenth and eighteenth centuries hung on the walls on either side of me. Ahead was a superb baronial staircase in white marble. And clattering down it in his spotless black Italian shoes came my new friend Signore Luigi Vanni.

'Welcome, welcome!' Signore Vanni greeted me, arms outstretched. 'I am so pleased you have come!'

We embraced and I hastened to apologise for the previous evening.

'Thank you so much for inviting me. I have to say how sorry I am for the embarrassing scene I caused last night–'

Signore Vanni cut me off straightaway. 'Not at all, not at all. I will not hear another word. Let us forget everything about it and rejoice only that it led to your being here today.'

'That's very generous of you. Thank you.'

'Come, follow me. There is nothing to see down here but it is much more interesting upstairs. It will give me great pleasure to show you round.'

'I had no idea you lived in a palazzo like this,' I confessed as we proceeded up the stairs. 'It really is a most marvellous building.'

Signore Vanni grinned with pleasure. 'It is the reward of much successful business. And it also helps to impress the people I deal with.'

'I'm sure it does. Is it very old?'

'Not really. Early sixteenth century, I believe. But it has been restored many times.'

I was about to ask him what line of business he was actually in, but we had arrived at the top of the staircase and my attention was immediately distracted by the sumptuousness of our surroundings.

The staircase opened into a grand vestibule off which there was a series of state rooms with big white doors and much gold-lined white panelling. The walls were covered with a deep red, textured cloth and adorned with more works by old masters, typically views of the city but also portraits in heavy gold frames of unsmiling Venetian donnas. The carpets underfoot were wonderfully deep and soft.

Signore Vanni led me through one spectacular, spacious room after another, all decorated in a similarly lavish style. There was even a white and gold grand piano, for heaven's sake, and a grand dining room with enough beautifully carved antique chairs to seat eighteen people.

But the greater glory was yet to come.

After the dining-room Signore Vanni ushered me into the only room on the floor that we had not yet seen. It was a long, comfortable living-room with yellow walls, white curtains that fell all the way to the floor, and stupendous views through the tall windows of the Grand Canal. In front of a vast white marble fireplace were arranged armchairs and a sofa clad in tasteful embroidered fabric. One of the armchairs, I saw, was occupied.

'I would like you to meet my wife,' said my host, leading me over towards the seated figure. 'Teresa, this is Tremayne Truelove, the English chef I was telling you about.'

Teresa Vanni put her book down and rose from her chair. She was tall, elegant and the epitome of a classic Italian beauty, with long dark hair and black, knowing eyes. Even with my powers of descriptive rhetoric I struggle to communicate her perfection. My God, she was lovely! I shook the slender hand she held out to me and hoped my mouth wasn't hanging open with naked lust.

'I am so pleased to meet you,' she said, in perfect English. Her manner was, like her appearance, cool and elegant.

'Likewise,' I stuttered, forcing myself to release her exquisitely soft hand. 'A real pleasure.'

Signore Vanni waved for us all to sit. 'Our lunch will be ready for us in just a few minutes. But first do tell us all about yourself, Signore Truelove. The life of an international chef must be very exciting.'

Now if there's one thing I don't need to be asked twice, it is to talk about myself. I know I should be embarrassed to admit it, but it is a minor flaw in the otherwise blameless character that I was born with and there's nothing I can do about it. It also meant I could postpone hearing the details of Signore Vanni's dreary life in business, which I'm sure neither the lovely Teresa Vanni nor I wanted to sit through. Anyway, Signore Vanni and his fabulous wife seemed genuinely keen to know all about me, so who was I to disappoint them?

Thrusting aside my hangover, which had miraculously dwindled in severity since the appearance of the stupendous Teresa Vanni, I told them all about my background, my absent father, my spendthrift mother, my schooling, my early successes at cookery school, the years of drudgery in kitchens around the world until I got my breakthrough after meeting Barry and then my first series on the BBC. It was all fascinating stuff.

The conversation continued through lunch in the huge dining-room. The fare that was served to us was of surprisingly indifferent quality and quite at odds with the sumptuous surroundings. Signore Vanni and his wife were clearly acutely aware that it might not be to up to the standards I was used to.

'We must apologise for the food,' Signore Vanni told me, with a regretful look on his face, 'but the truth is it is very hard to find a good cook in Venice these days. We move about a good deal for reasons of my business and it is asking much to get someone to travel from place to place with us. So we have to accept whoever the local catering agencies send us. Sometimes they are fine, but other times they are...' He gestured at the dishes set out before us. 'Well, you can see for yourself. We haven't had a decent meal for days.'

Teresa Vanni smiled coolly at me over her glass. 'Perhaps Signore Truelove would be kind enough to cook for us, if he is not too busy?'

'I am sure he has far too many other things to do, my dear,' Signore Vanni countered at once. 'A famous international chef like him, with his own television series…'

'No, no, not at all,' I interrupted. 'I'm always in demand, of course, but your husband has been so kind to me. I am in your debt. I would like to cook for you both. When shall it be?'

Signore Vanni blushed with pleasure. 'That is so generous! But I fear we are asking too much of you…'

'No, no, let Signore Truelove cook for us,' Teresa Vanni broke in, before looking coyly across at me. 'That is, if he really would like to.'

I don't know what it is with me, a sort of sixth sense I suppose, but I can tell when a woman is flirting with me – and I was getting the signals now. Could this ravishing black-haired beauty really be interested in me? Or was she just toying with me? It would be fun to find out.

'I would love to cook for you both. Really I would.'

'That is settled then,' said Signore Vanni with decision. 'We are free tonight. Would tonight be too soon?'

'No, tonight would be perfect, Signore Vanni.'

'Please call me Luigi.'

'And I am Tremayne.' I turned towards his wife. 'And may I call you Teresa?'

'Naturally. Tremayne.'

Lunch finished, Luigi led me back downstairs and ordered his boatman, whose name I learned was Bruno, to take me up the Grand Canal to the Rialto market. The short boat ride helped me to see off the last effects of my hangover and I felt almost sprightly as I wandered happily through the stalls, picking out fresh vegetables and seafood for the evening meal. It's one of my favourite markets, and I always savour the atmosphere there.

I looked forward to cooking for my two new friends, who were apparently a lovely couple, but I was still finding it hard work summoning up any enthusiasm for the actual business of cooking. I had a long list of assured standards of mine that I knew would delight both of them, but I was less sure they would delight me. There was no getting away from the fact that my celebrated palate had grown dull, perhaps fatally so, and seemed incapable of being roused by the prospect of eating.

I paused in front of the window of the horse butchers with its helpful diagram naming the various cuts available. Ever since the royal horsemeat scandal previously mentioned I had become something of a champion of the stuff. But even this failed to excite my culinary imagination this time. Even the piece of meat labelled 'burro' didn't tempt me in; it was, in any case, hardly a suitable dish for a dish like Teresa Vanni. Suitable for royalty, perhaps, but not for the gorgeous wife of my new friend.

After a reviving coffee at a place overlooking the canal, where I mused thoughtfully but inconclusively upon this latest and unexpected turn in my life and where it might lead, if anywhere, I ambled back to where Bruno and the speedboat were waiting for me and was then whisked back down the Grand Canal to the Vanni residence, flashing past crowded waterbuses and vaporetti.

Well, the creative impulse might not be firing on all cylinders, but I would enjoy an evening in the company of my two new friends, especially the one with the deep black eyes and soft, soft hands...

As Luigi was at a business meeting when I returned, Teresa broke off her reading to show me to the kitchen on the ground floor. It was one of the most theatrical spaces I have ever cooked in, with a vast cooking range coupled with an impressive array of modern kitchen gadgets and devices, some of which even I had not seen. Heston would have salivated at some of the electronic wizardry on offer. The whole room was gorgeously tiled and there was even an old master that slid aside to reveal a television screen behind if you were in the mood of some small-screen entertainment. I wasn't, of course. After my recent experiences at the BBC, I doubted I should want to watch television ever again.

I assured Teresa I had everything I needed to get started and she left me, padding like a cat back upstairs to her book. I couldn't help taking a sneaky glance at her legs as she ascended the stairs. Magnificent, slender calves she had and the shapeliest ankles. Oh, to see more! But that was hardly my place, of course. I tut-tutted at myself and my lack of decorum and set about the task at hand.

I wanted to produce something really wonderful for my hosts and dedicated the next two or three hours to preparing it for them. I didn't have any of my books to hand, of course, or my trusty old wok, but I was giving them tried and trusted recipes that I knew by heart so that was no problem.

I enjoyed exploring the stupendous kitchen and took a professional delight in the top-of-the-range traditional saucepans and utensils with which it was equipped. I won't give you an item-by-item record of what I made for them, but you may be assured I prepared each course with the utmost care and attention to detail. The ingredients I had gathered from the Rialto market were of the best quality and I had every spice and herb that I could possibly require available to me.

As the time ticked by I began to feel just a touch of creative excitement stealing over me, though it was nothing like the inspirational fury with which I dreamt up innovative new recipes in days gone by and I couldn't help feeling just a little sad that the old thrill was lacking when everything else – the ingredients, the kitchen, the people I was going to feed – was so very perfect. But sometimes you just have to set your own feelings to one side and get on with it.

Teresa popped down a couple of times to check that I had everything I wanted. Usually when I am cooking a complicated meal I hate to be disturbed by anyone for any reason (just ask my colleagues at the BBC), but in Teresa Vanni's case the interruptions were something I savoured to the full. I invited her to taste one or two of the sauces I was preparing and held my breath in erotic ecstasy as she bent to slip the spoon between her lovely lips. Who says cooking isn't sexy? You've only got to consider the comments Bettina gets in the online media any time she bends low over her cooking pots in one of those low-cut tops she's always wearing, the shameless hussy. The women have an unfair advantage in these things of course – if I slipped on a jockstrap while sniffing the aroma coming out of a saucepan I daresay

I'd get complaints by the stock pot. There's gender equality for you!

But the sight of Teresa Vanni closing her eyes as she appreciated to the full the flavours of what I was preparing for her and her husband was reward enough for me for all my trouble. When she finally left me alone in the kitchen I redoubled my efforts to produce a meal that would please her, concentrating fiercely upon what I needed to do to present my creative self to her in the best possible light.

After about three hours of hard work I decided everything that could be prepared in advance was done, so I allowed myself a doze in a comfortable chair in the corner of the kitchen. I was suddenly very tired after being so busy and the effects of the night before had not worn off completely.

It was very pleasant, sitting on my own in the warm kitchen, my work done, with the sounds of the unseen canal outside drifting through the window above me. I even heard a gondolier singing as he went past – not something you hear very often on the canals of Venice these days. I could almost content myself that all was well with the world, or at least my little bit of it. I quite forgot my present woes and recent setbacks. If I could have believed I could stay like that, in that kitchen, with a fantastic meal all prepared for one of the most beautiful women I'd ever laid eyes on – well, I would have been a happy man.

I think I probably nodded off for when I woke from my drowsy state I should be getting on the with actual cooking of what I had prepared earlier. I was in the process of heating up the oven and boiling pans of water when Luigi himself arrived in the kitchen, evidently newly returned from his meeting.

He gave a sigh of pleasure when he saw the array of dishes that were waiting to go into the oven. He positively clapped his hands with delight when he spotted the carefully presented first course that was already waiting on one of the polished granite surfaces.

'Ah, what marvels!' he exclaimed. 'My dear Tremayne, I believe this kitchen has never witnessed such beautiful dishes in all its five hundred years! This will be a splendid evening indeed!'

I beamed at him. 'I certainly hope so. It is the least I can do for two such lovely friends.'

Luigi blinked at me and I am not sure that I didn't see the glint of a tear in his eye, but then he gave me a warm embrace before breaking off and wagging a finger at me.

'This looks so good,' he told me in a conspiratorial manner, 'that it deserves the finest wine I have in the house. I have a very special vintage that I shall fetch immediately. When shall we be ready to eat?'

'About three-quarters of an hour?'

'Excellent.'

He disappeared upstairs and I got on with my work, humming with happiness.

When I finally went upstairs with some spectacular hors d'oeuvres on a silver tray I found Luigi and Teresa waiting for me at the door to the dining-room. Both had dressed for dinner, Luigi in a white dinner jacket and red bow-tie and Teresa in a dazzling gold dress with cleavage open to her waist. I nearly dropped the tray, such was the effect upon me. I also felt seriously underdressed in blazer and cravat.

We went into the dining-room together and I laid the tray on the table, then placed the dishes reverently before Teresa and then Luigi, who gasped with admiration.

'What a beautiful thing! Tremayne, you are a great artist!'

'Oh, I don't know about that...'

Teresa gave me one of her cool half-smiles and I settled in my own place, hoping I wasn't blushing with schoolboy pleasure.

Their reaction to the opening course was all I could have hoped for. Luigi rolled his eyes as he tasted his first forkful and no one said anything for a good minute as we surrendered ourselves to the experience. Then Luigi was up, napkin still tucked into his collar, congratulating me and at the same time heading for an open bottle of wine on the sideboard.

'This food is so magnificent I had quite forgotten to pour the wine!' he exclaimed.

He filled our exquisite Venetian glasses to the half-way mark and bid us try it. He hadn't been joking when he had promised me something special. The wine he had produced for us was possibly the best I have ever tasted. I didn't ask him what he had paid for it, because I just knew from the quality of it that the sum would have made my eyes water. Especially as we polished off two bottles of the divine stuff before we rose from the table a couple of hours later.

Course followed course to equal rapture from Luigi. Teresa, who never, it seemed, said more than she deemed necessary, honoured me with admiring looks that spoke volumes and made me squeal to myself in silent exultation. I try not to brag about my culinary skills and to let the food do the talking, but I have to admit that when I really put my mind to it I even impress myself sometimes.

It was a delight to serve up such fine fare, made with quality ingredients sourced locally, to such warm enthusiasm in such magnificent, historical surroundings. After all the hounding and harassment involved over the past few years in cooking for the entertainment of countless unseen television audiences (an unholy rabble for the most part as far as I could make out) it did my soul good to be here, rediscovering what cookery should be all about. I'd recommend some of my fellow telly chefs to follow my example and get back in touch with real cookery, for real people in real places, like I was doing. Cooking for fellow celebs in fake kitchens doesn't count. I hope you're listening, Ainsley.

I had prepared some six courses in all, each one complementing the previous one and guiding the diner up a new avenue of taste sensation. They were all familiar dishes to me, as I've already said, so I could not share in the sense of novelty the others were experiencing, but my heart swelled to see how much they were enjoying it all.

After the last course Luigi sighed with deep satisfaction before standing up and pulling his wife's chair back for her to rise. He then ushered us both into the living-room, where a small fire crackled in the massive hearth. It was entirely unnecessary in the comfortable warmth of the Venetian evening, but it did add considerably to the intimacy of the atmosphere that enveloped us like a warm blanket as we settled into the armchairs in front of it.

Luigi handed Teresa and me balloon glasses containing a good measure of excellent brandy and then poured himself one too and sat down.

'I cannot remember when I had a meal the equal of that one, my dear Tremayne,' he told me after he had taken a first sip. 'You have demonstrated your mastery of your art beyond all our expectations. I am sure I speak for both of us when I thank you from the bottom of my heart.'

I turned to Teresa. 'I do hope you enjoyed it. I wasn't sure the tomatoes I bought at the market were quite as good as they might have been, but in the end I think they tasted pretty good.'

'They were perfect,' she replied, looking steadily at me over her brandy, 'as I am sure you know.'

She raised her glass to me and we all drank together.

Teresa picked up her evening bag as the sound of a mobile ring tone emanated from it. She extracted the phone and looked at the screen.

'Please excuse me,' she said, getting up. 'I must take this call. It is from our daughter.'

She got up and walked to the far end of the room, where she stood elegantly framed before a mirror and began a conversation in subdued and rapid Italian. I reluctantly forced myself to stop looking at her and turned to her husband.

'How many children do you have?' I inquired of Luigi.

'Just one daughter. She is nearly grown up now and of course she wants to live her own life. But sometimes it worries me that she does not act responsibly.' He frowned. 'Children behaved with more respect for their parents when I was young.'

'I suppose each new generation of parents thinks the same thing.'

Luigi glanced at me severely. 'Maybe in England, but it is not the same here in Italy. Children should respect their parents for their wisdom and experience.'

'I'm sure she does really.'

Luigi shrugged. 'Perhaps you are right. But it is not obvious to me sometimes.'

'Being a parent isn't always easy, I suppose.'

Luigi sighed. 'Not always easy, no. Often in the school holidays we don't see her for days at a time. I insist that she telephones us regularly so we know she is all right, but even that is too much trouble for her sometimes it seems.'

Teresa finished her call and came back to join us before I could say anything more.

'What did she have to say?' asked Luigi.

'She has gone to stay with a friend in Rimini for the rest of the week.'

'Rimini? Who does she know in Rimini?'

'A schoolfriend. They are a good family. I think we met them once.'

Luigi grunted. 'We are not seeing much of her this holiday. She is always visiting some friend or other.'

Teresa sat down, seemingly unconcerned. 'She's growing up and wants to make her own choices. It's natural.'

'Many fathers would be angry at her lack of consideration for her own family.'

Teresa shot a swift look at her husband. 'If you get angry with her it will only make her more determined to defy you. You know that.'

Luigi pulled a face. 'I fear that is true. Like all young people, she can be wilful, but I suppose I have no choice but to forgive her however angry she makes me.'

'I have no children myself,' I informed him, 'but I cannot imagine you staying angry with anyone for very long.'

Luigi laughed. 'I think you are making me a compliment, for which I thank you. But listen,' he added, suddenly earnest in his manner and leaning forwards towards me, 'I wish to say something to you, to ask you a very great favour.'

'Oh? What is it?'

'It is on behalf of both of us.' Luigi glanced at his wife, then back at me. 'As I mentioned earlier, we rely upon local catering agencies to supply us with kitchen staff, and they often let us down quite badly. Your cooking here tonight has reminded us how much we need to change the situation. Now, I know you have a wonderful international television career to return to in due course, and we cannot hope to talk you out of that career, but – if you are willing – we would consider it a huge kindness if you would consider cooking for us for a period of, let us say, three weeks or so. I have a number of very important business meetings coming up here and in other places and it would be a great comfort to come home to meals like the one you just prepared for us – though perhaps not quite so many courses.' He laughed and patted his belly. 'I have my figure to think of, you understand.'

'You would like me to cook for you?' I responded, trying to take in what was being proposed.

'Of course, we will make it worth your while.'

He went on to mention a sum that was so large I had to ask him to repeat it, which he did. He had my whole attention now.

Luigi's tone became more confidential. 'You hinted that you may be taking a break from television in Britain... well, I have contacts high up in the Italian media and I am sure, quite certain in fact, that they would be very happy to give you your own series in this country. The company with which I have connections often syndicates its programmes throughout Europe and sometimes many other countries around the world as well. I imagine there would be much money to be made out of it for you.'

I refrained from licking my lips. 'Just so I understand,' I repeated, 'you'd like me to cook for you for a few weeks, for which you'll pay me the sum you mentioned and arrange a series with an Italian television company. Have I got that straight?

'Yes, indeed.' Luigi looked anxiously across at his wife then back at me. 'Is it something you would at least consider?'

I put my brandy glass down carefully on the side-table at my elbow. It was a beautiful little piece, with inlaid marquetry, that was probably two or three hundred years old and properly belonged in a museum of fine art. 'Yes, I think I could definitely consider it. In fact...' I stood up and with a dramatic gesture held out my hand to my new friend, who would now become my patron too, '...in fact, I'm happy to accept your offer here and now!'

A huge smile spread across Luigi's face. 'Really? You will agree to cook for us? Really?'

'I certainly will.'

Luigi grasped my hand and shook it eagerly. 'That is tremendous news! Do you hear that, my love? Tremayne is going to look after our kitchen for us!'

Teresa nodded. 'That is very good news. This latest cook the agency sent us was one of the worst we've ever had.' She looked almost as pleased as her husband did.

We all laughed and drank a toast to our new relationship. At the back of my mind a miniature version of me was doing a spiteful little clog-dance. A tidy sum of cash would shortly be wending its welcome way to my bank balance and I would be gaining a pan-European – nay, worldwide – audience to boot. That would be one in the eye for Barry and the BBC!

We carried on for another hour or so talking about their favourite dishes and some of the meals I had in mind to prepare for them. Eventually, however, the brandy bottle ran dry and I decided the time had come for me to make my excuses. It would be tactful, I felt, not to overstay my welcome on this momentous evening.

I started to lever myself out of my chair. 'It's been a most delightful evening. Truly delightful and surprising as well, in the nicest possible way. But I suppose I really ought to leave you in peace and be on my way back to my hotel.'

Luigi spread his hands out wide. 'But there is no need, my dear Tremayne. Your bags are already here.'

'Sorry?'

Luigi looked apologetic. 'I told Bruno to bring them here in the boat. Forgive me, but I was so confident you would find our offer irresistible – and we just couldn't bear to see you go, could we, my love?'

Teresa smiled coolly in agreement.

'Well, that's – that's terribly kind of you,' I stammered, 'but what about my hotel bill?'

'Oh, that is all settled,' Luigi answered. 'All your things have been brought here and you will find everything laid out in your room, waiting for you. Now, please tell us you will stay.'

I looked at them both in turn, at these two new friends who were fast becoming as dear to me as any friends of mine had ever been (certainly more than Barry Cullis, rot him). It had been most thoughtful of them to think ahead and have my things brought over to save me the trouble of going back and forth. I saw the twinkle in Luigi's eye at the thought of our future collaboration, and then the depths of secret longing (unless it just the brandy making me imagine it) in Teresa's.

'Yes,' I told them in a voice breaking with emotion, 'I'll stay.'

Eating In

I slept extremely well that night. The great food, the superlative wine and the excellent brandy, combined with contentment concerning my immediate prospects, soothed me and granted me a solid ten hours of blessed oblivion, which I sorely needed after the excesses of the previous couple of days. My brief, incidentally, did not extend to preparing breakfast, which my hosts were happy to get for themselves, so I did not hurry to get up.

Instead I sprawled on the pillows and congratulated myself on the recent turn of events. After two days of alcohol-fuelled despair I seemed to have landed squarely on my feet, with a new international television career opening up before me, good friends and patrons here in Venice, and the delectable Teresa Vanni to flirt with whenever I got the urge (which, I predicted, would be every time she made an appearance when her husband wasn't about). And I had achieved it all without the slightest help from Barry Cullis. If the little toad thought he was getting a percentage of any earnings I made from this new state of affairs he had another think coming. Of course, he'd be having kittens at not having the faintest notion where I'd got to, but as far as I was concerned he could gather as many feline friends as he liked. As far as I was concerned, he could open a cats' home.

My well-appointed room – a self-contained apartment really, with bathroom and other facilities – was at the back of the house. It commanded a broad view, visible from the bed, that took in a canal and the superb baroque frontage of one of Venice's many splendid churches. In fact it was the tinkling of the bells of that church that had finally roused me from my restorative slumber. I stretched luxuriously and wondered idly whereabouts in

Italy the TV companies might have their studios. I wouldn't mind at all if they happened to be in Venice.

Neither Luigi nor Teresa seemed to be about when I finally emerged from my room so, after a bit more exploring of the magnificent old building, I descended to the ground floor and set about tidying and rearranging things in the kitchen until everything was where I liked it in what I now felt entitled to consider my new (if temporary) fiefdom. My old wok was given pride of place beside the stupendous cooking range and had never looked more at home anywhere.

I discovered during my wanderings that there were more apartments in an annexe that adjoined the rear of the house. These were apparently occupied by Bruno, the boatman, and a couple of other men whom I took to be caretakers or odd-job men or something of the kind. As they had their own facilities they only came into the main part of the palazzo when summoned, so I could effectively ignore their presence.

I planned a few meals for the days ahead, all things that would allow me to show off my culinary skills to my hosts, and then made a long shopping list of things I would need. That done, I set about preparing a light lunch for anyone who might turn up for it.

In the event it was just me and Teresa, who had been out clothes shopping, it transpired. Luigi, she told me, was at one of his innumerable business gatherings and wouldn't be back for lunch. That suited me just fine, as you can imagine. I set lunch out for us both on the balcony overlooking the Grand Canal and we sat there in the warm sunshine, contemplating the busy scene before us.

Teresa listened in silence while I brought her up to date with my suggestions for dishes she and her husband might enjoy in the coming days. After a bit more chitchat from me, largely food-based, I set about eliciting more information from her. Most women, I find, enjoy talking about themselves, the shallow articles, and that always helps to win them over. Teresa Vanni, however, proved a hard nut to crack in that respect. Though she answered all my enquiries with polite enough responses, I ended up feeling at the end of it all that I knew no more about her than when we started. It wasn't that she was evasive exactly, just very, very private.

Teresa's manners were impeccable and the air of serene detachment that she maintained was both admirable and infuriating. She could have taught our royals a thing or two. She gave an impression of friendly but remote unapproachability, typically responding to even my wittiest and most insightful comments with no more than a nod or a half-smile on her beautiful lips. Her responses were those of some all-knowing Grecian goddess, who found the follies of mankind a source of sardonic amusement.

Her hands and fingernails were perfectly manicured and even her severest critic (if there was such a beast) would have had to acknowledge that she knew how to present herself to the very best advantage. If she had a grown-up daughter she would have to be in her late thirties herself, if not considerably more, but you'd never have guessed it. You'd probably have said late twenties or early thirties at the very most. Her figure, as previously noted, was enough to take your breath away and she knew how to beguile the observer with a glimpse of flesh here and there without the least trace of immodesty. I told myself that she must be a considerable asset to Luigi when it came to entertaining business associates, as they must sometimes do, and an even more considerable comfort to him when he came home and the door was shut to the lamenting world outside. He was a lucky man indeed.

After coffee Teresa thanked me and said she was going to spend the afternoon reading, which was clearly a passion for her. I took that to mean she intended to spend the afternoon alone, which was fair enough as it was her house – even if it did happen to contain me, who would have been more than happy to spend a few hours sharing her company. But no matter. It was a lost opportunity, but perhaps it was written in the stars that I'd never get beyond mild flirtation with her. She clearly wasn't interested in what I'd got to offer. Hard to believe, but it does happen sometimes, even to me.

Anyway, I had a harvest of ingredients to gather in, so I spent an absorbing afternoon going hither and thither looking for the very best provisions the city had to offer. I soon gathered a veritable hoard of goodies that I looked forward to transforming into succulence of one variety or another, even if the creative process had lost some of the thrill it used to have.

In the course of my harvesting I wandered somewhat further afield than I had intended and suddenly realised my route was about to take me immediately past the restaurant where I had had the unfortunate altercation from which Luigi had rescued me a couple of days previously. I stopped in the middle of the street, not twenty yards away, and wondered what to do.

If I tried to find another route past the restaurant I would probably have to go quite a long way back along the path I had just taken and, in the process, bearing in mind my notorious sense of direction, risked getting hopelessly lost in the maze of alleys.

I hesitated, unsure quite what to do for the best.

Then I had a brainwave, I remembered I had just passed one of Venice's ubiquitous mobile souvenir stalls, which had been loaded high with cheap carnival masks to flog to visitors – possibly the very one I had seen being wheeled past the restaurant window on that fateful night. All I had to do was nip back, buy myself a mask, and no one would know who I was when I walked past the restaurant. Even though it was long past the carnival season, lots of tourists bought masks and wore them as they wandered the streets and canals.

I retraced my steps to the stall, selected a rather dramatic mask in the form of a death's head skull, and put it on. Thus disguised I resumed my route past the restaurant without fear of being identified.

When I drew level with the restaurant itself I noticed that the place seemed to be shut up, with no one sitting at the tables inside. A notice on the window caught my attention and I paused. It was a picture of the chef I had had the unfortunate contretemps with, only this time he was smiling and not looking at all belligerent. The scrawl underneath informed disappointed customers that the chef was missing and until he was found or replaced the establishment would remain closed for business.

I wasn't sure what to make of this. Before I could cogitate at length upon the matter, however, someone appeared on the other side of the window and looked out at me. I recognised him at once as the manager of the restaurant. The man's mouth dropped open in what appeared to be terror when he caught sight of me. He staggered away from the window, knocking over a chair, and disappeared into the shadows behind him.

I was nonplussed. Then I realised it must have been the mask I was wearing. I looked at my reflection in the glass. Well, I suppose it could be off-putting to look up and see death staring at you through your front window. Mind you, such masks were ten a euro in Venice at any time of the year, so it seemed a little odd that he should be so alarmed at the sight of one. Then it occurred to me that perhaps my disguise was not all it could have been: I was wearing the same blazer and trousers I had worn that night when I had been the innocent cause of so much unpleasantness. Could that be why he was so perturbed? I decided it was best not to linger to find out and continued on my way, determined to put the whole distasteful business out of my mind. Once I had reached a safe distance from the restaurant I took off the mask and discarded it on the parapet of a bridge for some tourist or other to acquire as a souvenir.

Luigi turned up in time for dinner, which was on a more modest scale than the previous evening, but was nonetheless equally well received. He was, however, in a less loquacious mood than before and I speculated that he had had a less that satisfactory day at the office. I didn't like to enquire if anything was wrong, and Teresa didn't either, but he seemed in a better mood after he had eaten and we enjoyed a chat round the fire after the meal just as before.

Again I tried, subtly, to get more out of Teresa but once again without much success. I concluded that she was just one of those people who prefer to keep the conversation on lighter topics that skirt round touchy issues. She didn't seem at all keen to tell me about her origins or childhood, though my queries were innocent enough. She was, however, happy enough to tell me stories of Venice's history and to discuss its culture, its problems, its climate... I didn't much mind what she talked about, to tell the truth, as it was reward enough just to sit next to her and admire her beauty. Naturally, with Luigi present, I avoided giving any signal that I was so enchanted by her, but it was difficult sometimes to pay attention to what she was saying when she looked as ravishing as she did.

Before I knew it the fire had died down and Luigi was yawning. He thanked me for the meal and we all said good night. As I tidied the kitchen I was philosophical about my situation: if they were happy to keep things at a friendly but not overly intimate level I would just have to be happy with that too.

So life in the palazzo continued for the next couple of days, with me sleeping in as long as I liked, then happily going out to buy ingredients and preparing meals in the marvellous kitchen. I enjoyed light lunches in the company of the fabulous Teresa, and glowed in the Vannis' combined approval after dinner in the evening, which always ended with some pleasant if inconsequential chat before the fire. It was all very relaxing and I felt a contentment growing in me that I had not felt for many years.

I might have known it would not last.

Luigi was a remarkably busy man and he was always off to some meeting or other. When he was in the house he was frequently interrupted by the chirruping of his mobile, which often necessitated him having to go out again, always chaperoned by Bruno and sometimes the other denizens of the annexe. I still wasn't sure what their role was, but as it didn't affect me I saw no reason why I should bother my head with it. They were evidently very loyal to Luigi Vanni, however, and were at his beck and call day and night. I supposed Luigi made it well worth their while to be so attentive, as he did for me by feeding hearty amounts of cash regularly into my bank account, as I discovered when I checked it.

Once or twice people arrived at the palazzo to discuss business with Luigi. They never stayed to eat, however, so that was no concern of mine. Some of them struck me as rather stolid, brawny types who didn't fit the conventional business mould to my mind, but they were all unfailingly polite and courteous if we met on the stairs, and there's no judging by appearances after all.

But, as I say, the idyll that I was just getting used to was destined to come to an end, as I discovered one evening, after Luigi had returned from his day's business who knows where. He had a serious expression on his face at dinner, I noticed, and hardly paid his evening repast the attention it properly deserved.

I was in the kitchen tidying up after we'd all eaten when he appeared in the doorway.

'My dear Tremayne,' he began, 'I must apologise if I seemed distracted tonight. The food was superb, incidentally, and I should have told you so before now.'

'Not at all, Luigi,' I assured him. 'I could see you had a lot on your mind. Is business going well?'

Luigi shrugged. 'Oh yes, but there are pressing matters that I must attend to, so I am afraid we must close up the house for the time being and go to Rome.'

'Rome?'

'Yes. I have a place near the Colosseum where I often hold meetings with business associates. There is a big deal that requires my personal attention there.'

'Do you want me to come to Rome with you?'

He looked at me with a pleading expression. 'Do you mind? I believe I told you that my business means we have to move a lot.'

'No, of course not. Just tell me when to pack my bag and I'll be happy to tag along.'

Luigi clapped me on both shoulders. 'Thank you, my friend. I am very grateful. With all this going on it will be a relief to know that we shall at least be well fed.'

'It's no trouble. It's a long time since I was in Rome, so it will be good to see the city again. But you'll be sorry to leave your beautiful home here, I dare say.'

Luigi smiled. 'Oh, this isn't my real home. This is – what do you call it in English – a holiday house? Yes, a holiday house. I have several such places.'

'Ah, I see.'

Well, if he called this a holiday house, who was I to argue? Where I came from a holiday house was usually a little wooden chalet or a shared apartment, not a huge palazzo on the Grand Canal. But, as the wise man said, the rich live in a different country to the rest of us. He was full of surprises, our Luigi.

'I have told Teresa that I will fly to Rome early tomorrow morning with my staff,' he continued. 'However, she says she would prefer to drive so I propose you come down with her. It's a six or seven hour drive, depending upon the traffic. Would you like that, or would you prefer to come with me on the plane?'

That didn't take much thinking about.

'I'd love to go by car, given the choice. A drive through your beautiful Italian countryside would be a treat.'

Luigi nodded. 'That's settled then. I'll tell Teresa. She is on the phone to our daughter at the moment so that she will know where we are. I have told her I expect her to join us in Rome. Whether she will or not, who can say?'

Then he was gone. I looked rather forlornly around the kitchen, of which I had become very fond in such a short time. I would miss it. I hoped it would miss me.

But tomorrow I would have the company of the lovely Teresa Vanni all to myself for a whole six or seven hours – and that was sufficient compensation for anyone.

I turned out the lights.

Meals on Wheels

I heard Luigi and his staff leaving the palazzo around six in the morning and turned over and went back to sleep. When I woke up once more it was past nine and I thought I had better get up and grab some breakfast before Teresa announced it was time to leave for Rome. She joined me in the kitchen shortly after I got there and accepted some coffee and pastries.

'The car is kept on the mainland,' she told me when I asked her (not unreasonably since there are next to no roads within Venice itself) where the car was. 'We shall have to take a water taxi since Bruno has gone on the plane with my husband and the others.'

Half an hour later we convened in the front porch, me with my single sturdy wheeled suitcase, somewhat battered after many years of travel around the globe, and she with a tiny leather travelling bag with Ralph Lauren written on it in gold. She certainly believed in travelling light, but then in all likelihood she had a complete wardrobe and set of belongings waiting for her in Rome. I was beginning to understand the kind of lives these Vannis led, you see.

Teresa locked the door behind us, slipped her sunglasses down over her eyes, and then stepped aboard the water taxi that was waiting for us. I lugged my old bag in behind her and clambered in after her, rather less elegantly than she had.

As always it was a very pleasant ride up the Grand Canal and across the water to the mainland. I was enjoying it, though it was hard to make out exactly what Teresa was making of it as her glasses made it impossible to see her eyes at all. I wondered if we would be coming back to Venice after our stint in Rome, but she probably didn't know the answer herself so I didn't ask.

A short walk from the jetty where the water taxi left us brought us to a row of garages next to an international hotel. Teresa took out a set of keys and pressed the electronic button on the fob. At once one of the doors in front of us stirred into life and rose up with a whispering, whirring noise to reveal our transport for the day.

I should have known it wouldn't be a Ford Anglia. Parked in the shade of the immaculate garage, spotless and gleaming, was a sleek red two-seater sports car. I'm not a car buff myself, but even I could tell this was something special. I read the badge on the front of the bonnet.

'Dino. I don't believe I've heard of them.'

Teresa cast me a withering look. 'It's a Ferrari,' she told me.

'Well, I hope there'll be room for our bags,' I said, dubiously looking for the boot.

We managed to stow the luggage away, though it was a tight fit, and then I headed for the passenger side. I don't drive, so I wasn't about to offer to take the wheel of this svelte miracle of Italian engineering. It was clear, in any case, that Teresa had no intention of inviting me to drive as she was already lowering herself into the driver's seat.

It was surprisingly roomy inside the car but unnerving being so close to the ground. I fastened my seat belt as Teresa turned the key and the engine burst into life with a powerful roar. We eased out of the garage and the door slid closed automatically behind us. Teresa steered the car away from the garages and towards the main road, where a large traffic sign listed a number of major Italian cities, among them Rome. With a huge growl and a squeal of tyres we erupted onto the highway.

Now, being a non-driver, I am well used to being a

passenger while others drive. Some drivers scare me more than others. Somehow Teresa did not scare me at all, though God knows she drove about three times as fast as anyone I had ever been driven by before. I thought at first that maybe it was just because we were so low to the road, which tends to accentuate the impression of speed, but when I sneaked a look at the speedometer I was startled to see just how fast we really were going.

I'm normally a fairly nervous passenger, yet with Teresa at the wheel I felt strangely comfortable, though it was some time before I relaxed my steely hold on the inner door handle. Her serene composure and air of complete confidence in herself convinced me that I would be entirely safe with her at the wheel, even as we executed overtaking passes that with other drivers would have had me screaming and squeezing my eyes shut.

I didn't venture to make any comment to her until we were well beyond the urban sprawl of greater mainland Venice, anxious not to distract her from the task in hand, but once we were on the motorway clear of heavy traffic and feeling reassured by her competence at the wheel I finally dared to speak up.

'This is a magnificent car. I like the leatherwork. Is Luigi a Ferrari enthusiast?'

Teresa kept her eyes on the road. 'He has shares in the company.'

She didn't offer anything more so I took the hint and settled into my seat to watch the Italian countryside slip by at dazzling speed. Honestly, I complained to myself, it was a bit much risking my life at this velocity in order, presumably, to cut to a minimum the time she would spend apart from her beloved Luigi. I mean, I liked Luigi well enough, but it was a trifle hurtful to the feelings for my compensatory companionship on the journey to be apparently so little valued.

We drove south-west for a good stretch, flashing past Padua and Ferrara and reaching Bologna in under an hour and a half. They hadn't even had time to get the flags out to welcome our arrival. I thought Bologna would be a good place to pause for lunch, but Teresa showed no sign of turning off the main road and we continued to rocket southwards through Emilia-Romagna. About twenty-five miles southwest of Bologna, however, she caught me unawares when she slowed slightly and slipped into the slow lane, which we hadn't visited since setting out – perhaps, I speculated, she fancied a change of scenery. She then took the slip road and in seconds we were heading off at right angles to the motorway, entering a very rural-looking area of sleepy sun-baked villages and scattered farmsteads.

I glanced at the fuel gauge, thinking maybe we were running short of petrol, but it looked to me that the tank was still pretty much full so it couldn't be that. I looked questioningly at Teresa but she studiously avoided my gaze and said nothing to explain where we were going. Maybe she needed a toilet break, or perhaps she had decided to treat me to the scenic route.

It certainly was scenic too. As this is billed as a travel book as well as a record of my culinary adventures, it would be quite wrong of me not to say a word or three about the landscape we drove through that sunny Italian morning.

What can I possibly say to do the verdant vistas through which we passed anything approaching sufficient justice? Beneath immense blue skies the traveller in that part of the world dips and soars through valleys and hills, through lush woodland and close-cropped green fields grazed by cows, goats and other edible livestock. The terracotta tiles of village rooftops cluster round ancient campaniles and lend an air of history and rustic style to the view. And there are many more delights to surprise and delight, like little stone bridges, sloping vineyards studded with cypress trees, romantic castles, trickling streams, roaring waterfalls and rolling fields of crops.

Here one can easily imagine Virgil licking the point of his stylus and giving a contented purr before putting poem to parchment, or Dante kicking off his slippers and throwing himself full-length in the long grass, hands behind his head, to savour the view before him. How I wish I'd paid more heed in my Latin lessons all those years ago so I could delight you further with these pithy, well-informed historical insights...

But enough of the purple prose. I'll leave your imagination to furnish you with the details I haven't already listed. My more immediate concern was where the hell we were going in this undeniably beautiful setting. I'd been told the journey to Rome would take six or seven hours, but that presumably did not take into account lengthy diversions like this one was promising to be.

The road we were travelling along had got steadily narrower and gave the distinct impression it had no intention of ending up at any particular place on the map. It was also unlikely country for a car like ours and as the potholes grew bigger and more frequent I began to wonder if Teresa had thought she knew a shortcut but had missed a turn somewhere so we were now lost. Well, it wasn't much use her turning to me for advice. I've already explained how hopeless I am concerning matters of direction.

I wasn't quite ready to give up all hope in my driver's knowledge of her whereabouts, however. It was lunchtime, after all, and maybe she knew of a cosy little trattoria tucked away in the hills that she wanted to take me to. It was a good while since breakfast and my stomach was rumbling. I pictured the kind of place I hoped she had in mind. It would be a whitewashed villa picturesquely located high on a slope with a grand view over the vineyards and valleys. The building itself would be clad in flowering greenery and there would be a beaming moustachioed host with a round belly and hearty laugh bidding us welcome. Everything would promise fine local cuisine and delicious wine made with grapes grown within a stone's throw of our table.

It was a surprise, then, when Teresa finally pulled up outside a modest and rather dilapidated cottage on the outskirts of an equally dilapidated hamlet. I gazed at it through narrow eyes. It didn't appear to be an eatery of any kind. No view to speak of, no flowering greenery up the walls, no beaming moustachioed host. We climbed out of the car, me groaning as I stretched my back after so long folded up in the leather seat.

Teresa turned to me and then indicated the house before us. 'I shall introduce you to my grandmother.'

She took off her sunglasses and started up the flight of steps to the front door. I followed, somewhat bewildered.

Her grandmother? Then I began to twig what was going on. So this, as likely as not, was where Teresa originally hailed from. You would never guessed it. I had thought from her air of polished refinement that she was a product of Milan or one of the other fashionable northern Italian cities, but not a bit of it. I glanced about and began to understand why she hadn't wanted to flout her origins when I had asked about them back in Venice. She was just a plain little country girl by birth.

Teresa climbed the flight of stone steps leading to the front door, which looked like it hadn't seen a lick of paint since around the end of the nineteenth century, and knocked. Apart from a couple of ancient rose bushes the patch of garden below us was filled with wild flowers and weeds. Pink shutters kept the sun out of the upper rooms, although one pair of them was open on the lower floor.

The door creaked open just as Teresa was about to knock again and a wizened old woman in what I'd estimate to be her late eighties peered suspiciously out at us. Then she recognised Teresa and embraced her with a burst of high-pitched, voluble Italian that I couldn't follow. Finally releasing her, she opened the door wide and ushered us inside with squeals of pleasure.

It was hard to imagine this diminutive, button-eyed little Italian crone could have contributed some of the genes that went to create the stupendous beauty that was Teresa Vanni, but there was a brightness in the eye and a certain quality in her posture that felt faintly familiar. Her hair, though now white, was soft and abundant and I could easily imagine it the lustrous black that adorned Teresa's head.

Unfortunately for me, it quickly transpired that the old lady didn't speak a word of English. Instead she jabbered away so fast in Italian that I struggled to pick up more than the odd phrase or two. I think I detected a strong regional accent, which didn't help matters. She was obviously very surprised and pleased to see her grand-daughter, so this was clearly an impulse visit we were making. When the old woman finally managed to tear her attention away from Teresa and give me a closer inspection things became even more confusing. I soon realised, from her frequent use of the name Luigi, that she thought I was Teresa's husband. Teresa's attempts to correct her in this appeared to have no effect because she still kept adding Luigi to the end of her sentences when addressing me. I guessed from this that Granny and Luigi hadn't met very often, or at least not recently, as Luigi and I were not exactly similar in build and appearance (I hoped!). Teresa gave up trying to explain who I really was and I resolved to let the old lady continue in her misapprehension if that was what she wanted.

After five minutes of rapid Italian exchanges between the two relatives, of which I picked up very little, Teresa broke off as she spotted what her grandmother had laid on the rickety wooden table in her sitting-room. The old lady was evidently about to have lunch when we arrived, for there was a small sideplate with some bread and cheese and a couple of olives on it. Teresa's face said it all. She addressed her grandmother in despairing, admonishing tones and it wasn't difficult to imagine what she saying. Do you call that lunch, Granny? But it isn't enough to keep a bird alive. You know you should look after yourself at your age and it is important that you feed yourself properly.

And so it would have continued if I hadn't held up a hand, silencing Teresa in mid-flow, and offered to cook something for everyone.

Teresa looked at me for a long moment, for just about the first time that day. I repeated the offer so she, evidently lost for words, led me into the humble kitchen at the back of the cottage. Granny followed us, obviously wondering where we were going and why.

Having established that it was indeed a kitchen I was in, and not just an empty storeroom, I ordered Teresa and her grandmother out. Well, a chef needs his own space to work his magic in. The two of them backed out reluctantly and I closed the door on them, leaving them to catch up on each other's news in the front room.

There was precious little in the way of foodstuffs visible on the surfaces and it didn't take long to go through the cupboards to see what else there might be to work with. I heaped what I had assembled on the sideboard and rubbed my chin. I felt like I was on that ghastly programme Ainsley does where celebs are challenged to make something magnificent with a couple of potatoes and a packet of blancmange or a similarly limited choice of ingredients. There must be more than this, I told myself. I looked at the shelf above the little window. At least I had a good range of herbs and spices to help me on my way. Then I happened to look up and spotted the kitchen garden at the back of the building. I found the back door and climbed down the steps for a quick rummage. There were all kinds of things growing out there in the neglected plot and by the time I returned I had more than enough to get me going in the right direction.

It was an odd assortment of fruit and vegetables that I had gathered together, but I racked my memory and eventually came up with a recipe that I had not cooked for years, but which seemed ideal for the occasion – a simple enough concoction that would take the tomatoes I had found and Granny's bit of cheese as its starting point. The olives and the herbs I had found would have their role too. You'll find the recipe along with many others in the Mediterranean cookery book I expect to be commissioned to write in the near future.

I began to warm to the task, realising that I had all the makings of a really very appetising and nourishing lunch in front of me. You see, Ainsley, all it needs is a little imagination and you're away. Can't think why he hasn't had me on his programme yet. Perhaps he's afraid I'll show him up.

I got to work and soon the room was filled with delicious aromas. It didn't take long to get everything prepared. Like most Italian kitchens, that of Teresa's granny had a small but very serviceable set of utensils and old pans – no gadgets, but everything ideally suited to its allotted task. The knives were sharp, the spoons were deep, and the pans were seasoned from many years of trusty use. Granny's cooking range was old-fashioned but easy to control and within half an hour I had a beautiful lunch ready, with the cheese bubbling and lightly browned on top of a truly mouth-watering dish. This was cooking as it should be! My heart rejoiced at the first stirrings of enjoyment in the art of cooking that I had felt since I don't know when.

I carried everything through to the other room, where Granny greeted her Luigi with more squeaks of surprise and excitement. I laid the food on the table, while Teresa goggled a bit then fetched plates and cutlery and some home-made lemonade that she managed to find from somewhere. We sat Granny down, still jabbering away in incomprehensible Italian and clapping her hands with delight, and then we took chairs opposite each other and we all tucked in.

Granny's face as she ate was a picture to behold. You'd think she hadn't tasted cooked food for months on end, and I suppose maybe she hadn't. It brought a lump to my throat and even Teresa looked like she was moved. Well, she dabbed at her eye once or twice with a hankie so she was either moved or she had a fly stuck in there.

When Granny accepted a second helping Teresa stared at her in mute astonishment. It made me think. If Jamie could get such priceless publicity out of dollying up school dinners, perhaps I could do the same with old folks' homes. It wouldn't be a bad idea to run past Barry when, and if, I ever saw him again.

We polished off our repast with some fruit and coffee, then the three of us gathered in the kitchen to do the washing-up. Granny chattered away without pausing throughout the whole procedure and though she was still carrying on at about ninety miles an hour I got the gist of some of what she was saying – that Luigi was a marvel in the kitchen; that she had no idea he could cook like this; that Teresa was a lucky girl indeed to have a miracle worker like me about the place. Etcetera, etcetera.

We were all getting along famously and I was glowing in all the adulation when we were interrupted by a knock at the front door.

Granny bustled off to answer it.

'She's quite a character, your grandmother,' I confided in Teresa as she handed me a plate to dry. 'I take it your grandfather is no longer living?'

Teresa shook her head, but I could see she wasn't listening to me very hard. Instead she was giving the lion's share of her attention to the sound of the voices coming from the other room. She looked tense and serious. I stopped talking and listened too, tea towel still in hand. I could hear Granny jabbering away in her usual style, but with a pleading note in her voice this time, and then another voice, that of a somewhat younger woman I surmised.

Teresa wiped her hands on a towel and then smoothed down her skirt before glancing swiftly at me and then walking out of the kitchen towards the front room. I put away the tea towel and followed, not quite sure what to expect.

I found Teresa standing before a woman in her sixties – rather a striking woman with long, grey-streaked black hair and a face that I could tell had once been very good-looking, though now lined and tanned by years of sun. Granny stood between them and the resemblance between the three women was unmistakable. I hardly needed to hear Teresa say 'madre' in a subdued undertone to know beyond doubt who this must be.

Mother didn't look quite as delighted to see Teresa as Granny had been. Instead she stared at her daughter with narrowed eyes and pursed lips. She didn't look pleased at all and from her frosty expression I sensed that it was a very awkward situation I had walked into. Call me psychic if you like, but I could just tell.

I don't know what it is about women. We men have our ups and downs of course, but once we've done a bit of shouting and thrown a punch or two we consider the matter closed and everyone moves on. At least, that's how life is conducted in most commercial kitchens. No such frank exchanges were going to clear the air here, however.

Mother greeted Daughter with icy formality. Daughter greeted Mother with the same, only quieter. Mother enquired after Daughter's health. Daughter said she was fine and asked after Mother's health. Mother said she was fine too. Granny said something unintelligible but still in a pleading tone, probably something like 'Please, girls, let's all try to keep our tempers here' or 'I want a good clean fight with no kicking, spitting or gouging'. Whatever it was, the other two woman showed no sign of having heard it.

Daughter informed Mother that she was looking well. Mother asked Daughter if she was staying long. Daughter answered that she had just called in on the off-chance and was just going as it happened. Mother said I see, very well. Daughter said well, then and the two of them stared at each other a bit longer like rival tigresses eyeing each other up, Granny looking apprehensively first at one, then at the other like a nervous zookeeper.

Then it was all over. Teresa broke eye contact, hugged Granny rather peremptorily and then turned and gestured to me to lead the way out. I paused to kiss Granny on the cheek and gave Mother as cheerful a nod as I could muster in the circumstances, getting a severe look in reply, and made a hasty getaway through the door and down the steps outside.

Teresa followed just a moment or two later. When she reached the car she paused to fish her sunglasses out of her bag and put them on. I gave a half-wave of farewell to the two women watching us from the doorway, then clambered into my seat.

Teresa was already fastening her seatbelt. I couldn't be sure because of the sunglasses, but to me she looked hurt and angry. I secured my own seatbelt without saying anything and a moment later she had started the engine, turned the car around, and we were retracing our steps back towards the main road, only noticeably faster this time. I hung onto the door handle as we careered round blind bends, praying to God that we didn't meet a tractor or any other material object in our path, because there damned well wouldn't be much time for them to get out of our way.

We'd probably lingered at Granny's for about an hour and a half and now it felt as though Teresa intended to make good the time lost by breaking the land speed record. I felt more than a little frightened, in a way I hadn't earlier in the journey. Teresa had the air of someone who didn't much care whether our mad progress ended in success or failure.

I breathed slightly more easily when we arrived back at the autostrada, where the traffic on our half of the road was all going in the same direction at least. The tense atmosphere in the car didn't show any sign of easing, however. Teresa remained tight-lipped and unspeaking, her eyes fixed on the road ahead. I had the distinct impression that if I said so much as a single word about our ill-fated visit to Granny she would bite my head off.

It wasn't long before the signs for Florence appeared and then vanished behind us as we continued at light speed down the A1, which goes all the way south to Naples via Florence and Rome. It's Italy's longest motorway, popularly known as the Autostrada del Sole (the Motorway of the Sun), but I wasn't getting much leisure to enjoy its scenic beauties with every high-speed overtaking manoeuvre forcing my eyes shut. I almost longed for the traffic police to pull us over so that Teresa might be obliged to come back to her senses.

To distract my attention from my probable early demise I lifted up a roadmap of Italy that I'd spotted tucked into the well behind my seat and tried to see how far we were from our destination. I found where we were and estimated that we were still a good three hours away. What were our chances of surviving three hours' driving at these speeds? I swallowed. I wouldn't have put much money on a happy outcome.

A couple of minutes later, however, Teresa was forced to slow down as the traffic slowed for roadworks. It then became clear that the road ahead was closed for some reason and big yellow signs indicated a diversion off the main route. Teresa muttered her frustration in taut but expressive Italian and followed on the tailgate of a big, dirty truck, realising it was futile trying to get past it. The road we had been put on was winding and narrow and seemed to be interminable. Teresa swore again under her breath and glanced at me, then pointed at the map.

'Find us a way round,' she instructed.

Now, if she had known anything about my lack of any sense of direction, she would probably have thought better of asking me to map-read, but as the car, being a classic, had no satnav and I had thrown my mobile away there wasn't much alternative. I endeavoured to do my best.

'There's a turn-off on the left about a mile further on,' I told her after screwing my eyes up to decipher the squiggles and symbols on the map resting on my knees. 'I think if we follow that for a few miles we should be able to rejoin the autostrada further down, hopefully below the closed section.'

She nodded and started looking for the turn-off. It came rather sooner than I had been expecting, but without hesitation Teresa gunned the engine and we shot across the road and down a country lane that dipped into a lush wooded valley dotted with small hamlets and farms. We went along smoothly enough until the lane came to an abrupt dead end before a small lake. We both stared in surprise at the water that barred our way.

I consulted the map. 'Ah, I think I see what we've done. We turned off too early. If we go back I think I can get us on the right road.'

Without replying, Teresa spun the car around so that it faced back in the direction we had come and we shot off back up the lane. It took about five minutes to regain the road where we had turned off, but we again found ourselves in a long line of traffic slowly proceeding southwards through rural Tuscany.

I looked anxiously for the next turn-off. Teresa's fingers were tapping impatiently on the steering wheel. I hoped our little detour hadn't annoyed her too much. As before it was hard to tell exactly what she might be thinking.

Another turn to the left approached.

'This one?' Teresa inquired, somewhat curtly.

'Yes, this one.'

This road looked more promising at first but, just like the first one, it turned out to be a callow deceiver, petering out after a few minutes in a farmyard, from which a large mud-bespattered pig looked curiously back at us. It may not have seen a classic red Dino Ferrari before. Without saying a word, Teresa turned around and focused her attention on getting us back to the main road. I busied myself with the map.

'Here we are,' I said, stabbing the map with my forefinger. 'I see what I did. Take the next left and we'll be fine.'

Teresa made a small noise that could have meant anything but dutifully turned off again when the next left appeared. This time the road wound its way deep into the hills to the south, relatively long straight stretches alternating with series of tortuous bends. It was a burning hot day and the inside of the car was very warm, even with the windows down. I hoped to goodness I had put us on the right route at last.

I should have known I was being optimistic.

Teresa slowed as we approached a crossroads.

'Which way?' she asked.

I hurriedly consulted the map, but damned if I could see any crossroads anywhere along the road I thought we had been travelling along.

'Which way?' Teresa repeated, bringing the car down to walking pace.

I fumbled with the map, trying desperately to identify our location on the blasted thing. 'I – er, well, let me see – just hold on a moment…'

Teresa brought the car to a standstill, its engine humming. I squinted at the mesh of lanes on the map, quite unable to pick out where we were.

'Just give me a minute and I'm sure I can work it out…'

Teresa turned off the engine. Everything suddenly felt very quiet and my crinkling of the map unnaturally loud, deafening even.

'I'll soon work out where we are,' I assured her. 'It's

just this crossroads, which shouldn't be here…'

I heard a small choking noise coming from my left. I looked up nervously and saw that Teresa was shaking slightly.

Oh Lord, I thought, I know that sound. She is – she's crying.

But then I realised she wasn't crying at all. She was laughing. I stared in bewilderment as her shoulders rocked and she burst out in helpless guffaws of laughter. She positively shook with mirth and tears began to roll down her cheeks from behind her sunglasses.

Make a woman laugh, and she's yours to do with as you please, my mother once told me. Well, she's been seduced by enough comedians over the years, so she should know if anyone does. I suppose I should apologise on her behalf to the rest of the sisterhood for letting the cat out of the bag, though on second thoughts I'll leave that to her. In this particular case, I wasn't at all confident what to make of the sudden outburst of merriment. I waited for a clue.

The uncharacteristic sobs of laughter finally ebbed and Teresa removed her sunglasses and dabbed at her face with a tissue. Then she took several deep breaths. At long last she turned to look at me. Even with red-rimmed eyes she was breathtakingly beautiful.

'I'm sorry. But I want to thank you for what you did for my grandmother. You see, I am worried that she does not eat enough.'

'There's absolutely no need to thank me for anything.'

She kept looking at me with her big black, red-rimmed eyes.

'You are so unlike Luigi. He would be very angry with me if I laughed at him. Everything has to be just so with him. Everything has to be just as he wants it. But you… you don't expect other people to act in a certain way all the time. You just accept whatever comes to you.

You don't try to change everything. I like that.' She looked at me thoughtfully. 'Yes, I think I like that.'

The way she was looking at me made my toes curl with pleasure. I didn't mind her laughing at me a bit if this was the reward.

Teresa chewed her lip in thought for a few seconds. Then she opened her door.

'I have to get out for a moment.'

'Here? Why? We're in the middle of nowhere. At least, I think we are.'

But she was already climbing out of the car.

I watched her as she walked round to the front of the bonnet. She tapped the screen of her mobile, then held it to her ear as she looked absently at the hills surrounding us. She was such a beautiful woman it robbed me of breath just to look at her. You could easily become obsessed with a woman like that.

Teresa spoke briefly on her phone then closed it and got back into her seat. She started up the engine and turned to me.

'I just called Luigi to say we won't be arriving in Rome until tomorrow.'

A Bit of Sauce

I put my pathological need for attention down to the fact I wasn't bullied at school. If I had been perhaps I wouldn't need everyone to notice me so much. I suppose that's why I sought a career as a celeb in the first place. I suppose that's why I'm always getting into scrapes with the opposite sex too.

Anyhow, whatever my underlying psychological motivation, I wasn't absolutely sure what Teresa Vanni had in mind for me that afternoon lost somewhere deep in the Tuscan countryside between Florence and Rome – but you can bet I was up for it, whatever it might be.

Instead of trying to retrace our route back to the main road once more, Teresa chose one of the roads in front of us apparently at random and we penetrated deeper into rural central Italy via its side roads. It was a circuitous route we followed, to say the least. Sometimes we appeared to be going back on ourselves, but we carried on regardless and slowly but surely I got the impression we were progressing in approximately the right direction. None of the little hamlets and villages we went through appeared on my map at all – and judging by the looks we got from the locals it wasn't often an urban beast like a red Ferrari sports car like ours ventured down their high street. In a couple of places we even had small children running after us in a state of some excitement.

Mind you, it didn't bother me too much where we were. I was enjoying the proximity of Teresa Vanni too much for that, an enjoyment that was redoubled by the fact that neither of us seemed to have any idea where out journey might end up.

But end up somewhere we did. Teresa spotted it

before I did. We were on the outskirts of a pretty little village deep in the hill country and I think we both felt like we had gone far enough for one day, what with all the ups and downs and changes in direction. The cosy little rural albergo in front of us looked just perfect. In contrast to Granny's cottage, this one was indeed clad in flowering greenery and enjoyed a grand view of the surrounding vineyards and fields, being situated towards the top of a gentle rise. To my amazement there was even a moustachioed host dozing in a wooden chair by the door, though the vision varied from what I had imagined in the small detail that the moustachioed he was in reality a moustachioed she.

Teresa glanced at me and I smiled uncertainly back at her. She brought our car in a slow sweep and parked it alongside the railed verandah in front of the restaurant and turned the engine off.

The woman in the chair woke up with a start and beamed when she spotted us getting out of the car. She rose and beckoned us in, welcoming us like long-lost country cousins as I heaved our luggage out of the boot.

It wasn't a big place. There weren't above half a dozen guest rooms, but it was neat and authentic and I liked the smell of cooking that was coming from the direction of the kitchen. It smelt like real country cooking, heavy with herbs and traditional secrets handed down through the generations.

I let Teresa sort out the accommodation and sign us in, then we both followed the moustachioed woman up the stairs to a large and well-appointed room on the top floor. It had stunning views of the valleys below and of the hills opposite, though what really took my eye was the double bed it contained.

Things were definitely looking up.

The old lady disappeared after another word with Teresa and we were alone together. Teresa checked the ensuite and then dropped her little bag on the bed. I heaved my suitcase up onto a chair and wondered what was to happen next.

Teresa stepped over to the window to inspect the view. I thought I might be imagining it but she seemed a trifle nervous. I walked up behind her and, taking a deep breath, laid my hands gently on her shoulders. She didn't react, but then again she didn't pull away either, so I left them there.

'It's an impressive view,' I murmured in her ear as we both looked out at the vista in front of us. 'We've done rather well to find this place.'

She nodded. Encouraged, I let my hands drop to her waist and then slide round her middle to the front. She relaxed a little into my embrace, but did not turn her head for the kiss I was waiting to bestow. Instead she laid one of her hands lightly on top of mine. We stood like that for a long moment, rather awkwardly, then I ventured to slip my hand between the buttons of her blouse, where my fingers met the smooth warm flesh of her belly. For just a couple of seconds she let my hand stay there, but then she pulled away.

'Stop,' she said quietly. 'That woman will be back in a moment with the champagne I ordered.'

I frowned. If she was trying to tease me she was doing a very good job of it. But, then again, that's a lady's prerogative, I suppose.

The silence that was growing between us was fortuitously broken by the moustachioed woman coming in with two glasses and a bottle of bubbly. When she was gone I poured us a glass each and we drank a silent toast to each other. Then I sat on the edge of the bed, which was invitingly soft, in what I hoped was a subtly provocative manner. Teresa responded by putting her glass down on the dressing-table and telling me she needed a long hot bath after all the driving.

Accordingly she disappeared into the bathroom and I was left slumped on the bed like a deflated balloon, questioning whether I would ever get any further with my gorgeous but exasperating companion.

When Teresa said a long, hot bath she meant it. It must have been an hour later that she finally emerged, and it felt a lot longer. To my disappointment she already had her underwear on and immediately sat herself down at the dressing-table to mess around with her hair and make-up. It was a lovely view – Teresa Vanni in her skimpies – but I was clearly going to have to wait my turn for her attention, if it ever came at all. Perhaps, I taunted myself, we were going to lie on the double bed tonight with the bolster between us to stop anyone getting up to any hanky-panky. Anything was possible with Teresa Vanni, it seemed.

I took myself off to the bathroom, doing my best not to feel peeved at being made to wait like this and rather grumpily did what I could to make myself presentable by having a shower and general brush-up.

When I came out again, clad only in a towel, Teresa was ready, looking as supremely elegant as she always did. She had put her hair up and I couldn't help admiring the long curve of her neck beneath her glossy black locks. I also saw she had a pair of high heels on – how women get so much into their tiny little bags I have no idea.

My task now was to get myself dressed, which felt very awkward with her looking on fully clad herself. I opted to pull on undies and so forth while still keeping my towel round my waist, but it was a clumsy job I made of it and I'm sure I was blushing furiously by the end of it, making me feel even worse. It was like trying to put your swimmers on at the beach when you're eleven. The embarrassment factor was increased tenfold by the fact that I could see she was clearly enjoying my discomfiture and making no pretence of looking the other way. The familiar half-smile that had crept onto her lips was absolutely infuriating.

Somehow I managed to complete the job and, feeling hot and bothered, stood aside so that she could lead the way from the room. Instead she walked over to me, smiling in the friendliest way, and straightened my lapel for me. It was a small enough gesture, but enough for me to forget my irritation at her behaviour completely. Her perfume enveloped me and all I could think of was that I was going to spend the whole evening with this lovely woman.

It was seven o'clock when we entered the little dining-room of the albergo. That's early for Italian restaurants, so it was no surprise to me that we were the only people present apart from our host and a young waitress, who relayed our orders to the kitchen. That suited me fine, as I was revelling in having Teresa all to myself. Our relationship had changed so much during the course of the day it was hard to believe. I only hoped it would continue to develop further.

We were seated in a little alcove that promoted the intimacy of our meal together. I'm pretty good at remembering what I've eaten at particular restaurants over the years, but in this case I remember very little of what we ordered. I doubt if I even paid it that much attention at the time, which is extraordinary for a professional foodie like me. If I'd had my wits about me I would have pressed Teresa to choose dishes on the menu that I knew to be renowned aphrodisiacs, but I let her make her own selection, for heaven's sake!

I did, however, make a point of choosing from the wine list, which wasn't long but included some fabulous local products that more than amply met my expectations. Maybe it was the wine or the combination of the wine, the food, the surroundings and my company that did the trick, I don't know, but for the first time I managed to get Teresa Vanni to talk, just a little bit, about herself.

By the end of the first course I had elicited the information that she had indeed spent her childhood in the tiny village where Granny still lived. But she hadn't been back there much in recent years. It had been an idyllic rural upbringing that had included paddling in local streams, attending the tiny local school, making friends among local families. But she had always hankered to see the city and, just when she had been about to settle down and marry a local farmer's son, along had come Luigi with his money and his connections and all that those brought with them. It was clear to me that he had bought her, just as he had bought everything else that surrounded him. I didn't blame him for that, incidentally – if I'd been in Luigi's place I'd have mortgaged everything I owned to call her mine.

We paused for thought while the waitress took our plates away and refilled our glasses for us. Then the conversation turned to Luigi himself. She was still very guarded about telling me what he actually did, and it finally occurred to me that the truth was she really didn't know much about it. They had been married for getting on for twenty years and she'd simply stopped trying to get him to explain it to her a long, long time ago. Perhaps high-flying financiers can only be understood by other high-flying financiers.

But there was something more going on than just that. I sensed that Teresa's tight-lipped reluctance to talk about her husband said more than she realised about her feelings for him. I couldn't say exactly how I realised it but it seemed to me from her manner that over the years she had come to resent the impact he had had upon her life and the control he now wielded over it. It surprised me not a little as, knowing my new patron as I was beginning to and finding him always so charming, affable and accommodating, I would never have expected her to have anything but warm and grateful feelings for him.

Part of the trouble, I discovered over the main course, was that Teresa's family had disapproved strongly of her marriage to Luigi Vanni. They didn't understand the world he came from and had had a real soft spot for the farmer's lad she had spurned not too many yards before the altar. The lad's family were close friends of her parents and it had caused a deep and lasting rift between the two clans. Which was why the conversation I had witnessed early that afternoon had been the first she had had with her mother in over five years.

This last revelation was quite a conversation stopper and we finished the main course in ruminative silence. But at least it was a shared silence, not one we pursued separately.

The dessert course arrived and this time it was my turn to spill some personal beans. Teresa had heard quite a lot about my professional career, how it had started and turned into a job in television and so forth, back in Venice, so this time she delved into my off-stage life. I told her about the various wives and how each of them had finally given up on me for one reason or another. I told her how I didn't blame them, not a jot, and how I'd have left myself more than once if that had been an option. But I also told her how I missed each of them in their peculiar, infuriating way every day of my life.

She listened attentively to everything I told her, never taking her eyes off my face. Over the coffee I explained to her that I really couldn't see how I could ever rebuild the bridges I had burned with my former partners, and how I had pretty much stopped imagining that I would ever feel I could marry again or embark on a serious, long-term relationship of any kind with another woman. I even told her about my ill-fated dalliance in Venice with a girl half my age and how it had ended – and consequently what it had meant to me to find new friendship such as hers.

This really seemed to touch her for she reached across the table and laid a hand on mine in sympathetic understanding.

Then she leaned forward towards me. 'I think it is time to go,' she informed me softly.

'Don't you want to finish the wine? It's only nine o'clock.'

She leaned closer still. 'We can take the wine upstairs with us. I wish to make love to you.'

I thought I had misheard at first. Then I saw I had heard her correctly and my heart leapt. 'Oh. Oh, I see! Rightho then…'

So there it was. Of course, I'd known all along that she had the hots for me. Never doubted it for a moment.

I rose awkwardly from the table and grabbed hold of the bottle. Teresa collected up her purse, rather more elegantly, and slipped out from behind the table. After thanking the waitress we headed for the door out of the dining-room.

At the last moment Teresa seemed to remember

something she'd forgotten and turned back to the waitress to ask for it. We waited while the girl hurried off to the kitchen. When she returned she handed over a bucket of ice and a full bottle of extra virgin olive oil.

'I don't think we need ice,' I observed. 'We're drinking red.'

But she ignored me and led the way upstairs. I followed, my heart hammering like a pile-driver all the way up.

I may not have remembered what we ate in the restaurant but I certainly remember in vivid detail everything that took place in the bedroom that night. You needn't think, dear reader, that you're going to get all the juicy details either. I like to think I am a gentleman when it comes to such things, and Teresa was every inch a lady. But I'll treat you to one or two highlights from the banquet we shared together.

For hors d'oeuvres, Teresa waited until I was completely (and hastily) naked before removing a stitch of her own clothing. She told me to sit on the bed while she took her turn to undress. The moment she slipped the first strap off her shoulder I was up and advancing on her, but she insisted on my sitting back down and watching while she slowly, and very sexily, continued to remove her clothes. She made it very clear that touching was forbidden. It was absolutely maddening.

Once she was naked before me and she thought she had given me enough time to drink it all in we moved on to the first course, with her ordering me to lie face down on a bath towel that she had spread on top of the duvet. She then treated me to the most sensual massage I have ever had, drizzling me with the olive oil and then lowering herself on top of me and writhing about until we were covered in the warm, slippery stuff. It was quite the most arousing experience I could remember having in years. I knew that the ancient Egyptians, Greeks and

Romans had all favoured the use of olive oil in their lovemaking but only now did I properly appreciate the erotic potential of this wonderfully rich and potent unguent. I thought I would explode with lust – and eventually, as I'll leave you to imagine if you really must, I did. A number of times. If you want to continue with the food metaphor, we gorged ourselves on one fabulous main course after another, and then cleared the menu of dessert dishes. A fair few of them ended metaphorically all over the walls and ceiling.

The ice, I discovered, was there to revive me when I was showing signs of lapsing into a sexually satisfied coma and it certainly worked, though quite what Teresa did with it I've no intention of sharing with you. We old-fashioned types don't. It didn't end up in a glass, I'll tell you that much.

For the second time since I had arrived in Italy I saw the light of dawn seeping into the room before a wild night of passion finally came to an end. What is it with Italian women, I wondered through a haze of exhaustion? Maybe it's something to do with the water. Or the tiramisu perhaps. Whatever it is, it should be bottled and shipped all over the world. Someone (Jamie probably) would make a fortune.

I know I should be ashamed of what I did, her husband Luigi being my patron and friend, but even now I cannot bring myself to regret the bedding of the truly spectacular Teresa Vanni.

Second Helpings Anyone?

It was mid-morning by the time we surfaced and got ourselves back on the road. We'd both been too tired for a repeat of the previous night's shenanigans when we woke up and we finished our journey to Rome that day at an appropriately sedate pace, taking a leisurely lunch along the way in the old town of Orvieto, perched high on its dramatic summit, which was once an Etruscan acropolis. It was the middle of the afternoon by the time we arrived in Rome, which was baking in the summer heat. I wasn't sure what Luigi would have to say about the dust we had got all over his classic Dino Ferrari in the course of our rural adventure, and that wasn't the only concern I harboured about our extended journey…

Where should I begin to tell you about Rome? You may have been there, of course. You may know the Eternal City well, with its contrasts of old and new, grand and humble, friendly and hostile. If you haven't been there, well, you really are missing something. If there's a site more redolent of history in all its best and worst aspects I doubt if there's anywhere to rival the Forum and its environs.

Here the shade of the swinish Brutus is sentenced to spend eternity stabbing the arguably equally swinish Julius Caesar, while the ghosts of one mad emperor after another flit screaming in silence through the shadows cast by the pine trees on the Palatine Hill in perpetual rage at the excesses (or lack of them) committed by the city's modern residents. Today's Romans constitute a colourful and contrasting population that seems to include representatives of all the Italian regions and much of the rest of the world besides, with at least fifty per cent of them apparently tourists with nothing better to do than get in your way. I suppose it was ever thus. (You know, when this food-cum-travel book finally hits the shelves I shouldn't be at all surprised if I pick up a prize or two for the descriptive passages alone.)

The traveller may rest assured that Rome, with its fascinating history, bloody and romantic by turn, will transport them through the ages and leave them changed people at the end of their stay, however long it may be. And when the feet are too weary and sustenance is required there is the usual range of fashionable and more reasonably priced eateries to satisfy that need, from world-class restaurants to cheap and cheerful pizzerias. (I wonder if I mention this passage to that mercenary devil Barry Cullis we could get some cash up front for naming particular establishments? I'll have to bring it up with him.)

Anyway, putting the travelogue aside, we arrived in the outskirts of Rome, as I say, around mid-afternoon and threaded our way through the convoluted streets to the ancient heart of the broiling hot city. Teresa told me that Luigi and his associates were meeting at a venue within a stone's throw of the Colosseum. The building in question turned out to be a rather smart hotel with a basement car park, in which we duly left the dusty Ferrari.

I was feeling a bit jumpy about meeting up with Luigi again after my liaison with his wife. Teresa hadn't shared with me what her excuse had been for staying overnight on the journey south, but I guessed it was some hogwash about the car breaking down or her staying over with Granny perhaps. Given my ignorance of her story, I decided it was a subject best avoided.

In the event, Luigi seemed completely unconcerned by our delayed arrival when we were all reunited in a luxurious suite on the top floor of the hotel. He didn't even ask about the reason for it, which was a considerable relief. Instead he just seemed delighted that we were there at last. He give Teresa a kiss on the cheek, and then pumped me by the hand and asked if we had had a pleasant journey. Yes, I told him, feeling just a little guilty, it had been very pleasant indeed.

I'm sure Luigi would have continued in his enquiries for the sake of politeness but for a timely interruption by one of his many lieutenants, a bald-headed and physically daunting chap named Pasquale whom I hadn't met before. He whispered something in Luigi's ear and then took a deferential step back. Luigi shrugged and looked apologetically at us both.

'I am so sorry, but I have guests arriving for a meeting and I must take care of things. Teresa, show Tremayne to the guest room, will you? I must go downstairs.' He turned back to me. 'If you are not too tired after your journey perhaps you would like my wife to take you for a walk through the Forum? I am going to be very busy here, I am afraid. I am hosting a business dinner here for various colleagues this evening.'

'Can I help with that?'

Luigi shook his head. 'Thank you for offering, but there is no need. I have caterers coming in. It is only a meeting of people who work for my company, so your great talents would be wasted. But I may call on them next time, if I may?'

'Of course. I'd be delighted.'

He turned to go then paused and turned back. 'Perhaps when you have had your walk, if you're not too weary, you wouldn't mind taking my wife somewhere to eat? The food the caterers provide here in Rome is not always so very good.'

'It will be a pleasure,' I assured him.

Luigi trotted down the stairs, leaving Teresa to show me to a modest but comfortable room at the end of a short corridor. It contained two or three pieces of furniture and a single bed. An internal door opened onto a tiny ensuite with a basin, lavatory and shower. When I craned my head out of the window I could just get a glimpse of the stonework of the Colosseum itself. It wasn't the palazzo in Venice but it was still very acceptable.

Teresa left me to freshen up while she went back down the corridor to the rooms she and Luigi would be sharing, with instructions for us to meet at the top of the stairs ten minutes later. As I got myself sorted out I became conscious of a lot of activity going on elsewhere in the building. I heard feet going loudly up and down the stairs, men calling to each other, various other miscellaneous sounds as of chairs and tables being moved about. Clearly the evening's meeting was a big one of some importance. It had been the right thing to offer to help out, but I was privately glad that Luigi had declined my services. The alternative, a stroll through the ruins of ancient Rome with the delectable Teresa, followed by dinner with her, was immeasurably more attractive.

I joined Teresa at the top of the stairs as arranged and we made our way down to the ground floor, dodging

Luigi's business associates as they hurried about the place, carrying dining chairs and the like and looking serious. The bald-headed man named Pasquale was standing beside the front door as we approached, talking to two men in whites whom I took to be the caterers for the evening meal. They had a large hostess trolley between them, presumably containing the food that was being provided for the dinner. My professional curiosity aroused, I paused before the trolley and reached out a hand to lift one of the lids to see what was inside.

At once Pasquale seized my wrist in an iron grip and glowered at me. He clearly didn't like people interfering in the course of his duties.

'Sorry,' I stammered, squirming helpless in his grasp, 'I just wondered what–'

Pasquale growled, eyes glittering dangerously, and gave my wrist a sharp twist, making me yelp and bend double in an attempt to relieve the pain of his grip on my arm.

Teresa snapped something in Italian and two long seconds later Pasquale released me, somewhat reluctantly I felt. He glared as I backed away hastily and rubbed my wrist, which bore several red fingermarks. Teresa took me by the elbow and led me on through the open door.

'Come on,' she muttered. 'We are not wanted here.'

I grimaced at the ache in my wrist. 'That was uncalled for. I only wanted to see what they were bringing to eat. I'm surprised the hotel don't complain at all the commotion your husband's men are creating.'

Teresa tossed her head. 'They're hardly likely to. It's his hotel.'

'You mean he owns it – the whole building?'

Teresa nodded. 'Yes. He does a lot of his business here.'

We headed away from the hotel and towards the

Colosseum, which despite the shimmering heat was crowded as usual with coach parties and souvenir sellers. The pain in my wrist faded and I transferred my attention to the busy scene around us.

The Colosseum, Rome

'You have been to the Colosseum before?' Teresa asked.

'Yes, several times. Is it always as busy as this?'

'Always. Let's walk on the Palatine Hill. It's usually quieter there.'

We bought tickets at the entrance gate and climbed up the slope upon which the emperors built their palaces. As the heat of the day slowly began to ebb the number of tourists on the hill fell off and after a while we found we had the ruins largely to ourselves. We selected a spot where we could sit overlooking the Circus Maximus, where the ancient Romans used to flock to watch chariot races.

I yawned ostentatiously. 'Last night is catching up with me, I'm afraid. I'm tired.'

Teresa shot a cool look at me. 'Last night was last night. Today is another day.'

I held her gaze and gave her a smile. 'Of course. Mind you, it might be nice if…'

She turned away and I understood that the subject was closed and second helpings were most decidedly not on the menu. Oh well, I told myself, perhaps she was right. It wouldn't do to spoil things for us both with Luigi. There again, things might change later on perhaps.

'The meeting this evening is clearly an important one,' I remarked, trying to lighten the somewhat tense atmosphere. 'Do you know what it's about?'

Teresa shook her head. 'No. Just that another organisation is threatening to take business from my husband's company. I believe he and his partners are meeting to decide what to do about it. Luigi thinks both sides should meet soon, so tonight they will discuss what they will say to them at that meeting.'

I nodded absently. I always find discussions about business and money tedious in the extreme, and they struck me as incongruous topics for such a location and with such company. Mind you, when you considered the dark and labyrinthine intrigues that were hatched by emperors on this very spot in defence of their business and other interests, they weren't so very wide of the mark in reality.

'I hope you don't regret what happened last night,' I ventured after a pause, taking the risk of bringing the conversation back to a more enticing subject. 'I certainly don't.'

Teresa looked at me long and hard, until I began to feel uncomfortable.

'I don't wish to talk about it.'

She got up and I hastened after her, suitably cowed. We strolled around the ruins without speaking. Teresa remained moody and distant in manner, which was a shame as I knew it would be difficult to snatch many times like this alone with her. But women and their moods have always been a mystery to me – a delightful one, but a mystery nonetheless.

At length we descended into the Forum below the Palatine Hill and meandered down the Appian Way between the stumps of columns and broken-down walls. The Forum always strikes me as rather a melancholy place, lost in dreams of a far-distant and much more glorious past that we can only grope towards appreciating. By the time we reached the Curia Julia, where the Senate used to meet, and the formidable Arch of Septimius Severus we both, I think, felt quite subdued, even sombre in the presence of so much lost history. The fact that we ended up almost in the shadow of the Tarpeian Rock, from which the ancient Romans hurled notorious traitors and deceivers to their deaths did little to improve the ambience.

'I think we need a drink and something to eat,' I observed. 'And I know just the place.'

Teresa nodded and let me lead the way. We left the Forum behind us, skirted Michelangelo's Piazza del Campidoglio with its back forever disdainfully turned on the ruins of ancient Rome, and headed in the direction of a very good restaurant I knew within easy walking distance. I hadn't met up with Paolo, its proprietor, for ages, but I was confident of a warm welcome.

Considering the freedom we had taken with each other the previous night, it was an odd meal we shared that evening after I had renewed my acquaintance with my old confederate and had derived much gleeful pleasure in introducing him to my gorgeous companion. The table Paolo gave us was the best in the place and the food and wine were extremely good, but the atmosphere was strained and Teresa said very little. The fact that there was a bottle of extra virgin olive oil on the table, smack bang between us, did nothing to lighten things, so I took the opportunity when it arose to shift it to the side when

Teresa wasn't looking.

We took our time to appreciate what was placed before us and I enjoyed some banter with Paolo when he came over to see how we were doing. But my heart wasn't really in it when all the time I knew we must inevitably return to the hotel where I must dutifully hand Teresa over to her husband. Perhaps she was thinking much the same thing, I don't know. At one point I thought I caught the glint of unshed tears in Teresa's eyes, but I couldn't be sure.

We lingered over coffee and liqueurs, but finally, though it was still early, I concluded that there was nothing further to be gained by putting off the evil hour and suggested we go back to hotel and catch up with the sleep we had missed the night before.

As if this was a signal Teresa burst into muffled sobs. I watched, startled, as she scrabbled for a hankie and wept silently into it.

'What is it?' I asked as sympathetically as I could after her sobs had subsided a bit.

'I hate my life!' she told me in a tiny voice. 'I want to go back to where I came from, to live with my mother and my grandmother, like I used to. But he will never let me... he won't even let me speak to them...'

The 'he' she was talking about was presumably her husband. I was nonplussed. Luigi was such an easy fellow to get along with, even if some of his colleagues lacked social refinement. He wouldn't want her to be unhappy, surely?

'I'm sure your husband doesn't mean to upset you,' I told her as I sidled closer to her and slipped a comforting arm around her shoulders. 'Does he know that you want to see your family?'

Teresa sniffed impatiently into her hankie. 'Of course he knows. It's because of him I never see them! Oh, you don't understand. How could you...'

I gave her shoulders a squeeze and for a moment she sagged into my embrace. I became conscious of Paolo watching us from the other side of the room and, as decently as I could, withdrew the arm. Teresa wiped her eyes, apologised and then excused herself to go to the ladies to tidy herself up.

I settled up for the meal, as Teresa had paid for everything at the albergo in the country, and assured Paolo that the meal had been wonderful.

'I believe I have met your lady friend before. Is she all right?'

'Yes, she's fine, Paolo. A bit too much wine maybe. She just needs some fresh air, that's all.'

A minute later we were off on foot, retracing our steps towards the Forum. The tourist sites were all closed by now and it was quite dark. As we made our way past the ruins we glimpsed the black shadows of feral cats hunting among the stone blocks and pillars. What with that and Teresa's mute presence alongside me I felt quite depressed by the time we got back.

All was not so quiet, however, when he fetched up at the hotel. There was an ambulance parked at the front entrance and Luigi's men were hovering about anxiously as someone was lifted through the back doors on a stretcher. We heard the patient groaning in pain as we approached.

'What on earth's going on?' I asked Teresa, but obviously she had no idea either.

We spotted Luigi in the midst of his men as we joined the figures clustered around the ambulance. I peered over the shoulder of the man in front of me and recognised the bald dome of the patient's head. It was that oaf Pasquale, writhing and clutching at his stomach. Then the ambulance doors were slammed shut and the vehicle started off, siren sounding. I heard Teresa asking Luigi in Italian what the trouble was.

'It's nothing, really,' Luigi replied in English, presumably for my benefit. 'Come inside and I will tell you.'

He ushered us in through the door of the hotel. I couldn't help noticing how he cast a wary look out into the night behind us as we stood briefly silhouetted in the light. His business colleagues, looking equally ill at ease, crowded in behind us.

Once inside Luigi dismissed his men and started to lead us upstairs, explaining as we went.

'As you know, I was hosting a meal tonight for my business partners. We needed to discuss a forthcoming deal, you understand. I think I told you I had arranged for a local catering company to provide the food. We had hardly sat down and begun to eat when Pasquale started moaning and holding his stomach. Of course, as soon as we realised he had been taken ill, we sent for an ambulance.'

'What are his symptoms?' I asked.

'Apart from the pains in his stomach he was also holding his throat and he was having some trouble breathing.' Luigi looked at me. 'We have no idea what might have caused it.'

I pulled a face. 'I'm no expert but it could be food poisoning.'

'Food poisoning? You think so?' Luigi stopped as we reached the landing. 'Come, my friend, you probably know more abut such things than me. Would you be kind enough to take a look at what we were eating and tell me if you think that had something to do with it?'

'Of course I will. Though you'd need proper scientific examination to confirm it.'

Luigi led us into the dining–room, which showed all the signs of an abrupt interruption to the evening, with upturned chairs and items of crockery tipped onto the floor. One or two of Luigi's associates were still in there, looking jumpy and concerned. I took a good look at what was on the plates and nodded knowingly to myself.

'Where was the food prepared?'

'Through here,' said Luigi, leading me through a side door into a small ante-room where there were several hostess trolleys still with food on them waiting to be served. I went straight to the largely empty one on which the starters had presumably been laid out. There was a big serving container with a few leftovers still inside. I took a close look at the contents and sniffed them.

'Hmm. My first thought was that it might be out-of-date seafood of some kind that was to blame,' I told him, 'but I can see that you were having mushrooms for starters. And we all know what a reputation they have if not responsibly handled.'

I picked up a serving spoon and started prodding the mixture in the bowl. 'They look innocent enough, but it's terribly easy to confuse edible mushrooms with poisonous fungi. My guess is that a few of the more deadly variety accidentally got among the safe ones when they were picked – with predictable results. You have to be so careful. Just an ounce of certain varieties such as death cap fungus is enough to kill.'

Luigi peered suspiciously over my shoulder into the bowl. 'So you think it was food poisoning?'

'Possibly. It's odd though. I wouldn't normally expect any symptoms to show themselves until eight to twelve hours later. My understanding is it takes a while for the toxins to get into your system. Once they do, of course, it's a serious matter. In severe cases you can end up with liver failure and death within a week. One other thing...'

'What?'

'They really shouldn't have been served it with so much tomato. It completely overwhelms the taste of the mushrooms.'

Luigi grunted. 'Perhaps that was what someone meant

to do.'

I blinked. 'What? You're not suggesting someone did this on purpose?'

Luigi looked non-committal. 'It is unlikely, but there is a lot of money involved in the business we were discussing.'

'But – deliberate poisoning? Surely not. It's an easy enough mistake for someone who doesn't know their mushrooms very well. Mind you,' I conceded, 'I'm surprised professional caterers couldn't tell what was safe and what wasn't.'

Luigi ruminated for a moment then clapped me on the back. 'You are probably right, my dear Tremayne. It was a mistake, of course.'

Well, I said to myself, that's what comes of getting caterers in instead of calling on the services of yours truly when they're offered!

Teresa, who had been listening to everything, piped up quietly in the background. 'Will Pasquale be all right?'

'I'm sure every possible care is being taken of him,' Luigi reassured her briskly. 'Come, let us go upstairs and forget this whole unpleasant business.'

Luigi held out an arm for Teresa to take and she slipped her hand through his elbow. I followed a pace or two behind. As we walked back through the dining-room I happened to glance through one of the other adjoining doors and got a glimpse of the two men I had taken to be caterers earlier on sitting on chairs surrounded by Luigi's associates, Bruno among them. The two men looked sullen and scared. Then someone saw me looking and closed the door.

I followed the others up to the top floor, my mind whirring. What was all this about? Had someone deliberately tried to poison Luigi's friend tonight? Who would want to do such a thing? And what kind of business did they do anyway to invite such criminal interference?

Luigi sighed when we were all assembled outside the Vannis' suite. 'This has been a most trying evening. But I hope you will join us in a minute or two, Tremayne, for a small nightcap before we all retire to bed.'

'Yes, of course. Thanks, I think we could all do with a drink after that.'

I headed off to my room while Luigi and Teresa disappeared into their apartment. It was very muggy inside the small bedroom and I decided to open the window wider to let in the evening air, warm though it was. As I did so I looked down.

My bedroom overlooked the rear of the hotel and my eye was distracted by activity in the little courtyard below. Even as I looked down I saw Bruno and a couple of Luigi's other associates bundling two figures in caterers' whites out of a back door and into the back of a van. As soon as the van's doors were secured Bruno and two others got into the cab and the vehicle drove off at speed. I couldn't be sure in the dim light – in fact I was sure I must be imagining it – but I got the impression that Bruno was carrying something in his hand that looked distinctly like a gun. But no, I scolded myself as the van vanished out of sight, I was definitely letting my imagination run away with me. It was probably just a mobile phone or something.

I secured the window on its latch and, after a quick trip to the bathroom, headed thoughtfully back down the corridor to Luigi and Teresa's apartment. I wouldn't say I felt exactly carefree, what with the business between me and Teresa, the calamity in the dining-room, and now the incident in the courtyard leaving so many unanswered questions, but I tried to ignore the feeling of unease that was creeping over me.

I would have found it a good deal harder to do so if I

had known what was awaiting me.

I knocked at the door of the apartment and Luigi opened it. To my surprise there were already three people in the room I walked into. There was Luigi, who was holding out a brandy for me. There was Teresa, who was looking distinctly happier than she had been when I last saw her two minutes before. And, staring at me with a look of shock on her face, there was the girl I had gone to bed with at my hotel in Venice.

'Ah, my friend,' said Luigi as he passed the glass to me, 'I have a delightful surprise for you – please allow me to introduce Mariana. Our daughter.'

Bubble and Squeak

I'm not sure what the correct etiquette is when introduced by an unknowing father to his young daughter with whom you've shared the heights of sexual ecstasy barely a week before. There probably isn't one, so I just had to make it up as I went along. That it was the same girl there could be no doubt. She even had the diamond-studded black necklace with her name fashioned into it round her neck. I stuck a hand out for her to shake, which she did, a little reluctantly I felt, and then I launched off into the most appalling run of gabbled nonsense.

'Ah, so you're Mariana! Ah-ha! Well, well. Splendid. Indeed, yes. What a surprise! Aren't you just – who'd have thought it – but you don't have a brandy. Let me get you one.'

'Oh no, my friend!' Luigi espostulated, laughing and staying my hand. 'She's only seventeen, you know.'

Seventeen? What? Seventeen! I'd thought she was easily in her early twenties. I looked at her again, confused. She had taken off the purple lipstick and all the other goth-themed adornments and I had to admit, painful as it was, that she looked a lot younger without the warpaint. She was standing right next to her mother and now I saw them together I was amazed I hadn't noticed how like her daughter Teresa was – the same long black hair, the same dark, knowing eyes and, yes, that distinctive, infuriating half-smile. They both had the full set. And yes, there was no denying it, they were both extremely beautiful.

I laughed my faux-pas off as best I could and accepted the brandy Luigi offered me. I needed it.

Mariana looked at me with an inscrutable expression

on her appallingly young face. For a dreadful moment I wondered if she was about to expose me as her seducer, but instead she transferred her gaze to her mother and embarked on a conversation about something girly and trivial, the exact details of which I have forgotten.

Well, at least the dear child apparently had the decency to deceive her parents for my sake. Or perhaps she didn't want them to know what she'd been up to with me – though in any other circumstances I would prefer to think that any female would be more than proud to claim me as a paramour.

Teresa, all unbeknowing as far as I could ascertain, took Mariana by the elbow and sat her down to ask her all kinds of questions about how she had spent the last few days with her friends in Rimini, where they'd been and what they'd done. I knocked back a big swig of the brandy and hoped I'd get the chance to slip away to the safety of my room before attention switched back to me. Luigi, however, apparently had something he wished to discuss with me, for he motioned to me to join him out of earshot of the two women.

He looked like a man who was somewhat troubled as he swilled the brandy in his glass.

'Dear friend,' he began, 'in the light of what has happened this evening, I am wondering if you would do a great favour for me. I know you only agreed to cook for Teresa and me, but the fact is I am planning to host another important meal, for some business competitors of mine, in a few days' time and it is imperative that I find someone I can rely upon to prepare good food for them. As you may appreciate, I simply cannot trust professional caterers… It would be disastrous if anyone came down with food poisoning because of the carelessness of the chef I had hired. The deal could not possibly go ahead. Do you understand?'

I cleared my throat. 'Is this meal to take place here?'

'No. I must explain. What has happened here this evening changes everything. It was probably an accident, but then again... Well, I have decided that for safety's sake we should go to Napoli tomorrow. I have a place on Capri so we can prepare things from there.'

'This meeting is to take place in Naples?'

'Yes. Nothing is arranged yet, but I hope it will take place within a week or so. But first we go to Capri. I own a villa there. I will give you more details of the arrangements nearer the time. That is, if you are willing to help me in my hour of need?'

Put like that, I couldn't decently refuse his request, whatever my misgivings about recent events. And an invitation to stay at a villa on Capri is not something you turn down without very good reason.

'Very well. When do we go to Capri?'

'As soon as possible. Tomorrow would be best, Yes, tomorrow.'

So there I was, in dire danger of being exposed as an incorrigible womaniser who had had liaisons with my patron's wife and daughter and now obliged to live in close quarters with all three of them on a tiny island for several days at the very least. It was an unsettling prospect.

'I am so sorry you have not had time to see more of Rome,' Luigi said, looking apologetic. 'But I am sure you will love Capri.'

'Ah well, it can't be helped, I suppose.'

I finished my brandy and bid a brief farewell to all present, then slipped back to my room before any of them could deliver any rejoinder that might complicate my life even further.

As I lay in bed I pondered my best course of action. In the morning I could, I told myself, just tell Luigi that I had changed my mind and remembered I needed to be back in London for something, but there were risks in doing that. He might not like to be disappointed and might hand me over to Bruno and the others to get me to change my mind. Or Teresa or her daughter might take offence and forget their own interests just long enough to taste revenge at my expense by telling Luigi what I'd been up to. And that in turn would put paid to the prospect of the new career in international television that Luigi had suggested he could fix for me. No, on balance, the price for packing up at this point was just too high. I'd go along with them to Capri, mind my ps and qs while I was there, cook for this blasted business dinner of Luigi's and only then, if his promises showed no sign of coming to anything, make my excuses and leave. It was, all things considered, the sensible course to take.

Except, naturally, it wasn't.

About three-quarters of an hour after I had left the Vannis to finish their nightcaps I jerked out of the doze I had fallen into. I listened carefully for what had disturbed me. For several seconds I heard nothing, then there was a tiny click and my heart gave a lurch as I realised my bedroom door was slowly opening.

I'm not the most courageous of people and I couldn't think what to do apart from pull the duvet up to my chin and hope this wasn't happening. I held my breath as a shadowy form slipped into my room and closed the door behind it.

Then someone switched on the small lamp on the bedroom table. It was Mariana.

I opened my mouth to express my astonishment, but the cheeky article pressed a finger to my lips and shook her head in warning. Then she sat down on the bed next to me.

'What are you doing?' I hissed as quietly as I could. 'Your parents are just down the corridor!'

'They've gone to bed,' she whispered back. 'What are you doing here in Rome? Are you pursuing me?'

'No!' I exclaimed, shocked. 'I had no idea Luigi was your father. I met him by chance and he asked me to cook for him and your mother for a few weeks.'

She stared at me and chewed her lower lip. Even in this fraught situation her youthful beauty was impossible to ignore. I registered for the first time that she wasn't wearing very much, just a two-piece set of pyjamas with a rather childish penguin and polar bear pattern on it. She made quite a contrast to the smouldering goth chic I had encountered in the Venice bar what seemed a couple of thousand years ago. I would have bet her father had chosen the pyjamas for her and that he had no idea at all about the small tattoos she had secreted in various locations about her body.

Mariana noticed that my attention had wandered from her face. She gave me the half-smile I was getting to know so well and stood up. Then, to my horror, she began to unbutton her pyjama top.

'Don't do that!' I hissed fiercely.

'Why not?'

'Because someone may come in!'

'That's not very likely,' she countered, 'as long as we are quiet.'

She had her pyjama top open now and the view was bringing back all kinds of intoxicating and utterly inappropriate memories.

'Button yourself up!' I urged. 'We can't possibly do this now – not here!'

'I don't see why not.' She opened her pyjama top wider and looked at me with half-closed eyes, lips pouting.

'We just can't. Besides…'

'Besides what?'

'You're seventeen, for God's sake! And I'm–'

'What?'

'Not seventeen.'

She stared at me, her expression freezing over a little. 'That wasn't a problem for you in Venice.'

'I didn't know then. I thought you were older.'

'The law thinks I'm old enough.'

'I doubt if your father does.'

'This has nothing to do with my father.'

'No – and I don't want it to either!'

She looked sullen and more like the rebellious girl I remembered, but I noted that she had paused in the act of undressing.

'Anyway,' I continued, with just a suggestion of hurt creeping into my voice, 'you said yourself I was too old for you.'

She stared at me, looking annoyed.

'I'm sorry, Mariana,' I assured her. 'Really, I am. You're a lovely girl and I'd love to–'

Well, that did it, of course. No girl likes to be rejected when she's gone out of her way for you and then be told she's lovely by way of compensation. It sounds too much like you're pitying them.

She pulled her pyjama top closed and fastened the buttons with ferocious twists of her fingers. She looked absolutely furious with me, and I only hoped that in her rage she wouldn't make some loud noise that would rouse the family.

Before I could say anything more to soothe her, or reassure myself that she would be careful not to bring the household down on us, she had stood up and, without a last glance for yours truly, had stormed out of the room. Thankfully her storming out was of the seething, soundless variety and after a few seconds I dared to lower myself, with a sigh of relief, to my pillows. It had been a narrow escape indeed.

My dreams that night were troubled and alarming. Mariana, in various states of undress, and her mother, similarly disrobed, fought over me with shrieks of jealous fury, then made it up and turned their anger on me. Just when it seemed they would tear me bloodily limb from limb I found myself being bundled into a van by Bruno and Pasquale and whisked off into the night. I was just congratulating myself on my getaway when I looked through the tiny window separating the back of the van from the cab and saw who was driving.

It was Luigi.

Thought for Food

Ah, Capri! Capri, where the olive trees slide in stony confusion down scrubby slopes to the azure Tyrrhenian Sea. A sea, we remind ourselves, that not so many thousands of years ago was ploughed into furrows by the oars of Greek triremes en route from Athens or Piraeus to Pyramus and Thisbe. Standing in a velvet breeze coming up off the shining copper-coloured sea in the twilight of an August evening it is easy to imagine a Homer or Achilles or Pythagoras bent over the oars, looking forward to a slap-up meal at soon as the ship has reached its haven. They lick their lips in anticipation of an evening ahead in a candle-lit harbour-side trattoria where the crew may dine on food literally scooped from the salt waters in front of them that very afternoon, still writhing in briny life. Ah, the innocence of golden times long since passed!

Honestly, reading this back now months later I question whether a really talented writer like myself needs an editor at all. (You'll leave that in, if you please, Mr David bloody Pickering! Never mind the expense involved, not that he gets much out of Barry in the first place. Anyway, he'll only spend it on booze – and you should hear him on the subject of split infinitives!) But I'm drifting off the point.

Lovely Capri, with its majestic cliffs and golden beaches, its Blue Grotto and its luxury shopping outlets – it really does have something for everyone. As long as you've got the cash, that is. You see the day-trippers blanch at the cost of a humble Diet Coke and marvel that anyone can afford to stay in the place even overnight. It was a favourite resort of the ancient Romans, who built holiday palaces here, and today's emperors of business still consider it a special place, if you can disregard the shoals of the great unwashed who come ashore each day like so much flotsam.

Most people live in the town of Capri itself, but many of the finest residences are much higher up, some of them situated on the top of the island's limestone ridges, from which they enjoy spectacular panoramic views. Needless to say, the Vanni residence was one of these – a spotless and very spacious whitewashed modern villa with unbelievable views extending over the sea in nearly every direction. The most attractive vista was to the north and east, where distant features of interest visible through the heat haze over the Bay of Naples included Naples itself and, looming over the whole coastline, Mount Vesuvius, destroyer of Pompeii.

Reached by a single-track road, the villa was reassuringly remote from its neighbours and the high fences enclosing the extensive grounds guaranteed the undisturbed privacy of its occupants. Perhaps its most impressive feature was its enormous infinity-edge swimming-pool, where you could almost fool yourself you were swimming in the Tyrrhenian Sea itself, though that was many hundreds of feet below this vantage point. The addition of a few genuine Roman pillars and bits of marble salvaged from the ancient ruins thereabouts added a final touch of class to the whole effect.

We arrived at the villa not by car or by boat but by helicopter, having driven down to Naples from Rome. The helicopter was apparently one of Luigi's more expensive toys, though he didn't venture to fly the thing himself. When we got out of the aircraft after the breathtaking flight from Naples and walked the short distance to the villa itself we found that most of Luigi's associates were already in residence and had got things prepared for our arrival. I was in a guest annexe just off the pool and I have to say I was thoroughly satisfied with the set-up, even if I was less certain what perils the next few days might have in store for me.

This was the kind of treatment an internationally renowned celebrity chef like me deserves. My God, even Jamie and Heston probably didn't get luxury like this every day! I could certainly get used to it, given half a chance, which fate – that fickle beast – has given me all too rarely over the years.

After settling in and enjoying an excellent light lunch prepared for us by the team of diminutive Filipino kitchen staff resident at the villa, I excused myself from the company of the others and had a look round the business end of things. I ascertained that the place boasted a superb stainless steel kitchen as well as an impressive walk-in store cupboard that was crammed full of interesting ingredients to play with, so my duties as guest cook were unlikely to present me with great difficulties. And with the team of bustling Filipinos at my disposal to tidy up in my wake I envisaged myself working in even easier circumstances than I had in Venice.

But what, I pondered, was I to cook for the big meeting Luigi was hoping to arrange in Naples? If the arrangements worked out, it clearly needed to be something impressive in order to get his business rivals in a receptive frame of mind. I was finding it very hard to come up with anything that went beyond the obvious. I needed ideas that were novel and challenging to give my imagination something to feed on.

It was even hotter in Capri than it had been in Rome and I decided a swim in the amazing pool to wake up the befuddled brain might be in order. In any case, Luigi was in conference with his business partners behind the closed doors of the dining-room so was unavailable for consultation about arrangements for the big meal, whenever it was to be. Accordingly, I changed into my swimwear, which hadn't made it out of my case since leaving London, and padded out into the blinding sunshine outside.

Teresa and Mariana had obviously had the same idea and were already out there. I sucked in my stomach and tried to look more muscle-bound than I know I really am as I strode manfully out to join them.

Teresa was lying on a sun-lounger by the side of the pool reading a book. She was wearing her dark sunglasses so that it was impossible to tell if she was looking at me as I approached or whether she never lifted her eyes from the page. Mariana, meanwhile, was lying flat out on another lounger a few feet away, apparently asleep. Both of them were wearing swimming costumes and had wraps loosely gathered around them. The amount of firm, tanned flesh on display was enough to make my head spin, but I didn't see any avenue to indulge myself with either of them just then. Mariana had been distinctly frosty during the journey over, while Teresa had also kept her distance. Neither of them had said more than a couple of words to me the whole way.

'What are you reading?' I asked Teresa in as breezy a manner as I could muster.

'It's by an Englishman. I like to practise my English by reading novels written in the language.'

'Your English is very good. What's it called?'

'Running in Corridors, by someone called Frankie Fulwood. You won't have heard of it. It's about a gypsy who keeps getting into trouble, usually because he cannot keep his hands off other men's women.' She paused and that wretched half-smile crept onto her immaculately painted lips. 'It's rather good.'

At the sound of our voices Mariana stirred on her sun-lounger then rose on her long, smooth legs and, without a glance in our direction, headed for the house, gone to fetch a drink or something. I waited until she was safely out of earshot.

'Well, I can't say I've heard of it. I don't know why, but I expected it to be Jane Austen or Dickens or something.'

'That's what my husband would prefer me to read, too,' she murmured, 'but I like to choose my own reading. Things no one has heard or, things I don't have to share with anyone else.'

'I bet I can think of something you'd rather do than read a book,' I whispered in her ear.

Teresa moved her head away from me. The sardonic half-smile had crept back onto her lips again.

'Don't laugh at me,' I protested. 'I'm being serious. I want you to take me seriously.'

She sighed with impatience and lowered her glasses to give me a long cool look. 'Isn't that what everyone wants?'

I gaped at her, deeply affronted. It's not often people suggest I'm like everyone else, but that was precisely what this eyetie doxy was now doing to me, as though I was just some nameless oik who'd drifted in off the street, damn her beautiful hide.

'I've a good mind to carry you off to my room this instant and give you a few very good reasons to take me seriously,' I teased her in a low voice.

Teresa's smile faded away and her eyes narrowed. 'You need to think of something else. If you embarrass me in front of my daughter I shall never speak to you again.'

I could see she meant it, so I decided to lay off. I daren't start anything with her in any case, what with Mariana and Luigi and his minions in the near vicinity.

Teresa replaced her glasses and waved with a languid hand at the vista before us.

'Why don't you go and enjoy the view. There's no better anywhere in the world. Once it was only emperors who could enjoy it.'

I cast a quick glance over the panorama before us, though feeling it was a poor substitute for looking down at Teresa's stunning figure. 'I don't know much about all that. I'm not a history buff, to tell the truth,' I told her. 'I've been to Pompeii and Herculanium, of course.'

Teresa nodded. 'History is all around us here. You'd be surprised at the things that have happened here over the years.'

'What things?'

'There are plenty of books inside if you want to find out.'

'I prefer you to tell me. It's too hot for reading, in my opinion.'

'I think it is just perfect.'

'Too hot for me.'

'That is because you are an Englishman.'

I plumped myself down on a plastic seat beside her. 'Go on, then, if you're so determined to stop me thinking about things I shouldn't. Give me a history lesson. Just the highlights, mind.'

Teresa lowered her book with a gesture of mild exasperation. At least she was looking at me now.

'You want me to summarise two thousand years of history, just like that?'

'Give me just one thing, then. But make it exciting or I shall lose interest.'

She sighed again, then pursed her lips for a moment. 'Very well. There was the battle of the Gulf of Naples. On the fifth of June 1284 two great fleets of galleys met in battle within sight of this island. The Neapolitan galleys of Charles of Salerno were outmanoeuvred by their enemies and many were captured. Charles himself was made prisoner. It was part of the War of the Sicilian Vespers.'

'Never heard of it.'

'No? It began as a rebellion against French rule in Sicily. In the end, your King of England, Edward I, talked to the two sides and helped restore peace and the release of Charles.'

'I grant you, that is quite interesting,' I conceded, 'but I still want to carry you off to my room. Tell me something else, something more up to date.'

She muttered something to herself in Italian. 'All right,' she resumed, carefully. 'About twenty years ago there was another Operation Sicilian Vespers, this time between the Italian army and police and criminal organisations on Sicily. Two judges had been murdered, together with their police bodyguards and one of the judge's wives.' She paused. 'You see how history repeats itself? People have fought for control of this region for thousands of years. Many of those who became involved in it have lost their lives.'

'You Italians are a bloodthirsty lot.'

'Blood. Yes, that is what life is all about here. This has always been a place of violence and conflict, back to the time of ancient Rome.' She transferred her gaze from me to the great expanse of sea and coastline before us. 'You must not be deceived by the beauty that surrounds us. There is great danger here, too.'

I stared at her, trying to work out what she was hinting at, if anything. 'Do you mean,' I replied after a short pause, 'that you think that your husband's business affairs may be putting him, all of us, at risk from criminal elements? Is that why you told me that stuff about the Sicilian Vespers?'

Teresa stared back at me but didn't reply. She was clearly in a less than frivolous mood and all this talk of battles and murders wasn't exactly conducive to establishing an intimate, seductive atmosphere between us. Mind you, what with all the reading she did, she certainly seemed to know her stuff. I wondered fleetingly if I should ask her to help me with the book I was supposed to be working on. Some local colour would help a lot.

Further discussion between the two of us had to be cut short when Mariana padded back outside to resume her stint in the sun. It was probably just as well.

I reluctantly left Teresa to resume her reading and plunged into the water for a swim. I'm not a bad swimmer and I rather hoped the two females were watching as I executed a few lengths in front of them. Neither of them, however, seemed to be paying much attention when I checked so eventually I hauled myself out and towelled myself dry, acutely conscious all the while of their apparent disinterest in me.

Once dry, and still not getting any attention from anyone, I opted to do moody. I went inside and loafed about the house for a bit, feeling unloved and unappreciated. Then, because there was no one about to rescue me from my listless despondency and it was really too hot for me outside, I wandered into the kitchen, my old refuge in times of stress. Besides, I reminded myself, I really ought to be applying myself to the question of what I was to prepare for Luigi Vanni's big dinner.

My conversation with Teresa set me thinking as I placed my trusty old beast of a wok on the oven. If she was finding literary gold reading things no one else had heard of, perhaps I should be doing the same thing with my cooking. Perhaps I too should be looking beyond the obvious and considering ingredients and combinations of ingredients that the rest of the world passed over or had never even considered in the first place.

I inspected the knife block, which housed a dozen or more top quality blades of differing shapes and sizes. I absently removed one of the bigger blades and tested its sharpness against my thumb. Then I found myself thinking about the conflict that Teresa had been telling me about. The whole history of this area, she had explained to me, was one of warfare and violence. Perhaps I was guilty of being too safe in my cooking. Perhaps, in keeping with my surroundings, it should incorporate more violent clashes of taste and texture than conventional cookery allowed – sweet with sour, bitter with bland, strong with mild.

The fashion for years now had been for fusion of complementary cooking styles, but maybe it was *fission* that would prove the more exciting, the bringing together of traditions and ingredients that at first glance would appear to be at war with each other. Perhaps it was a path I could follow to wake up my jaded palate and get my dormant creativity going again. Might it even prove the base of a new culinary trend – a revolution even? It was worth thinking about.

But what would such a cuisine look like? What contradictions in taste, texture and cultural expectations could I surprise the world with? Hadn't everything been done? Well, no, of course it hadn't. Experimentation always stopped where the food didn't please diners' palates. But then that begged the question, why didn't it please their palates? How did we decide what did and didn't go together? Who decided it?

I began to feel a creative excitement stealing over me. I waved the knife I held in the air, as though sparring with an imaginary monster in front of me.

The only reason experimentation stopped where it did, it occurred to me, was the hidebound caution of my fellows in the culinary establishment, who dictated to the world what was deemed good food and what wasn't. People decided something tasted wrong because that was what they had been told was wrong, not necessarily because there was anything intrinsically wrong with it. Of course, you didn't eat things that were inedible, but the rest was based on cultural narrowmindedness rather than taste alone.

I rubbed my furrowed brow. Why, I asked myself seriously for the first time, don't we pour custard on our roast beef? Or pour gravy over our ice cream? Or add cream to a glass of beer? Or add a drop of beer to a cup of tea? When I stopped to think about it, the whole question of our modern approach to food seemed absurd and built largely on inherited prejudices and artificial principles. My God, what had we been doing all these years? There was so much out there that had never been attempted, except in a very timid way as an eccentric experiment (chocolate wine came to mind for some reason).

I sat down on a stool and stared without seeing at the oven in front of me. I felt like I was experiencing a moment of almost religious enlightenment. Whole new avenues of culinary possibility were opening up before me. Why the hell did we dismiss things automatically on the unthinking grounds that they just did not go together? Opposites attract – wasn't that something that held good in just about every other sphere? Why not cookery too?

It all seemed crystal clear to me. Our sense of taste had to be untrained, liberated. The tongue was a battlefield to be fought over, ravaged, despoiled, exploded. Like a forest it needed to be subjected to a burnt earth policy so that it could spring up anew, vigorous and full of vitality. And the only way to achieve this reawakening was through the tastes of fire and smoke and, yes, just as Teresa had said – blood.

This was a historic moment, I felt. This was where a whole campaign for a new cuisine might begin. It would be the opposite of fusion – it would be a whole new style in which the more ingredients were in contrast with each other, both in terms of taste and expectations, the greater the progress we would make towards a new understanding of taste – eating – life itself!

My mind in a whirl of inventiveness, I tried to focus on a few sample dishes that might encapsulate my thrilling new theory of cooking. What classic dishes might be invigorated by the inclusion of ingredients that would startle our jaded, prejudiced tastebuds into a new, vivid consciousness? Queen of puddings with the addition of trout and horseradish, apricot mousse with soused herring and pâté de foie gras, Victoria sponge with pepper and mustard. The image of a single Weetabix topped with sandwich spread and three wedges of a chocolate orange flashed up in my memory. My God, my mother had been so much wiser than she had realised!

Ideas for new dishes tumbled about in my head. What I needed to do was to get outside in the fresh air and go for a walk so I could start to make sense of them. A brisk hike along the limestone cliffs below the villa would be just the job.

I made my way out through the villa's front door and headed down the driveway towards the main gates, which were manned by a couple of Luigi's men They watched me warily as I approached. In my excitement and feeling full of love for them and the world in general, I grinned and raised an arm in greeting. I had quite forgotten I was still holding the knife from the kitchen.

At once one of the pair gave a cry of warning and both of them suddenly crouched and produced automatic pistols, which they levelled expertly at me. I came to an abrupt halt before them, heart pounding. They couldn't shoot me – they couldn't – not now, not when I was just about to unleash on the world my huge new idea, my gift to mankind! Life couldn't be so unfair! Could it?

Somehow I forced my fingers to open and let the knife drop to the ground with a clatter. The sudden noise only made the two men look even more alarmed, squinting over their barrels at me with apparently lethal intent.

The guns were terrifying. I've never had much to do with them in my line of work. Of course, when I was in the US, everyone seemed to have one. I remember enjoying an extended moment of intimacy with a lady friend in a quiet corner at a party one time when my hands came up against a hard lump under her jacket and I found she had a loaded revolver tucked into a holster under her left armpit. It killed the moment, I can tell you. It's not relaxing to know that if your partner is at all dissatisfied with the service you're providing she is sporting the means to make that dissatisfaction pointedly, and permanently, evident. Advice to my American readers: call a halt to this ludicrous addiction to guns and you'll get laid one helluva lot more often, well, by me at least.

Fortunately for me, at the precise moment that it appeared my life was about to be cut short due to a misunderstanding over what is to me just a humble kitchen implement, we were distracted by the sound of engines coming from the direction of the villa. I glanced nervously over my shoulder and saw two sleek black limousines descending the driveway towards us. The lead vehicle came to a halt just behind me where I stood, my arm still raised.

Luigi emerged from the rear door and came over to join our static little group.

'Is there a problem?'

'Your men here won't let me out,' I complained.

Luigi frowned and then spoke in rapid Italian to his men. They jabbered back in equally fast Italian and pointed angrily at the knife lying at my feet.

Luigi listened, then tut-tutted and picked the knife up. 'It seems my men were alarmed when you approached them holding this.'

I felt myself blushing. 'I'd quite forgotten I was carrying it,' I told him, rather lamely. 'But it's no excuse for them frightening me half to death with their – their – artillery!'

Luigi signalled to the men to put away their guns, which they did at once. He looked apologetically at me.

'You must forgive their enthusiasm,' he said. 'After what happened in Rome we are all feeling a little anxious. I am sure you understand. And I do have the safety of the two women to consider. That is why I have this extra security here. It is to protect us all from anyone who might wish to interfere with our plans for the forthcoming meeting I have told you about.' He shrugged. 'I am afraid we must just put up with it. We are all subject to it, even me. My associates have advised me never to leave the villa without bodyguards. You see how it is – I am only on my way to visit an old colleague of mine on the other side of the island and all these people have to come with me. It is very inconvenient, I know.'

'Do you mean we are prisoners here?'

'Not at all! You are free to go wherever you wish on the island. Only please let me know first so that I may inform my men to let you through. May I ask where you were going?'

'I was just going for a walk, to think about the meal you want me to cook for you.'

'Ah, I see!'

'I thought the view from the clifftops here might inspire me.'

Luigi nodded approvingly. 'Of course. There is a path that offers spectacular views just near here. You will find it a short distance past the first bend in the road going down to the village. How long will you be?'

'I don't know. An hour or two, I suppose.'

'Excellent, I will see you later then.' He looked down at the knife in his hand. 'I'll give this to one of my men to take back to the kitchen. I don't think you will need it.'

Luigi spoke rapidly to the two men on the gate. One of them took the knife and trotted back up the drive towards the villa, while the other pressed a button to open the iron gating.

'Goodbye, my friend,' Luigi called as he got back into the car.

A moment later the two vehicles eased through the gateway and then accelerated in a cloud of dust down the narrow road beyond and disappeared from sight. I took a deep breath and headed after them on foot, gritting my teeth as the remaining guard watched me go past with a sullen look on his face.

After the fright I had just had I needed the peace of the countryside to calm my thoughts and let me concentrate on the matter in hand. A clifftop walk overlooking the sea should restore my equilibrium like nothing else. Or so I thought.

I had hardly walked a hundred yards out of sight of the villa, rounding the bend in the road below, when three figures in white shirts and blue uniform trousers and caps emerged from behind a large rock and pounced on me.

Out of the Wok, into the Fryer

Barely ten minutes after being jumped by the three uniformed men, I was seated on a wooden chair in the police station in the nearby village of Anacapri across the table from a stern-faced Italian police inspector. A burly sergeant stood by the door as though to forestall any attempt I might make to escape. To my demands to know what I was doing there and what the devil they meant kidnapping me in broad daylight as I went about my lawful business I had received no response in the car in which they had brought me there. So now I waited to see what the inspector might have to say, when he was good and ready.

The inspector, who had a lean, vulpine face and piercing eyes, flicked through the cards in my wallet, which his men had found in my trouser pocket.

'Your name is Tremayne Truelove,' he said in heavily accented English. 'Is that how you pronounce it?'

'Yes.'

He examined another of the cards. It was evidently absorbing reading. 'You are a citizen of the United Kingdom?'

'Yes.'

'You live in London?'

'Yes.'

'You are a gangster?'

'Yes. I mean, no, of course not! I'm sorry, I'm feeling rather flustered. Please don't take anything I say seriously.'

'But I do take what you say seriously.' The inspector gave me a grim look. 'Very seriously.'

I lapsed into silence. The inspector laid the wallet down and opened a file of papers at his elbow on the table in front of him.

'You were in Venice recently,' he remarked, without looking up. It sounded more like a statement of fact rather than a question.

'Yes. How do you know that?'

'It is my business.' He read a bit more and his brow furrowed. 'You had a fight with a chef at a restaurant in the city. Is that correct?'

I stared at him. Was that what this was about? 'It–it wasn't a fight exactly. The man served up a terrible version of one of my recipes. Something had to be said, and the man lost his temper. Fortunately he was prevented from attacking me and I left before things got out of hand any further.'

'You did not go back to the restaurant later?'

'No. Well, I passed by it once, but I didn't go in.'

The policeman consulted the sheet of paper in the file open in front of him. 'Yes, you were wearing a disguise and stopped to read a notice in the window.'

I goggled at him. 'How the hell do you know that? Have you been watching me?'

'We have been watching you ever since you were first seen in the company of Luigi Vanni.'

'What? You've been following me all this time?'

'We lost sight of you for a time after Venice but then you were identified, again in company with Luigi Vanni, in Rome and now here in Capri.' He put the paper down and turned his piercing eyes on me. 'You spend a lot of time together, the two of you.'

I shifted uncomfortably. 'What's wrong with that? Luigi is a most generous patron of mine and a friend.'

The inspector considered me for a moment without speaking. 'Let us go back to Venice. You did not see the man you had the argument with again?'

'No. Judging by the notice in the window, I gathered he'd gone off somewhere. Isn't that so?'

'Not exactly. The man you refer to is still in Venice.' The inspector continued to level his unflinching gaze at me. 'He's lying on a slab in the city mortuary. He was found in a canal not far from where he worked.'

I stared at him, speechless with horror.

'Now, Signore Truelove,' the inspector continued, in a very cool manner. 'I wonder if you have anything you would like to tell us about that?'

'No! Nothing at all! You can't believe I had anything to do with this – this – event.' I scrabbled desperately for anything to clear myself of any suspicion. 'Perhaps he fell in.'

'We think not. He had been strangled.'

I looked helplessly at him as what he had said sunk in.

The inspector cleared his throat. 'You are currently staying at the villa of Luigi Vanni.'

'Y-yes,' I stammered. 'I'm cooking for him and his family.'

'Cooking. I see.'

'I'm an internationally renowned chef, as it happens, with my own–'

'Are you aware of the nature of the business Signore Luigi Vanni is involved in?' the inspector interrupted.

'No. I haven't asked and he hasn't told me. I believe it's something to do with high finance. I'm a chef. I know very little about such things.'

'I see.'

The policeman stared at me long and hard. I waited for him to continue but he just kept on staring.

'Why are you staring at me like that?'

'I am trying to decide whether you are telling me the truth or not.'

'Oh.'

I couldn't think of anything helpful to add to that, so I sat there in mute silence while he completed his examination. Then he gave a small sigh.

'Very well, Signore Truelove, I am prepared to give you the benefit of the doubt. I will try to make things clear to you. We believe Luigi Vanni is involved in a number of criminal activities. But we need more information about his operations before we can put him on trial and for that we need someone who is, as you say, on the inside. That person, it seems to us, could be you.'

'Now hold on a minute...'

'If you do not cooperate with us in this matter then we will conclude that you are a member of the Vanni gang and deal with you accordingly. You will be thrown into the prison here in Naples. It is not a good place for a cultivated person such as yourself. If you come out...' he paused for effect, 'then it is likely that you will be put on trial on several serious charges, maybe even murder.' He paused again. 'If, however, you agree to help us, then all may yet be well. You may even return to your country a hero. So, will you help us?'

Christ! Were they really telling me that the charming, generous Luigi Vanni was a gangster? It couldn't be true. Could it?

I licked my lips. 'Let me get this straight. You want me to go back to the villa and spy on Luigi Vanni. If I don't I will be arrested and charged with murder.'

'Precisely.'

I nodded slowly, not trusting myself to say anything either appropriate or sensible.

For the first time the inspector smiled. It was a thin, wan smile that didn't reach his eyes, but it was a smile nonetheless.

'I understand that this has come as a shock to you. Luigi Vanni is skilled at concealing his true character from the world. Sergeant, bring Signore Truelove something to eat. And a drink.'

The sergeant left the room.

'Look here, inspector, if what you say is true, I'm not

sure this is such a good idea. I'm not trained for this kind of thing. I'm a chef, for heaven's sake. All I know about is cooking.'

'We do not expect you to be a James Bond for us. We only ask that you keep your eyes open for anything interesting that happens up at the villa, so that it may be used as evidence when Signore Vanni and his associates appear in court. You don't have to do anything else, just be a witness to anything that does, or doesn't, happen.'

'But won't you want me to contact you? I've seen this kind of thing in films…'

'No contact at all, until it is all over. We have no wish to endanger your safety.'

'Neither do I.'

The door opened and the sergeant reappeared with a glass of water and a thin piece of what I suppose was meant to be pizza, but looked more like the heavily textured wallpaper my grandparents had decorated their living room with back in the fifties. I took a sip of the water then gave the pizza a tentative nibble and tasted – well, nothing at all really.

I looked up at the sergeant, genuinely interested. 'You like this?'

The sergeant grunted in the affirmative.

The inspector rose from his chair. 'Return Signore Truelove to the villa – discreetly. The sooner the better. We don't believe Luigi Vanni will be back until this evening, but we don't want anyone at the villa to know he has been in contact with us.'

The sergeant nodded and reached out to take the plate and pizza back from me. I let him take it.

'Seriously,' I repeated, 'you like this?'

It was only after they had deposited me from an unmarked police car some distance from the villa gates that it began to dawn on me just how much danger I could be in. The police inspector hadn't exactly made it clear what business Luigi was engaged in, but it obviously wasn't one the police approved of – and I had seen for myself that it was serious enough for those involved in it to carry guns and behave like twitchy racehorses before a big race.

I was acutely conscious of my own vulnerability. As I've already mentioned, as a species we chefs aren't terribly pugnacious. Frankly most celebrity chefs (even Gordo) fight like a girl when the French fries cooked with parmesan and garlic are down. For all the bad language and macho posturing you encounter in kitchens, when it comes to actual fisticuffs the worst injury you risk with most of us is a rap on the knuckles with a wooden spatula. And that's no defence at all against shady gun-toting operators like those I now found myself amongst.

It was all so unexpected. From the kick-off, when Luigi had rescued me in my cups from the rage of that Italian cook, I had thought him a genuinely lovely man. He was beautifully dressed, generous with his favours, adoring towards his wife and daughter – sincere, genuine, kindly. He had seemed the sort of person my mother would have referred to as 'utterly charming' and done her best to seduce. That should have warned me, I suppose. My mother has an unerring taste for men who are subsequently revealed to be untrustworthy, ungentle and uncaring for the welfare of yours truly. Now I had to face the unpalatable possibility that dear, honest Luigi was some kind of gangster, a rat, an unloving hoodlum whose taste for the finer things in life was a complete sham. If so, he had fooled me completely.

I stumped up the track towards the villa, feeling oddly hollow inside, the product of indignation and abject terror. It really was too much. There I was, hurt and on the defensive after my troubles in London – what had I of all people done to be singled out for such unfeeling treatment at the hands of the Vannis? It had been an unlucky day indeed when I had stumbled into that restaurant just at the moment that Luigi Vanni himself was finishing his meal.

And what of that cook? What had happened for him to end up in the canal like that? Surely it couldn't have been just because he had had a go at me? But the police seemed pretty sure that Luigi Vanni was a wrong 'un. If he was as bad as they seemed to be suggesting he was, perhaps he had even ordered the unfortunate chef's killing in order to ingratiate himself with me. But would anyone really commit murder just to obtain the services of a better chef, even one as talented and internationally renowned as me? It seemed a bit of a stretch... But then again, he also wanted me to cook for this wretched meal of his – and he had stressed how vitally important it was to him that it went well...

Not that it was just Luigi Vanni who had taken advantage of hapless little me. That police inspector was just as bad in his way, blackmailing me with the threat of prison and trial for murder in order to get me to become his spy within the Vanni household. It was intolerable when I thought about it. I was sure this kind of thing could never happen in England.

Unfortunately for me, however, I wasn't in England.

I felt very jumpy as I walked past the two guards loitering at the villa gates. They watched me go by without speaking. I don't know why, but I felt incredibly guilty, as though I was sure they knew all about the act of treachery I had reluctantly agreed to.

I reached the villa itself and made my way pensively to my room. I was trying desperately to think of a way out of the mess I found myself in, but nothing obvious occurred to me. If I backed out of the deal with the inspector I would be arrested and put away, to face a very uncertain future. Did they still have the death penalty in Italy? If I stayed I risked God knew what. The women were an additional risk, of course. If Luigi found out what I'd been up to with his wife and his daughter – I shuddered to think what the consequences might be if he was even half the villain the police said he was. I made a mental note to keep both females at a distance. Not that that would be especially difficult, it seemed, as both of them were already keeping a wary distance from me.

I sat on the bed and cursed myself for my naïvety. Why didn't I spot the danger I was in long before this? How could I have been so blind as to the likely true nature of Luigi Vanni's business? Many odd things made sense now, such as the Vannis' collective caginess about Luigi's affairs, their extravagant wealth, the presence of the burly associates, the secretive meetings, the fear of interference from business rivals, the guns…

I really had been a prize chump.

I remained in my room till the time came to prepare the evening meal. I heard doors open and close as Luigi Vanni and his men came home and waited tensely for him to storm in to tell me he knew what I'd been up to that day and to announce my immediate execution. But nothing happened and I steeled myself to finishing preparations for the meal and to facing my nemesis once more.

In fact, the atmosphere in the villa dining-room was relatively tranquil and unthreatening when I presided over the entry of the first course, carried in by my Filipino underlings, that evening. Luigi seemed sombre and distracted as the four of us tucked in and there was little conversation. Luigi didn't appear to be in a mood to chat, and God knew I wasn't either, so it was up the two women to make whatever observations they wanted to volunteer about their day, though there weren't many of them either. Teresa, it seemed, was enjoying her novel, while Mariana thought the filter in the pool wasn't working as well as it should. Luigi promised her he'd get someone to look at it and we lapsed into silence once more.

The reason for Luigi's distraction became clear after the Filipinos had cleared away the last course and we were relaxing, if you could call it that given my jumpiness, over coffee and hand-made chocolates. He cleared his throat and then looked up with a most disconsolate expression on his face.

'I'm afraid I have bad news,' he told us solemnly. 'This afternoon I received distressing information from Rome.'

My heart missed a beat and I paused in terror with my coffee cup in mid-air. Someone had told him about my talk with the police. I was sure of it. He was about to order me carried out to the lip of the terrace and tossed over it like Tarpeia herself when she was thrown to her death from the rock that now bears her name.

'I am sorry to have to tell you,' he continued mournfully, 'that my dear colleague Pasquale has died in hospital in Rome.'

The two women made small noises of surprise while I responded by rattling my cup in its saucer as I shook with relief. It was the demise of that oaf Pasquale he was distracted by, not the treachery of little me! I must admit that I'd entirely forgotten about Luigi's stricken associate since getting to Capri, but if Pasquale had been present I would in all likelihood have kissed the dome of his dead, bald head with gratitude.

'Yes, it is very distressing, I know,' Luigi went on, patting first his wife's hand, then his daughter's, though they didn't look all that distressed to me. 'The funeral is to be held in Naples the day after tomorrow, as that is where his family comes from. That will give us time to get his body back home and get the word out to everyone. We should all attend, as a mark of respect. I believe most of the others will wish to be present too.' He turned at last to me. 'Tremayne, you are under no obligation, of course, but I would appreciate it if you could look after Teresa and Mariana. As Pasquale's employer, I shall be expected to support his family and there will be many attending the funeral I must speak to on their behalf. I would be most grateful if I could rely upon your help.'

I nodded dumbly. Though Luigi was making it sound like I had free choice whether to attend or not, and that it would be a personal favour to him if I did come along, it didn't in truth feel like I had any real choice in the matter.

'Of course,' I told him, perhaps a little too jauntily. 'I'll be happy to.'

Between you and me, I was so relieved not to be at that moment hurtling downwards from the clifftops of Capri that I'm not sure I didn't even smile.

below from Capri

Salad Days

Life at the villa next day began pretty much as normal. Luigi left early in the helicopter, which soared off in the direction of Naples, off no doubt to supervise arrangements for the coming funeral. The two women took their places, as usual, by the pool. I decided not to join them and thereby put myself through the agonies of revelling in their proximity and being unable to do anything about it. Instead I pottered about the kitchen, getting in the way of the Filipinos and trying to focus upon the exciting new ideas about our universal approach to food that I had been absorbed with prior to being carted off against my will to the local nick. But it was an uphill struggle. World-changing though my notions promised to be, every time I tried to advance my theories on the subject the image of the unsmiling Italian police inspector rose up before me and blocked out the light.

I gave up trying to think creatively about my craft and instead spent a couple of hours leafing through the books on the shelves in the palatial living-room, attempting to distract myself with the history of the Bay of Naples, as previously delineated by the delectable Teresa. The more I looked into it, however, the more blood-soaked the history of the region revealed itself to be. And that did nothing to take my mind off the dangers to which I may currently be exposed. When I came to a chapter about the martyrdom of Januarius, the patron saint of Naples who was beheaded at the Solfatara volcanic crater (still actively spewing out sulphurous fumes today) in the fourth century BC, I returned the book to the shelf with a shudder and resolved to find something else to take my mind off things.

I found myself wondering if I should be doing something more proactive concerning gathering information about Luigi Vanni's operations. After all, I told myself, the sooner I could help the police uncover what was going on, if anything was indeed going on, the sooner my patron and his associates could be hauled off to gaol and the sooner I would be free to get the hell out of here and back to the safety of London, which right now held far more charm to me than the sun-parched slopes of Capri. Even if it was raining back in England, which it probably was.

I didn't think I'd get much more out of either of the two women outside, not to mention the risks involved in trying to get back into their confidence. Instead I pondered the possibility of learning something from Luigi Vanni's hirelings. The Filipinos were hopeless, having no English and patently very little understanding of what Luigi Vanni's world was about. That left his associates, whom I had by now worked out might be more properly described as his henchmen. Approaching them for information was a risky enterprise, I acknowledged at once, but there weren't many other avenues open to me, so it was worth trying. I could always back off if they started becoming suspicious of my motives.

I sauntered outside. There weren't many of Luigi's men about that day as several of them had gone off with him to the mainland, but then I spotted Bruno, the boatman in Venice, who had been left in charge in his boss's absence. He was patrolling the perimeter rather listlessly, clearly not expecting trouble with his patron absent.

I waited until Bruno's route brought him within a few yards of where I was loitering, leaning against the wall of the villa in a patch of shade and making a show of enjoying the stunning view. I knew from past experience that he had a little English, though it was halting and often inaccurate.

'Hot day,' I commented to him as he reached me. He had some kind of automatic pistol looped on a strap over his shoulder, but I did my best to ignore the beastly thing. 'There's not a lot of shade up here, is there?'

Bruno grunted and wiped the sweat from his forehead.

I took that as an encouraging beginning. 'I bet you'd like a cold drink. I could make one for you in the kitchen, if you like.' I mimed the action of lifting a glass and taking a long swig at it, then smacking my lips with satisfaction.

Bruno stared at me and for a moment I thought he was about to tell me what for, to stop fooling around and to go back inside. But then a trickle of sweat dripped into his eye, making him blink and curse under his breath.

'How about an iced lemonade?' I suggested. 'I'm sure no one would mind if you took a quick break. It is awfully hot, after all.'

Bruno considered for a moment, presumably weighing up the risk of heat exhaustion against the risk of anyone accusing him of dereliction of his duty. After a few seconds he appeared to come to the conclusion that my offer brought with it the smaller hazard.

He followed me into the shade of the house and through the living-room to the kitchen. I glanced apprehensively towards the terrace as we passed the big windows, but Teresa and Mariana seemed to be entirely unconscious of us.

Once in the kitchen I sat Bruno down in a chair and fussed over him with a jug of iced lemonade and a bite to eat, as I had already prepared something for the three of us for lunch and there was plenty to go round. Bruno was a man with a big appetite and I could see the food was of great interest to him. I had no idea what he and the other men were generally given to eat, as that task was left to the Filipinos, but judging by their general performance in the kitchen, it wouldn't have been anything to write home about. Bruno knocked back half a glass of lemonade in one go and then filled his mouth with meat and salad.

I watched him, noting the big brawny hands and huge muscles straining the fabric of his black cotton tee-shirt. He was the sort of thug you really wouldn't want to meet on a dark night. He wasn't, as far as I could tell, the sharpest fruit parer in the cutlery drawer, but I would do well to tread carefully.

'Not much for you to do with Signore Vanni away, I suppose?' I ventured.

Bruno grunted and helped himself to some olives.

'I expect he's over there getting things ready for poor Pasquale's funeral,' I continued, nodding in the vague direction of Naples.

Bruno made a noise of regret at the mention of Pasquale's name.

I know my cue when it comes. I sighed theatrically and endeavoured to look suitably stricken. 'Poor, poor, poor, Pasquale.'

Bruno paused in mid-munch, registering my distress.

Ah-ha! Now I knew how to play this. I built it up a bit more, sniffing ostentatiously and wiping my nose. I knew it had worked when a second or two later Bruno reached slowly across the table at which we were sitting and awkwardly landed one of his huge paws on my shoulder in what I took to be a clumsy gesture of consolation.

I nodded appreciatively at him. 'I know. Silly of me to get upset,' I told him. 'But it was a huge shock. To all of us.'

Bruno nodded and withdrew his hand.

'You know, I can't believe it was accidental,' I went on, a little conspiratorially now I appeared to have him on my side. 'It seems very odd, what happened. What do you chaps think about it?'

Bruno looked defensive. It didn't seem he was going to share that with me.

I shrugged. 'Of course, of course, that's between you and your friends. Wrong of me to ask. Well, it doesn't matter really whether it was accidental or not when we don't know who might have been behind it in any case. That's the important thing, if it wasn't an accident, I mean. But who on earth would want to do in poor Pasquale like that, and why, that's what I'd like to know.'

I shook my head sorrowfully, as though that was an end to the conversation, that out of deference to his wishes not to talk about it I would speculate about it no more. It would just have to go down in history as one of the unfathomable mysteries of existence, like the building of Stonehenge or the Bermuda Triangle.

Bruno had gone very quiet, forgetting the remains of the food on the plate in front of him. I avoided looking at him directly but instead topped up his half-empty glass. Then I rested the big jug on the table and waited for a response.

'The Albanians,' I heard him mutter a second or two later.

'The what?'

'The Albanians.'

I frowned at him. 'The Albanians? The Albanians were behind it?'

I hadn't the foggiest what he was talking about, but something told me this could be important. I stared at him, hoping he would elaborate in some way.

But now, abruptly, I realised I had shown just a bit too much interest in the matter, for Bruno's expression had tightened and he had drawn back from the table.

I held up my hands in apology and looked at the table

top. 'Sorry. I don't mean to pry. It's just that Pasquale's death – well, you know…'

I risked a glance up at Bruno and saw that he was frowning with concentration, apparently trying to decide what to make of me and my sudden curiosity. Suspicion was written all over his brutish face. I'd have to think of something quick to stop him from going any further down that path, for the sake of my health.

'I do apologise, Bruno, really I do. I'm always talking when I should be quiet. It's just that the news about Pasquale is so upsetting – and, I don't know, I felt I could talk to you, that you'd understand.'

His silence was deafening but I ploughed on.

'I can't talk about these things with Signore Vanni, you understand, as I'm working for him when all's said and done, just like you chaps. And I don't want to upset his wife or daughter by talking about it.' I looked up at him again. 'It's just that I feel you and I are – are – what's the word – simpatico. Am I wrong to think that?'

I don't quite know now where I was going with this line of approach. I think I was just trying to come up with something, anything, that would defuse the dangerous belligerence that was hovering about the big hoodlum's features. I really wasn't sure what he was thinking, whether he would nod and we'd be pals again or whether he'd be making a mental note to share his suspicions with Signore Vanni the minute he returned across the threshold later in the day, with all that might entail. My fate might well depend upon which way his thoughts tended at this very moment.

Before I could say anything more, however, Bruno leaned forward again and before I could move it out of the way he had laid both his massive paws on my own tiny white right hand and pressed it against the table.

'Simpatico,' he growled at me, an odd intensity of emotion glowing at me from under his hairy brows.

We stared at each other, him with some weird passion that was completely incomprehensible to me, and me with a pleading expression born of uncertainty and alarm.

He clutched my hand in his for several long seconds more then, seemingly satisfied, grunted and stood up. Pausing only to sweep the last morsel of food from his plate and up into his mouth he stalked out of the kitchen without a backward look and continued back the way we had come, leaving me startled and open-mouthed at the table.

What the hell was that about, I wondered. I had thought that bringing up the subject of Pasquale's death would be a good way to establish a connection with the man, but I had never expected quite such a strong response. Perhaps they had been closer than I had realised.

I shook my head as I cleared away the plate and glass. The important thing was, I had learned something that might turn out to be highly significant, if I could just figure out why. The Albanians were involved in Pasquale's death. All I had to do was work out who these Albanians were and what on earth they had to do with Luigi Vanni. Simple, really.

Lunch with the women was a placid and silent affair, with no one looking at each other more than necessary. Teresa brought her latest book to the table, while Mariana had her mobile phone at her elbow and spent most of lunch tapping out text messages, presumably to her friends. My prosciutto salad with roasted courgettes, fennel and goat cheese was wasted on them. I might as well as given them paste sandwiches and a cup-a-soup.

After lunch I tidied up and then sneaked about the villa, feeling very secret agent-like and looking for any clues that might put me in better stead with the police next time we met. There was nothing incriminating to be seen anywhere and eventually there was only one place left to check – Luigi Vanni's study. I had only been in there once, when taking him a mid-afternoon snack, and it was clearly somewhere that most visitors were barred from entering. On my previous visit I had noted how tidy he kept the place. Perhaps he was paranoid about prying eyes seeing information that he would rather they did not see. There was probably a large safe hidden somewhere so that all any casual visitor would find on his impressively large desk would be insignificant memos and other papers.

Nonetheless, I felt it would be remiss of me not to take a quick look round. After double-checking that no one else was nearby, I slipped through the door and into the empty study. There were a few bits of paper on the desk, as I expected, but it all looked innocent enough to me. I suppose it was asking a bit much to hope there would be an open diary on the desk in which Luigi Vanni described in minute detail the various crimes of which he was suspected by the authorities, but I nosed about a bit among the sheets of paper, hoping for something incriminating. Nothing.

In television detective thrillers, I recalled, they usually found the most interesting information in the wastepaper bin, so I picked it up and examined the contents, rather pessimistically. There wasn't much in it, but near the bottom there were two crumpled bits of paper with something scrawled on them in Luigi's hand, so I flattened them out on my knee to see what he'd written.

The first sheet bore just three words. '1 km Castellammare.'

The second sheet was more interesting. He had written what I translated as 'First shipment. 15 km south-west Capri. 2 a.m.' This was followed by what looked to me to be a location in terms of latitude and longitude, but it meant nothing to me.

I tried to puzzle out what it could mean. There was obviously a first shipment of something coming in from the sea, from the south-west, but there was no clue as to what it could be or what day it was arriving. I knew that Castellammare was on the coast midway between Naples and Sorrento – could that be where the shipment was to end up perhaps? There was no way of knowing anything for sure.

I crumpled the sheets of paper up again and returned them to the bin, then stole quietly from the desk back to the door and through it, closing the door softly behind me.

Satisfied that I had got away with it, I turned and then walked slap bang into Teresa. She stared at me.

'What were you doing in my husband's study?'

I groped for a plausible answer. 'I was – looking for a cup that's missing from the kitchen. I took him some afternoon tea and must have forgotten to collect it afterwards.'

'Did you find it in there?'

'No.'

I stared helplessly back at her. After everything that had passed between us, I felt I could trust her not to betray me willingly to her husband. But her husband he was, and I sensed there were limits to how far she might be prepared to go to protect me.

'Don't go in there alone again,' she warned me in a low voice. 'Luigi would not like it.'

I took a deep breath. 'Listen, Teresa, what's going on here? No one tells me anything.'

Teresa shot me an alarmed look, glancing over her shoulder to check we were not observed before turning back to me. 'You must not ask about Luigi's business! Never! It is private.'

'But you must know something about what he does?'

'I know nothing. Nothing at all. It is nothing to do

with me.'

'I believe you, Teresa. But why does it all have to be so secret–'

She stopped me speaking by placing a forefinger on my lips and staring earnestly at me. I looked into her lovely face and felt myself melting once more before her exquisite beauty.

She lowered her finger, 'You must not ask,' she whispered. 'Please.'

It was at that point that Mariana came through the big windows from the terrace, dressed as usual in her bikini and wrap. She stopped short when she saw her mother and me together. We were not touching and there was nothing we were doing that anyone could read anything into, but we were undeniably standing very close together and I suppose something about our expressions suggested an air of intimacy somehow, for Mariana's mouth dropped open and her eyes flashed surprise.

Teresa stepped back immediately but said nothing. I gave Mariana what I hoped looked like an innocent smile of greeting, but probably came over more as an anguished grimace, and then took myself off in the direction of the kitchen as swiftly as I could, leaving her no opportunity to accuse me of anything.

Whether mother and daughter exchanged any words after I made myself scarce I have no idea. But my heart was hammering in my chest as I closed the kitchen door and leaned back against it. No more risk-taking for me, I promised myself. If the inspector wanted to know more about Luigi Vanni's operations he would have to find out himself.

Cold Meat

Vomero, Naples

You may not have been to the funeral of a Neapolitan gangster, so I suppose I ought to fill you in on what happens. It had clearly been decided by someone (I thought I could guess who) that Pasquale's funeral would be a grand affair in the traditional Catholic tradition, with no expense spared. He might not have been that important a figure in Luigi Vanni's organisation but a message was going to be sent out that even Luigi's minor operatives had their value and were not to be lightly dismissed, by anyone.

Teresa, Mariana and I were ferried to the cathedral in Naples by helicopter and I was immediately impressed by the size of the crowd attending. There wasn't a spare seat in the gloomy but capacious and richly ornamented edifice, though we had good places reserved for us near the front among Pasquale's immediate family, who seemed to comprise almost exclusively elderly female relatives. The place was full of flowers and candles.

The massed females broke into sobs of grief as the casket was carried up the aisle by the pallbearers, Luigi among them, looking very grave. They laid the coffin on cushions on the floor before the altar and then retreated to their places in the congregation. An extravagantly large bouquet rested on top of the casket with a banner wreathed through the arrangement. The wording on it I translated as 'From his family and friends'. More immense bouquets were arranged on the steps leading up to the altar.

The priest conducted the funeral mass with due gravity, with that telling air of distance and disdain that I have noted in every Catholic priest I've ever seen in action, whether it be at baptisms, weddings or funerals. I suppose they've seen it all before and all they want to do is collect their fee and get back to watching the football or something.

After he had finished various people stood up to say a few words in the dead man's memory, their voices echoing round the huge space. First among them was Luigi himself, who, if my Italian served me right, called the late Pasquale his beloved brother, the friend of his bosom (I might have got that wrong) and his right arm. He had been carried off before his time but if that was how God wanted it we would all have to take it on board and get on with our lives. If anyone was to blame we must leave it to God to find them out and deal with them accordingly. He paused for a long moment after this bit and I got the distinct impression he was communicating something quite different to the assembled masses. You got the feeling that he wanted everyone to know that if the Almighty felt he wanted someone to lend him a hand with the finding them out and dealing with them accordingly bit then Luigi Vanni was the man he'd contact first.

Luigi was followed by a large man wearing a sash, apparently a senior representative of the state, possibly even the mayor of Naples. He looked to be on the edge of tears by the time he finished, though he didn't exactly say he had been a close friend of Pasquale's or even known him at all. I was beginning to think that I must have misjudged the stolid Pasquale, or come to the wrong funeral, because he had never struck me as one to arouse such emotions in his friends, in the unlikely event that he actually had any.

When everyone who had anything to say had said it, the pallbearers resumed their places and carried the casket back down the aisle and outside to the hearse. As if this was a signal, Pasquale's elderly relatives (whom I later discovered were mostly paid mourners in the traditional Italian style) broke into howls of anguish. This set off an elderly white-haired woman whom I guessed was Pasquale's mother. She let out a yell of grief and staggered towards the coffin until restrained by her neighbours. Her hysterical sobs echoed around us as the relatives gathered in a little knot and processed down the aisle towards the main door. The rest of us followed in a shuffling, subdued mass until we were all back in the sunshine, blinking after the sombre gloom from which we emerged.

An even larger crowd waited outside as we watched the casket being loaded into the hearse. I had never seen anything like that hearse. It was a terrifying, enormous carriage painted in the deepest satin black with gold fittings and drawn by six magnificent black horses with heads adorned with towering black plumes, fretting with impatience to be on their way to the cemetery.

I watched as the pallbearers began to heave the casket inside until a little old lady at my elbow broke off from loud weeping in order to start jabbering at me in rapid Italian. I glanced at Mariana, who was next to me, for an explanation.

'She warns not to look into the back of the hearse,' she informed me coolly, before rolling her eyes in youthful scorn. 'It is an old superstition here in Naples that it is very unlucky to do so. They say you will travel in one yourself before too long.'

I looked away hastily. Mariana might roll her eyes, and I'm not especially superstitious, but I was in no position to take unnecessary risks of any kind when my own prospects looked so insecure.

The funeral cortege set off for the cemetery, the horses swishing their tails and tossing their heads imperiously. As we walked down the road at a dignified, sedate pace I noticed dozens of posters depicting the dead man that had been stuck up everywhere to announce his demise. A lot of them began with a stock phrase that I struggled to translate, until Mariana observed me puzzling over it and gave me the English equivalent.

'He has serenely gone out like a candle.'

Recalling how I had last seen the unfortunate Pasquale squirming in agony on that stretcher I felt serenely was not the most accurate adjective that could have been chosen. But if that was what people wanted to believe, then fair enough.

Luigi, I saw, had taken a place of honour at the front of the procession, providing Pasquale's grieving mother with an arm to lean on for support. His men seemed to be everywhere, keeping a close eye on the crowd as they went past. None of them had weapons on open display, but I could tell from the bulges beneath their suit jackets that they had come prepared for any threat. I wondered uneasily from whom such a threat might be expected.

A police helicopter followed our progress from above and there were a lot of press photographers in attendance, though Luigi's men were quick to drive them off whenever they got into position to take a picture of Luigi Vanni himself. I glanced around nervously for any sign of the police inspector who had interviewed me on Capri but there was no sign of him. I did not doubt, however, that he was somewhere nearby, given his interest in the Vanni business empire. Perhaps, I speculated, he was in the helicopter above our heads.

Looking at Luigi's men I was appalled once again at my lack of any intuitive understanding on my part as to their real character. A more formidable bunch of thugs it would have been hard to imagine. Once you looked past the neat and expensive suits you began to notice the broken noses, the cauliflower ears and the scars. My God, I really had stumbled completely unknowing into a nest of vipers!

The cemetery we headed for was a large, well-kept area crowded with white stones and funerary monuments. We accompanied the chief mourners between the tombs to a wall with a niche that had been opened for Pasquale's casket, which was removed from the hearse at the cemetery gates and carried by the pallbearers to the family plot.

At Luigi's invitation Teresa stepped forward to place a single rose on the coffin lid, then we watched in silence as the casket was slid into its slot. Each niche, I saw, was decorated with a light and a vase and many bore a framed photograph of the deceased. A photograph of Pasquale was already in place beside his allotted niche. Even confined to a photograph in a frame barely five inches wide, Pasquale looked forbidding, as though daring anyone to go too close and risk some unpleasant consequence for their impudence. He wasn't smiling, and his bald pate shone like it had been polished.

As soon as the coffin was in place a pair of workmen began the job of closing up the slot with bricks and mortar. This acted as a signal for all those present to make their way out of the cemetery.

I had been warned that close friends of the family, which naturally included us, would be expected to play a leading role at the wake at a nearby hotel. As we walked the short distance I steeled myself to do whatever was necessary and not to attract any attention to myself. I was ready for a drink, too, as it was broiling hot in the cemetery and there was little shade.

It was at this point that I spotted the police inspector from Capri watching us. He was standing beside the cemetery gate, eyes hidden behind dark sunglasses and hands clasped in front of him. I cursed him for making no effort whatsoever to conceal himself. Luigi and the others gave no sign of knowing who he was but I scowled at him nonetheless as we went by.

The wake was not a jovial affair. The Italians are not like the Irish, who treat a death as a good reason to celebrate life and redouble their attempts to enjoy themselves while they have the chance. The atmosphere in the hotel's old ballroom was tense and hushed, with people taking their turn to express condolences to the dead man's mother and other relatives, who looked stony-faced now they had finally stopped their sobbing and wailing.

Luigi Vanni stood at the bereaved mother's side throughout, overseeing everything. Pasquale's mother herself had recovered sufficiently from her earlier emotional outburst to give attention to each individual mourner as they paid their respects in their turn, though I thought she looked nervous to have Luigi so close beside her. She, like several other family members of either sex, I noticed irreverently, were also very thin on top – baldness clearly ran in the family.

I was about to go and see what was on offer in the way of food and drink when the atmosphere suddenly changed. All at once, no one was talking and all Luigi's men were standing stock still, glaring and apprehensive.

The object of their attention was a small group of men in dark suits who had just entered the room. There were half a dozen of them, looking just as thuggish and rough-hewn as Luigi Vanni's associates, and with hands similarly hidden inside their jackets. At their head stood a tall, muscular-looking man with crew-cut hair and a rather flashy dark suit and shirt with a collar done up with a little gold chain in place of a tie. He was a handsome enough chap, but the effect was rather marred by a long white scar that ran from above his forehead and diagonally across his face towards the bottom of his right ear, as though he had been slashed by a blade of some sort. The man stared at Luigi Vanni for a moment then stepped forward with his hand outstretched.

Luigi took his own hand out of his pocket and extended it, taut-faced, in return, but the other man went straight past him and gripped that of Pasquale's mother instead.

'I do not speak Italian but I do speak excellent English,' the man told her in a heavy eastern European accent. 'I did not know your son, but I wanted to express to you my condolences for your loss.'

Pasquale's mother looked in confusion at Luigi Vanni. It was clear she didn't have any English herself and was relying on him for a translation. Luigi gave her a tight-lipped translation in Italian and the old woman nodded politely.

The stranger pulled a sad expression and gazed down at her while patting her hand. 'It is very tragic to lose a family member in such circumstances. Such a terrible thing should never have happened to your son.'

The stranger finally turned to Luigi. He looked him up and down for a long moment before speaking.

'You are Signore Vanni?'

Luigi Vanni nodded warily. 'I am.'

The other man held out his hand once more. 'I thought so. I have heard much about you. We are in the same business, I believe. You are famous, Signore Vanni, even as far away as where I come from.'

Luigi shook the hand held out to him but his eyes

never left the other man's face. 'I believe I have heard of you, too. You are Vaz Jakupi?'

The stranger nodded briefly. 'Just so. I came here today to say how sorry I am, how sorry we all are, about the unfortunate death of your friend.'

Luigi stared daggers at him. 'It was a shock to all of us. How did you hear about it?'

'News like that travels fast in our business, don't you find?'

Luigi looked glacial. 'Good news travels fast. Bad news travels faster. Which was it for you, I wonder?'

Vaz Jakupi laughed, but it was not the kind of laugh that makes you feel like you are invited to join in. It was the kind of laugh that laughs at someone, not with them.

'I like your country. You have a sense of humour. I think I and my friends will like to spend more time here. Much more time. We love the weather too.'

'I see. But I am afraid you will find it too hot here.'

'Oh no, my friend, not hot at all. Nowhere is too hot for us, is it, boys?'

Jakupi turned to his entourage who grinned and agreed.

'You see?' the stranger smirked, turning back to Luigi, 'We are all determined to stay in your beautiful country. And we hope to see much more of you.'

'We shall meet again soon, I am sure,' Luigi replied. 'Now, if you don't mind, there are others waiting to be presented...'

'Of course, of course. I know how upsetting this day must be, for all of you.'

'If you step that way you will find something to eat.'

Jakupi shook his head, with a slow, insolent, smile on his face. 'Ah no, I think not. Not today. I would not want to eat something that disagreed with my stomach.'

He chuckled and his men grinned. I saw Luigi's fists clench.

'We bid you farewell,' the tall stranger announced to everyone present. 'Or what is it you Italians say? Arrivederci. Yes, that's it. Arrivederci!'

With that, and before Luigi could say anything in reply, the man swept from the room and back outside, his men falling into place behind him, hands still gripping whatever they had concealed under their jackets.

Luigi made a show of picking up from where they had left off, greeting more mourners, but I could tell from the two red spots of anger high up on his cheeks that he was seething at the interruption. His men looked equally put out about it, exchanging dark looks but saying little.

I remained at my post between Teresa and Mariana and tried to work out what I had just witnessed. That accent – could it be Albanian? Could these have been the Albanians Bruno had referred to the previous morning? It seemed highly likely. Were these the men behind Pasquale's poisoning?

I didn't have any certain answers to my questions but I felt sure my friends in the Italian police would be more than interested to hear about it. The only trouble was, they hadn't provided me with any means to get in touch with them – and I certainly wasn't going to take any undue risks to make their job easier for them. No, let them work it out for themselves if they were so keen.

Once the line of mourners had all been greeted everyone gave themselves up to the business of helping themselves to food and drink, though it was far from a jolly atmosphere after all that had happened. Luigi glowered in a corner surrounded by his closest associates, locked in muttered conversation with them. It was not difficult to surmise what they might be talking about. Teresa dutifully took up her post among the women and looked suitably grave and sympathetic as the old biddies in black busied themselves making sure she had something to eat and a full glass in her hand.

Mariana, being younger, was apparently excused such doleful duty and lingered at the food tables with me – only, I think, because there was no more congenial company on offer elsewhere. She looked bored and resentful.

'I don't know why we have to be here,' she muttered. 'Pasquale was only one of Daddy's employees. He wasn't a real friend.'

'I think it's a case of public appearances,' I confided in her. 'Your father is an important man around here and he has to be seen to be doing the right thing when something like this happens.'

She pouted. 'I don't see why I have to come.'

'You're one of the family. Your father obviously thinks that it's important you all come.'

She looked at me squarely in the face. 'You must hate all this. It's not your family after all.'

'I'm happy to do whatever your father asks me to do.'

'There are a few things you've done that Daddy would never ask you to do.'

I gasped and looked quickly to left and right in case anyone had heard her.

'I don't think we ought to talk about that here,' I murmured. 'It could get us into a lot of trouble.'

'You seem to like living dangerously,' she countered. 'Like yesterday.'

There was a look of resentment in her expression that worried me. What was she trying to say? 'I don't know what you mean...'

'You and Mummy outside Daddy's study. What were you saying to her?'

'To your mother?' I floundered, trying to think of a reply that would deflect her curiosity. I decided the truth might be the best line to take. 'As a matter of fact, she was telling me off for going into your father's study without permission while he was out.'

Mariana's eyebrows rose a little. 'Why did you do that?'

'I was just looking for a cup I had mislaid the day before when I took him afternoon tea. That's all.'

Mariana's eyes narrowed and I couldn't make up my mind if she believed me or not. I hoped desperately that she did.

Out of the corner of my eye I spotted Teresa leaving the gaggle of elderly women across the room and coming towards us.

'Here's your mother now. If you don't mind, I'll leave you with her for a couple of minutes while I pay a visit to the gentlemen's. I haven't been since before the service, and it went on for a very long time.'

I peeled off in the direction of the lavatories, praying to God that the two Vanni females would find something to discuss other than my suspicious behaviour.

The hotel loos were empty when I entered, which was welcome news, but I had hardly got started when the door swung open and a man unknown to me came in and joined me at the urinals.

The man glanced round the room, then stared at the wall directly in front of him and startled me by mentioning my name.

'Signore Truelove?'

'Er, yes?'

'I must speak to you privately. I am a policeman. I have orders from the inspector you spoke to in Capri to find out if you have learned anything about the Vanni operation.'

I trembled with horror. The nerve of it! A policeman coming into the heart of the Vanni empire and risking exposing my connection with them to everyone! Then I reminded myself to be cautious. This man might not be what he said he was. This could be a trap set by Luigi

Vanni to test my loyalty.

'Why should your inspector, whoever he is, want to know that?'

The man gave me a withering look. 'If you don't give me a satisfactory answer before someone else comes in here I will have to tell him you would not cooperate. You will be arrested and put on trial for murder.'

Well, that was enough of being cautious as far as I was concerned. I zipped my trousers. 'All right, but make it quick. There are people out there who will notice if I am gone more than a minute or two.'

'What have you found out?'

'There are some Albanians here who may be responsible for the death of the man whose funeral this is.'

'Albanians?'

'Yes. I don't know what their connection is to Luigi Vanni, but it seems they are involved in the same business. They were here just a few minutes ago.'

The policeman's brow furrowed. 'A group of six men, some of them carrying guns? I saw them leave the hotel.'

'Yes, that was them. Their leader is a chap with a very short haircut and a scarred face. He's called Vaz Jakupi, or something like that.'

'I will tell the inspector.'

'There's another thing too. I found some scraps of paper in Signore Vanni's study that suggest there's a big shipment of something coming soon.'

'A shipment of what?'

'I don't know.' I told him as quickly as I could what I had read and what I guessed it might mean. 'But don't ask me where these Albanians fit into it because I've no idea, and I've already risked my neck to get this information as it is.'

The policeman nodded and stepped away from the urinal. 'It may be significant. We shall look into it. If you find out anything else you must pass it on to us.'

'No way!' I protested. 'That is it, as far as I am concerned! I took a huge risk to get you that information and I was very nearly caught too. You can't ask for more. It's just not fair. You told me I wouldn't have to do anything, that I wouldn't have to take any risks. And now here you are, ordering me to snitch on the very people I am staying with. My God, if Luigi Vanni finds out about it he'll toss me off the cliffs of Capri without a second thought!'

The policeman shrugged. 'The risk is a small price to pay to escape trial for murder.'

'But I didn't murder anyone!'

'That won't stop you being arrested and put on trial. If you get to court.'

I stared at him. 'What do you mean?'

'Luigi Vanni would not want someone in his employment, someone who has been living in his house, giving details in court of his private affairs. He might act to prevent it.'

'You mean... you're not serious!'

The man took a step towards the door. 'These are serious matters. Look what happened to Pasquale.'

My blood ran cold. 'All right! I – I'll do my best. If I find out anything more I'll tell you. Somehow.'

The policeman opened the door a crack and peered out, then drew back quickly. 'There is someone coming. Go back to what you were doing.'

I hurriedly repositioned myself at the urinal. A second later Bruno entered the room. As he held the door open the policeman ducked under his arm and slipped out before Bruno had time to look at him.

Bruno let the door close then crossed to occupy the booth next to mine. I nodded at him then made a show of zipping up my already zipped-up trousers. I had done nothing, I think, to arouse his suspicious, but it was a very odd look he gave me as I passed him on the way out.

A very odd look indeed.

Sweet and Sour

Despite the perils I was braving, it was a decided relief to get back to the villa at Capri after the stresses and strains of the trip to Naples for the funeral. Having prepared a light supper for us all, I made my excuses to Teresa and Mariana and went to bed early. I heard Luigi and his men return in the middle of the night, but after that the house fell into silence once more and I drifted back off to sleep.

After a quiet breakfast, at which Luigi seemed withdrawn and out of humour, we all announced our separate plans for the day. The women, for once, opted not to spend it in their usual places beside the swimming pool but decided instead to spend the day in town, shopping and having lunch. With Luigi taking himself off to confer with his associates elsewhere in the building and leaving no orders for food, that left me free to indulge myself for a couple of hours with a bit of a swim and some sunbathing on the terrace.

I needed the break. I had a lot to think about too, what with my turbulent relationships with Teresa and Mariana, my role as spy for the Italian police and my recent revelations about the philosophy of food to consider. In fact, it was all rather too much to tackle at the same time. As soon as I focused on one subject, the others started muscling in and I found myself utterly unable to make progress in any of them.

The surroundings didn't help either. The view from the terrace was just so beautiful that it felt sacrilegious to ignore it and devote my thoughts to such mundane, earthly matters. I gave up in the end and surrendered to the majesty of it all. I closed my eyes and revelled in the heat of the sun on my eyelids. When it got too hot I slipped into the water and idly drifted about, wishing I could stay like it for ever.

Around midday I was floating on an airbed in the pool under a cloudless sky, absolutely not thinking about menacing Albanians, implacable Italian policemen and resentful teenagers, when I was abruptly broken out of my reverie by Bruno coming out to tell me Luigi wished to see me in his study. I slipped off the airbed in haste and dried and dressed myself hurriedly, my complacent sense of security brutally shattered. Bruno waited while I made myself presentable then escorted me through the house to Luigi's study. He knocked once then indicated to me to enter.

I swallowed hard, fearing the worst. Luigi had somehow learned about my contacts with the Italian police. He had discovered about my liaison with his wife. Someone had told him about me and Mariana…

Luigi was seated behind his desk. I noted the ominous, serious expression on his face as he gestured at me to sit down opposite him. I waited nervously for him to explain why I had been summoned.

'My friend,' he said at last, after eyeing me for several long seconds, 'these are challenging times for us all. I am sure you have wondered who those people were at the funeral yesterday.'

'Ah. Yes, I did wonder…'

'They are the business associates with whom I need to negotiate the important deal I believe I have mentioned to you once or twice.'

I nodded.

He fiddled with his jacket cuff. 'When I say associates, really I mean rivals. Unfortunately one cannot always choose the people you have to do business with.'

'They are Albanians, I understand.'

'Yes. They are powerful men who seek to expand

their interests in this part of the world. Others who have opposed them have suffered greatly, so it is best that we try to reach a compromise with them. For the good of all parties.'

I shrugged. 'That seems sensible to me.'

Privately I was wondering why he was telling me all this. Luigi wasn't usually one to share his secrets so willingly.

He got up and paced restlessly about behind his desk.

'Sooner or later, preferably sooner, we have to meet and talk things through frankly, face to face. We need to state our positions and agree to work together instead of against each other. We need to meet on neutral ground, where no one feels threatened or influenced in an unfair way.' He paused and looked at me. 'But that is not so easy to arrange as you might imagine. I am sure we can find a venue for a meeting that we can all agree to, but what then? Normally, as the host, I would welcome business rivals, make them feel comfortable, treat them to a wonderful meal perhaps – but after the tragic incident with Pasquale...'

'You still think it may not have been a case of accidental food poisoning?'

'You said yourself that it was unlikely professional caterers would make such a mistake. And the behaviour of our Albanian friends at the funeral only strengthens my suspicions. But meet we must...'

I tried to work out where he was heading. 'So... your problem is how to host a big meeting to which all parties will agree to come, which they won't if they think there is the slightest chance that they too might succumb to a case of –'

'–accidental food poisoning. Precisely.' He paused again and looked down at me. 'Any chef I provided to cook a meal for us all would come under immediate suspicion. But if that chef was not actually one of my men and clearly had far too much to lose if he were ever discovered to be involved in, shall we say, legally questionable activity… then, maybe, it might just be possible that everyone would be able to trust each other.'

The light began to dawn.

'So you want me to…'

'If they saw that I was offering them a man who would clearly never contemplate such actions because of the damage his international reputation would suffer, there is a better chance that our guests will accept him. If it was explained to them that if that man's reputation was damaged his career as a major European television star would be over before it was even begun, that even back in his home country no one would let back on the screen again – well, then I think they might agree to the meeting.'

I took my time before answering. I didn't like the sound of this one little bit. I found all his references to reputations being damaged and careers ended unsettling to say the least. But, on the other hand, his description of me as a major European television star in the making was alluring and, after due consideration, proved just enough to sway my mind in his favour. 'It sounds a bit risky to me, to be honest, Luigi, but very well, if it will help you out, I'll be happy to cook for you and your Albanian friends.'

Luigi grinned and I could see he was relieved. He came closer and perched on the corner of the desk beside me.

'I was confident that you would help me. But I am afraid I must ask one more favour of you, if I may. As you saw yesterday, relations between the two parties are at this moment uneasy. Our Albanian friends might panic if they see me or one of my men arriving at their door. So, for the safety of all, the proposal for the meeting should, I think, come from a neutral person.

And who better than the very chef who is to cook for the big occasion?'

I held my breath as my stomach turned over. Was he seriously suggesting that I should go as his emissary to those thugs at the funeral yesterday?

'I–I'm not sure I could get them to do what you want, Luigi. This isn't really my field... I wouldn't want to let you down –'

But I could see Luigi Vanni had already made up his mind about it. There was no use in my arguing. He rose from the table and slapped me on the shoulder.

'You won't let me down, my dear Tremayne. I have every faith in you.' He checked his watch. 'But I must not detain you. The sooner you deliver my invitation to our guests the better.'

I felt the panic surge up within me. 'You want me to go now? This minute?'

'Luigi spread his hands out in mock surprise. 'But of course. The helicopter is waiting. There is no time to be lost. Bruno will go with you to where we think the Albanians are.'

Thus it was that, after a few more instructions as to venue and timing, before I barely had a chance to catch my breath, I found myself being led out to the helipad by my genial host. I was too stunned at the sudden turn in events to protest. I didn't want to believe what was happening, that I was to be delivered like some hapless lamb to the very door of the lions' den.

'You will be fine,' Luigi reassured me as I looked down at him from my seat in the helicopter. 'Just tell them who you are and deliver my invitation, then return with Bruno in the helicopter. You'll be back before you know it.'

The rotors picked up speed and Luigi slammed the door and retreated. I looked helpless down at him and he waved back, rather more cheerily than I felt was appropriate, as we lifted off the ground. In a moment we were swooping low over the island and roaring across the water towards the distant shore.

That journey was one of the most fraught I have ever taken. As we flashed over the Bay of Naples I tried desperately to remember everything I had been told to say and how best to deliver Luigi's message. I was a gibbering wreck by the time we landed and seriously thinking about making a break for it and throwing myself upon the mercy of the authorities as soon as we landed, but Bruno was keeping a close eye on me and there was a car waiting for me at the helipad with another couple of Luigi's hoodlums in attendance, so I was deprived of any opportunity to turn my plan into action.

One of the men opened the rear passenger door for us to get in, then joined his colleague in the front once I was safely installed. Bruno stabbed a number into his mobile phone and spoke briefly into it, presumably reporting back to Luigi that we had arrived safely and were now on my way to find the Albanians.

The car journey took longer than I expected. We negotiated the old heart of the city, then set off around the built-up conglomeration that follows the Neapolitan coastline right round the Bay of Naples towards Vesuvius in the east.

When you think of Naples, you probably think of the historic centre so picturesquely sited across the bay from Vesuvius, with its hotels, casinos and restaurants. You probably don't think of the busy multi-lane highways that snake their way eastwards through mile after mile of dreary industrial and residential suburbs dominated by dilapidated high-rises and factories and punctuated by brief patches of derelict, sunparched wasteland and heaps of uncollected rubbish. But this is where most people live and work, and this is where most of the business of modern Naples is carried on. I'm not saying that it's all depressing, half-derelict and dangerous – just that the bits I saw looked that way.

The guidebooks will tell you that the city is home to more than three million people but they usually gloss over the fact that a large proportion of that three million are unemployed and poverty-stricken. Consequently bribery, corruption and crime are rife, especially in the eastern part of the city to which I was now headed. I shrank lower and lower into my seat as we passed by graffiti-daubed concrete walls and vandalised hoardings deeper and deeper into this barren, dystopian landscape.

I realised from the signs on the motorway that we were heading for the port area and eventually I spotted the funnels and radars of large ships moored up at the piers. After a brief muttered conversation, the security men at the various checkpoints in the docks waved us through, mostly without a second glance. We drove past gleaming passenger cruise liners, ferries and other grand vessels and threaded our way, as I feared we would, to a more run-down part of the docks, which were grim, grimy and generally alarming. It was surreal to be among such menacing and unkempt surroundings when just across the bay you could make out the tourist landmarks of the historic city centre and, way across the water to the south-west, Capri itself.

We drew up beside the rusty hull of a particularly ugly cargo vessel with an unpronounceable name on its stern. A man armed with a nasty-looking snub-nosed automatic pistol straightened as the three of us got out of the car and walked calmly towards him.

The man slipped the strap of the gun off his shoulder and levelled the weapon in our direction, then called something up the gangway. We stopped. A man's head appeared at the top and turned towards us just long enough to take in the main features, then disappeared again, apparently off to spread the good news that they had visitors.

Bruno prodded me to go forward while he and the other two retreated to the car. Taking a big gulp of air, I forced myself to walk to the foot of the gangway and came to a halt in front of the man posted there, acutely conscious of the gun barrel pointing towards me.

'I–I'm here to speak to your leader,' I stammered. 'Is he in?'

It sounded such a silly thing to say, but it was amazing frankly that I could speak at all in the circumstances. Before the man could reply another figure appeared at the top of the gangway to give me the once-over. I recognised him straightaway by his crew-cut and hideously scarred face as the chap who had introduced himself to Luigi as Vaz Jakupi, the man in charge.

Jakupi considered me for a few seconds then glanced at my escort, who remained at a safe distance beside the car. He nodded and waved me up the gangway. The guard lifted his gun and let me past. As I ascended the ramp I hoped to God that Luigi knew what he was doing when he said I'd come to no harm.

One of Jakupi's men frisked me as soon as I stepped onto the deck of the rusting hulk, then Jakupi indicated to me to follow him inside the vessel. All this was done without a word being spoken, as though they already knew what I was there for.

I followed Jakupi down some steep metal steps and then along a long corridor till we came to a small cabin. Jakupi gestured to me to go in first. This was it, then, I told myself gloomily as I ducked my head to avoid hitting it on the low metal doorframe – they were going to lock me up in here then sail out to sea and dump me in the ocean to show Luigi they meant business here. In about a year's time a local fisherman would dredge up my tattered remains in his net and wince at the mess the fish had made of me. Chances were he'd probably throw me back again.

I looked up, expecting to find myself in a grim death cell with a bare mattress and a bucket my only luxuries till the time came for my execution. It was, then, a considerable surprise to me to find the cabin was comfortably furnished, with a large walnut desk, curtains over the porthole, and pictures of the Albanian countryside on the wall. Even more surprisingly, it came furnished with buxom young blonde perched on a corner of the desk and filing her fingernails with a look of great concentration on her face.

'Oh! Hello,' I mumbled.

The girl looked up and a very pleasing, young face she had too. With her short skirt, carefully made-up lips, expansive chest and wide, questioning eyes she appeared the quintessence of the beautiful dumb blonde. Before she could say anything in reply, however, Vaz Jakupi appeared from behind me and walked round behind the desk. The girl gave a yelp as he shoved her off her perch on its corner. He clearly didn't like people sitting on the furniture.

I sat down on the only chair on my side of the desk and tried not to look as frightened as I felt. Close up, Vaz Jakupi's appearance was even more off-putting than it was at a distance. He had an icy regard, thin lips, and a sharpness about his manner that suggested an uncompromising, easily angered personality. The long scar across his face did nothing to counter this impression.

The girl was busy scrabbling on the floor for the nail file she had dropped when pushed off the desk, but she yelped again as Jakupi reached out and grabbed her wrist, hauling her towards him and then depositing her, none too gently, on his lap. He muttered a few words to her in what I assumed was Albanian and then drew her attention to me.

The girl looked at me and smiled. It was a nice smile – unfeigned, genuinely interested. I bet she was a lot of fun if you had the chance to spend time with her out of the company of terrifying, scarred gang leaders.

Vaz Jakupi transferred his gaze to me. 'You are English?'

I nodded.

'I saw you at the funeral,' he murmured. 'A tragic occasion.' He paused to consider me some more. 'This is Luljeta,' he told me after a few seconds, stroking the girl's forearm.

'Hello, Luljeta,' I responded, rather meekly.

'Hello.'

'Luljeta – that's a pretty name.'

'Thank you. It means flower of life. Most people call me Lule. You can call me Lule.'

'What is your name?' Jakupi interrupted coldly.

I got the message that flirting with his girlfriend would be unwise and cleared my throat. 'My name is Tremayne Truelove. I'm from London.'

Jakupi's eyes narrowed. 'You have come from

Signore Vanni, I think.'

'That's right.'

'I have been expecting you. I knew he would want to talk sooner or later. What does he say?'

I took a deep breath and launched into it. I told him how, after recent events, Luigi saw the need for their two organisations to cooperate, of his concern that the new Albanian operation might unwittingly conflict with his own interests, which would benefit no one.

Jakupi's expression clouded over and he glared at me. 'Who is this Luigi Vanni to tell me how things are to be? It is for me to decide how I run my business, not him!'

'No, no,' I countered hastily, 'I'm sure Signore Vanni has no designs upon your operation itself. He is only concerned that you do not unintentionally damage each other's business interests so that everyone ends up worse off. He sees room for the two organisations to work side by side.'

Jakupi nodded slowly. 'Go on.'

I passed on Luigi's suggestion that they meet somewhere on neutral territory in Naples to negotiate a deal. It would be a social occasion during which they could discuss what each side hoped for and expected of the other. Everyone would be invited, including wives and girlfriends. It would be an opportunity for everyone to air their opinion without fear of offence.

'A social occasion?'

'Yes, Signore Vanni is offering to host a meal, to which everyone is invited. I personally will prepare the food.'

'You are to cook for us?' Jakupi barked a laugh. 'I don't think so. We would end up like that Pasquale!'

'No, no, you can trust me.'

'Trust you?' His eyes narrowed to slits once more. 'You are one of Luigi Vanni's men. How can I trust you?'

'You don't understand. I'm not one of his men. I'm just a guest of his on a purely temporary basis. I have nothing to do with his business affairs. That is why he asked me to come here today, as an independent intermediary. He asked me to cook for him and his family for a few weeks, that's all.'

'That is enough, I think. Why should I believe you? I think you are just trying to fool me so that you can poison us all.'

'No, nothing could be further from the truth!' I was appalled that he could think such a thing. I tried to master the fear that rose up when he turned his cold blue eyes on me. 'Let me explain. You may not know my face, but I can assure you I am a very well-known chef back in Britain, with my own television series and everything. My name is often in the papers and I know all the top chefs back home.'

The Albanian's face twisted in an unpleasant sneer. 'So what?'

'Well, don't you see? I wouldn't dare get myself implicated in any criminal activity such as poisoning people. It would mean the end of my career, the destruction of my reputation – I would lose everything!'

Jakupi looked genuinely surprised. 'You are famous?'

'Yes, I'm what they call a celebrity chef. I'm often on the BBC.'

'The BBC?' That seemed to impress him.

'You've heard of the BBC?'

Lule looked equally impressed. 'Everyone's heard of the BBC.'

I focussed my appeal on the girl in the hope that she might speak up on my behalf. 'I'm one of the biggest stars they have,' I assured her. 'As a matter of fact I'm in the middle of filming my next series for them right now.' All right, I admit that was an exaggeration, but the circumstances seemed to call for it.

'Why are you in Italy then?' asked Jakupi, inconveniently.

'Some last-minute research,' I lied.

Lule gazed at me with round, guileless eyes. 'I've never met anyone really famous before! Do you know lots of other famous people?'

'Oh, yes, lots. Chefs, television people, footballers, royalty–'

Lule gave a squeak of delight. In other circumstances, confronted by her bounteous naïvety, squealing enthusiasm and cute smile, I'd have been all over her in a flash. She was obviously quite overwhelmed by my celebrity connections; her seduction would have taken all of ten minutes. Sweet, prodigiously well-equipped physically, and evidently unworldly as she appeared to be, she was refreshingly different from the dark, complicated Teresa and Mariana, who had dominated the romantic scene of late. What the hell she was doing with a murderous creep like Vaz Jakupi was quite beyond me.

Lule turned to Jakupi, all excitement and eagerness. 'Oh, please let him cook for us! He has cooked for kings and queens! It will be wonderful!'

'Shut up!' Jakupi snarled suddenly. 'You're not here to talk.' He turned back to me. 'I'm sorry. She is as stupid as a rock, but she is very good in bed, so I put up with her.'

Lule's expression changed from one of excitement and enthusiasm to one of shocked hurt. Tears sprang to her eyes, but Jakupi made a show of ignoring her and turned back to me.

'Okay, Englishman. Tell Signore Vanni that we have a deal. I will listen to what he has to say. If he can choose somewhere public, in the middle of Naples, we will meet him the day after tomorrow.'

I nodded. Lule was starting to whimper so Jakupi

began to coax her with blandishments in their native Albanian. It sounded like he was soft-soaping her into forgiving him for his outburst and, judging by the way in which her natural cheerfulness was almost instantly reasserting itself, it rather looked like he was succeeding. She really was as dim as he accused her of being, bless her.

Jakupi slipped a hand onto the girl's knee and then up her inner thigh beneath her skirt and began to caress her freely. With the other hand he gestured at me to leave. I felt sorry for the poor girl but there was nothing I could do. I stood up and quietly made my way out.

'They have agreed to meet you for a meal the day after tomorrow as you suggested, as long as it is in a public place in the middle of Naples,' I reported to Luigi on my return to the villa.

'Good. You have done well, my friend. Very well.'

I sat down across the desk from Luigi in his study. Even after the car ride back to the helipad and the flight to Capri I was still shaking like a leaf after my meeting with the Albanians. Luigi seemed oblivious.

'I shall send them a message about the venue as soon as it is arranged. Now, we must give some thought to how we shall receive our guests. The meal itself needs to be something that will impress them, a meal that is unlike anything they have ever tasted before. I don't know what they eat in Albania. But you will know that, I am sure.' He leant back in his leather chair. 'My friend, your challenge is to give them something so amazing they will open their eyes in admiration and say, if Luigi Vanni's chef can work miracles like this, what else can he achieve? He would be a good man to have as a partner. He understands how to do things well and he is a person we can do business with!'

Talk about pressure. Despite my enormous trepidation

and my trembling nerves, however, it occurred to me that this might be a good time to promote my own interests.

'Oh, I'm sure I can come up with something that will impress your Albanian friends. Speaking of which, wouldn't it impress them even more if you could announce that the chef who is preparing their meal is about to host his own series on Italian and International television? I wonder if you've had time to set the wheels in motion at all, not that I'm suggesting I'm impatient or anything–'

Luigi waved his hands in the air. 'Of course, of course. I will set it all up for you within a matter of days. A week maybe. As soon as this business if over. You must understand that with all this going on it has been impossible for me to think of other things. But I shall talk to my contacts, who are very high up in Italian television and, indeed, the government, and you will not have to wait too long to hear good news, my dear friend, I promise you.'

Well, you couldn't really say fairer than that.

'That reminds me, my dear Tremayne. I have a small present for you.' He got up and picked up a large shopping bag from the carpet in the corner of the room and handed it over to me. I opened it and found a pristine set of chef's whites neatly folded inside.

Luigi grinned. 'We want you to look like the great chef you are. My guests will appreciate that. I think you will find they are the right size. I had Teresa guess what size you would need. She is very good at such things.'

I suppressed the thought that Teresa had good reason to know exactly what size I was. She had been up close and personal after all and seen my frame from a variety of angles, without the hindrance of clothing too.

Luigi became suddenly businesslike. 'When you know what you are going to cook you can give Bruno a list of everything you will need and he will arrange to get it all for you. Have you decided what it will be yet?'

'I have a few ideas.'

'Good. I will look forward to what you produce.' He turned to go back behind his desk, then changed his mind and swivelled on his heel. 'Oh, and one thing more. I know that the police have spoken to you.'

I did a classic double-take in the action of rising from my chair. 'W-what?'

'Of course.' He beamed at me. 'I like to know everything that goes on around me and it is only to be expected that they would want to check you out as a guest in my house. But do not concern yourself with whatever they have told you. I have connections high up that will prevent them from taking matters further. They are only trying to frighten you. In any case, you must not believe anything they have told you about me. It is just jealousy that motivates them, and my rivals in business are always seeking ways to gain an advantage over me by spreading lies. Some of them, I regret to say, get the police to do their dirty work for them.' He spread his hands wide in a gesture of apology. 'I am sorry you have been exposed to such pressure, but such things are inevitable in business in Italy. I hope you will forget all about it. Now go and think about our meal.'

I exited the study on hollow legs, barely able to support myself.

Food of the Dogs

With just one day to finalise my plans for the all-important meal between Luigi and Vaz Jakupi and their respective factions, I spent the following twenty-four hours or so in a ferment of terror and creativity. In order to distract myself from the heart-stopping prospect of what lay ahead of me I turned all my attention upon developing my ideas for the menu. It really had to be something special to meet Luigi's expectations, that was clear. But I was the man for the task, I insisted to myself. And in the long run, it wouldn't be the mollifying of two business rivals that the world would remember. No, the occasion was to mark the launch of a whole new way of cooking.

Fission. My God, my biographers would probably identify my invention of the concept as one of the momentous events in the history of world cuisine. The more I thought about it, the more convinced I became that I really had something. What I was proposing was a fundamental rethinking of mankind's approach to the whole business of eating. It felt to me as though I was asking questions that hadn't been properly asked, not even by Heston, since humanity first picked a berry from a bush and wondered if it might be improved by serving it up with a spot of cream or a sliver of mammoth meat.

If a thing wasn't actually poisonous, it stood to reason that it was capable of being prepared and enjoyed in a practically infinite number of ways. But had we actually been doing that? No! For millennia we had confined ourselves within boundaries based on such superficial grounds as cultural tradition, personal habit and similarities or complementarities of ingredients. Of course, along the way we had stumbled in a limited way upon the beauty of contrast in taste and texture in such dishes as sweet and sour pork, or baked Alaska, but we had hardly gone the full distance available to us if we cast off our old prejudices.

I wasn't being naïve about the challenges that might lie ahead if my new concept was to sweep the world. It would take a lot of time and effort to re-educate the collective palate of nations. For so long we had been used to accepting recipes on the grounds that particular ingredients 'go well together', but now I was proposing that the only reason we felt things went well together were artificial and the product of stuffy convention. Now I would be inviting people around the world to abandon all inherited notions about everything needing to be complementary in some way and to retrain their palates to appreciate tastes that are not only contrasting but in direct, violent, exciting opposition to each other. I was asking the world's gourmets, gourmands and gluttons to declare their mouths a battlefield in which wild and unpredictable things could, and would, undoubtedly happen.

If a person knew a berry to be rich, sweet and succulent I was challenging them not to pair it with other rich, sweet and succulent ingredients, or even with things that were bland or neutral in taste (the usual source of the 'everything tastes like chicken' complaint) but to go out of their way to find ingredients that had absolutely nothing in common with that berry, either in taste, appearance, texture or anything else. By bringing such opposed ingredients together, I was arguing, they would appreciate anew their individual qualities and rejoice in the very fact that there was nothing complementary about them at all. Our appreciation of every foodstuff known to mankind would inevitably end up being radically reassessed.

The possibilities were endless. Once people were

liberated from their prejudices, anything could go with anything. I saw visions of a table laden with such delicacies as chocolate-coated whitebait; banana wrapped in bacon; Victoria sandwich with a filling of anchovy and spring onion; rollmop and chocolate mousse... the only limit was our imagination.

It was difficult to know where to begin. It's not every morning you are faced with the challenge of constructing a menu on principles that are so entirely new to the world. Once I had assembled all my Filipino assistants in the kitchen I locked the door with a big flourish, which I admit alarmed them somewhat, and told them no one was leaving until together we had cracked it.

The first thing I did was to get every foodstuff available to us heaped up on the surfaces around us. In addition to those fetched from shelves and cupboards, Bruno had, on Luigi's orders, been to town early that morning and had returned with a prodigious amount of additional ingredients, a fair number of which were relatively unfamiliar to both me and my helpers. Each one had to be assessed and paired with foods with which it seemed to have absolutely nothing in common. That task alone took a good couple of hours.

Next, it was a matter of preparing ingredients in a variety of ways to see what happened when they were coupled with what I considered their most unnatural companions and then to sample what resulted. Some of the concoctions thus produced almost made me retch, but I admonished myself for this weakness. Even I, the founder of the fission movement, needed to retrain my palate in order to free myself of centuries of cultural complacency and learn how to taste things properly, in the new way. I can be quite humble sometimes, you'll observe.

Some of the combinations I stumbled upon startled me with the strength of the contrast between the constituent ingredients. Though I winced a lot at some of my creations, it was a morning of revelation for me. Even if something tasted impossible at first bite, I reminded myself that it was only my cultural prejudice that told me it was unacceptable, and I forced myself to take another mouthful. Often, strange to relate, it didn't taste so bad the second time around and I began to appreciate the contrasting qualities of the violently opposed tastes and textures.

I always work in a frenzy when faced with a big challenge in the kitchen and the Filipinos shrank away from me as I charged about, tasting this, adjusting that, in an almost religious fervour. I say almost, but of course to really serious chefs like me cookery is nothing short of a religion and we top chefs are high priests in our temples (or kitchens as the common herd refer to them). Anyone slow enough not to get out of the way when we're careering from sink to hotplate or fridge to wok is liable to be crushed like a worshipper under the wheels of an Indian juggernaut. But what, I asked myself, is the odd bruise or third-degree burn in such a great cause as the one I was engaged in? Insignificant, that's what.

The Filipinos were naturally curious to know what it was all about. Little did they realise that they were witnessing an historic moment in human history. Kitchens the world over would never be the same again. People, I expected, would look back on this moment as the culinary equivalent of the French Revolution or the discovery of electricity. Eventually, however, I got tired of having them getting under my feet and going too close to my precious wok (which no one is permitted to touch but me) and, after persuading them to prepare a light lunch for the other denizens of the villa, I ordered them all out at the top of my voice. When they didn't understand I waved my knife at them and they all scurried to the door with yelps of alarm. The door, of course, was locked, so I had to put the knife down in order to unlock it and let them all out, but it proved only a temporary interruption to my creative flow.

It was hellishly hot in the kitchen by early afternoon and the sweat was pouring off me as I wrestled to find new and more surprising contrasts, challenging my imagination beyond anything it had ever grappled with before. Looking back, I'm not sure that I wasn't very far away from toppling over the Tarpeian Rock of insanity.

Eventually I was forced to realise I needed to take a break before I passed out under the mental and physical stress I was putting myself under. I burst out of the kitchen and ran through the house and onto the terrace, then, with a roar of exhilaration, threw myself fully dressed and still wearing my chef's apron, into the pool.

The aquamarine water was wonderfully cooling and I let myself sink to the bottom, revelling in the refreshing sensation that swept over me. It was only when I got out again, water streaming from my clothes, that I became conscious of Teresa and Mariana lying on their sun-loungers as usual, both staring wide-eyed at me. I nodded to them both and, without pausing to dry myself off with a towel, stormed back to the kitchen, leaving a trail of wet footprints behind me.

It was the kind of thing the world must accept we geniuses have to do from time to time.

New, more extreme ideas, come to me as I worked through the afternoon. At some point I hit upon the idea of raiding the cuisines of Albania and Italy in search of ingredients that might properly represent two great culinary traditions with all their contrasting qualities. I continued to perfect the dishes that resulted until I had the first course completed and the basis of a highly complex and utterly original main course all assembled in the biggest bowl I could find. I covered the bowl with a cloth and wiped my brow, feeling obscurely heroic at the fact that I had met the challenge and come out victorious. All that I would need to do the following day was work on a few accessories by way of salads and so forth and then oversee the transfer of everything to wherever the great occasion was to take place.

It was tea-time, so I set some cold drinks out on a tray and carried them out to the terrace where the three Vannis were already assembled. Teresa and Mariana cast curious glances at me when I appeared among them, but said nothing about my eccentric behaviour earlier in the afternoon.

Luigi sipped at his drink before setting his glass down with the air of someone about to make an announcement.

'Tomorrow is a big day for all of us,' he told us equably, 'so tonight I thought we might give ourselves a small treat. Would you be free to accompany us, Tremayne?'

I nodded. There was nothing more I could do by way of preparation for the big meal at this stage.

'Very well. I have been given tickets for the opera tonight. I have decided we shall go.'

Now, I'm not a great fan of opera, though I don't mind tagging along if it's a freebie. Judging from the extravagant way in which Mariana groaned and muttered under her breath at her father's announcement, however, I gathered she wasn't a big opera fan either.

'Why do I have to go?' she complained.

'Because we have been asked, and because we have a position to maintain, that's why.'

'You do, you mean. I couldn't care less.'

Luigi's mouth tightened. 'You will come to the opera tonight, young lady, and you will make it appear to everyone that you are enjoying it.' He held up a hand as Mariana began to protest once more, this time in Italian. 'There will be no more discussion about it! Where are you going?'

Mariana had thrown herself off her sun-lounger and was stomping away from us. 'To my room!'

My patron glared at his wife. 'See that she gets ready in time. I don't want us to be late.'

Teresa put down her book, looking less than pleased with his request that she bully their daughter to do his bidding. Then she rose up on her immaculate long legs and stalked off into the villa after her.

'I am so sorry,' Luigi said, turning to me. 'But you know what teenagers can be like.'

I nodded. I knew exactly what they could be like, but I wasn't about to share that with him.

'What is the opera?' I asked by way of easing the tension.

'Lucia di Lammermoor,' said Luigi absently. 'It is a tale of forbidden passion and murder. You will love it.' He leaned confidentially towards me. 'It is important, particularly with what is to happen tomorrow, that the whole city sees us – to show that all is well within the family, that we are united, that we are afraid of no one. No one! I would be grateful if you would keep an eye on the two of them for me once again.'

I nodded, a little wearily. I was beginning to get used to being treated as a nursemaid.

Luigi shot me a look of concern. 'Is everything prepared for the meeting tomorrow?'

I assured him it was.

'Good,' he replied. 'We will go to Naples in the morning. You will come with me in the helicopter. Some of the others are already there getting things ready.'

I said nothing in reply. My mind was too full to think about anything much but my recent frenzy of creativity. Luigi's business interests were of minor significance to me.

In the kitchen not twenty feet away I had an amazing first course, the likes of which the world had never yet seen, all plated up, and a sensational main course marinating in the vast bowl I had found. I was ready!

Bread and Circuses

Mariana, chivvied by her mother no doubt, turned out as requested when the time came for us all to troop out to the helicopter to be whisked off to the opera. She didn't look at all pleased to be going, however, and stared moodily out of the window all the way there without speaking to anyone. Personally I was still so distracted by my ideas for the meal the following day I was finding it hard to concentrate on anything else, so conversation between our little party on the journey out was non-existent beyond Luigi telling Mariana to stop behaving like an infant a couple of times.

Once we arrived at the opera house we were greeted by various dignitaries and shown to the best seats in the auditorium. The place was packed with opera fans in their best outfits, and I was glad Luigi had managed to find me a dress suit from somewhere so that I was saved the embarrassment of sticking out like a sore thumb. During the first interval Luigi went off to talk with the great and good attending the event, leaving me to escort the women to the bar. We ordered champagne and stood listlessly about while everyone else bustled around us.

After a couple of minutes surveying the scene, Teresa excused herself to powder her nose, leaving me with Mariana. As the girl still looked sunk in gloom and resentment, I steeled myself to make some attempt to try to jolly her along a bit.

'Are you enjoying the opera?' I asked.

She grunted dismissively but didn't offer a reply.

'I don't think your father means to upset you on purpose,' I ventured. 'He's under a lot of pressure with his business right now.'

She grunted again.

'Making him angry will only make things worse, you know.'

Mariana's black eyes flashed with annoyance. 'He just wants to make my life miserable! No one understands me! No one asks me what I want.'

'What do you want?'

'To decide for myself! Not to be bossed about by my stupid parents all the time, especially by him.'

'I don't think your father is that bad—'

'You don't know him. You don't know what he's really like.'

We stared at each other for a long moment. I could have said more, but she looked so beautiful when she was angry I hadn't the heart to argue with her. In any case, the last thing I wanted to do was to antagonise her. God only knew how miserable she could make my life if she wanted to.

'Be patient, Mariana,' I urged her gently. 'You'll be leaving school soon and then you'll be old enough to make your own decisions.'

'Not soon enough for me!'

I frowned. I knew teenagers could turn into the devil's brood when the mood took them, but she seemed so desperate and so alone I wished there was something I could say or do to help her out. But there was nothing.

We sipped our drinks in silence until Teresa came back from the ladies. Mariana took that as her cue and headed off in that direction herself before her mother reached us. Mariana cast a cool look at her daughter as she brushed past, resentment and youthful beauty personified.

I handed Teresa her glass. 'I don't think Mariana is enjoying this evening very much. What about you?'

She shrugged. 'I like opera when I am in the mood. But I hate being ordered to come.'

'Your daughter was telling me much the same thing.'

Teresa pursed her lips. 'We are alike in many ways. But she shouldn't contradict her father. He does not like it.'

'The perils of parenthood, I suppose.'

Her face darkened. 'Luigi is not like other fathers. He must have his way in everything, even with us. I am not surprised Mariana cannot stand him, even if he is her father.'

'Don't you talk to him about it?'

She looked at me. 'You know him a little by now. You cannot talk to Luigi. You just have to do what he says. If you question him he becomes angry and you end up doing what he wants anyway. He is a bully that way.'

'I'm sorry to hear that.' I looked at her with new understanding. 'I didn't realise you were both so unhappy.'

Teresa avoided my gaze, as though worried she might burst into tears or something. 'Thank you,' she replied in a quiet voice, 'but there is nothing that can be done about it.'

I felt genuinely sorry for her, for them both. On an impulse I took Teresa's hand briefly, but she withdrew it almost immediately.

'Don't,' she murmured. 'Luigi is coming.'

I looked over my right shoulder, startled, and saw that Luigi Vanni was bearing down on us. My blood ran cold at the thought that he might have seen my clumsy gesture.

'It is almost time to return to our seats,' he informed us. 'Where is Mariana?'

'I think she's in the ladies,' I told him.

Luigi scowled and turned to Teresa. 'Go and tell her to hurry up.'

Without saying a word, Teresa put her glass down and set off.

Luigi transferred his regard to me, but said nothing for

a moment or two. I shifted uneasily and got the feeling he was assessing me, judging me in some way. I began to grow more certain that he had seen me holding his wife's hand, though the gesture had been innocent enough, surely, for God's sake…

'Tremayne,' he said at last, 'after the opera is over I would like you to help me with a job that needs to be done later tonight. I think it is necessary that you witness it, so you have a better understanding of the importance of my business here in Naples tomorrow.'

'Tonight? But–'

'You must have been wondering what nature my business is. Later tonight you will see for yourself. You will understand better what is at stake and how important it is for us to reach a good settlement with our Albanian friends. If we get in each other's way we could suffer greatly from the consequences.'

I didn't like the way he said 'we' as though it included me. Was he trying to embroil me in criminal activities of some kind? If so, it would make my standing with the Italian police somewhat precarious, to say the least. But how could I possibly get out of helping him with the ominous-sounding 'job' he said he had on tonight? I couldn't see a way.

I didn't pay much attention to the second act of the opera due to my perturbation over the discussion I had had with Luigi in the interval. The more I thought about it, the less I liked the sound of what he had proposed. Was the man bullying me into helping him as punishment for the liberties he was beginning to perceive I had taken with his family? I sincerely hoped not. My God, why hadn't I run for the hills when I had the chance back in Venice, or Rome even? I had the feeling Luigi's net was closing around me and I was damned if I could see an avenue of escape in any direction.

During the second interval I excused myself to answer the call of nature and made my way to the gents while the ladies drank more champagne. The lavatories were crowded when I got there but while I was waiting my turn the man behind me tapped me discreetly on the shoulder. I turned in fright and recognised the policeman who had accosted me in the toilets at the funeral. I opened my mouth to speak, but he signalled to me to say nothing and then jerked his head towards the door. I understood the message and followed him back out into the corridor outside. The man led me round a couple more corners to a less frequented area beside a window overlooking the square outside and made a show of studying his programme. I leaned against the wall close by and pretended to be looking out into the night view of the city.

'I have a message from the inspector,' the man murmured without taking his eyes from the programme. 'You absolutely have to find out what the subject of the negotiations between Luigi Vanni and the Albanians is.'

'I've already told you I've given you as much as I know. Why doesn't he do some work for a change instead of leaving it all to me?'

All right, it wasn't exactly what you'd hear James Bond saying, but then I wasn't James Bond, as the inspector already knew.

'You will do it, the inspector says to tell you, or we will treat you as an associate of Signore Vanni and lock you up.'

I repressed the urge to tell this bastard once and for all what I thought of his inspector's way of doing things.

'As it happens,' I muttered darkly, 'I think something's on tonight. For some reason I don't fully understand Luigi Vanni wants me to witness some operation of his. I've no idea what it is or how or when it is to take place, unless it's something to do with what was written on those bits of paper I found in his study.'

The policeman turned a page of the programme. 'That is good. It will give you a better chance to find out what they are up to.'

'I'm glad you think it's good. I don't think it's good at all. You don't seem to appreciate the danger you're putting me in.'

But the policeman, blast his hide, just walked away.

I didn't have time to go to the loo before the third act started so I spent the remainder of the performance trying to ignore my swollen bladder. The finer points of the unfolding plot were consequently lost on me. Luigi didn't seem to be getting much out of it either. He kept looking at his watch and from the way he was tapping his fingers on his knee I surmised that he was getting anxious about whatever plans he had for the rest of the evening.

It all came to an end at long last. The heroine went mad and died, while singing long and loud about it, and then her lover and various other people did a lot of lamenting and swooning about her loss and the lover did himself in too. The violence of the piece was a bit too close to home to be comfortable, to tell the truth. Once the endless curtain calls were finally completed I dashed out to the loos where, thankfully, there was no policeman in sight.

Five minutes later we were back in the helicopter and on our way back to Capri.

Mariana looked as broody and out of sorts as she had done at the start of the evening, while Teresa just looked sad, and gazed at the black sea below us most of the way. Even Luigi seemed tempered by the show we had seen and did not speak, except to give instructions to the pilot a couple of times.

When we got back to the villa Luigi ordered the two women to go to bed, then told me to change into something less formal and meet him outside in a couple of minutes. When I rejoined him, duly changed, I found him waiting for me with a gaggle of his henchmen, all dressed in dark clothing. At Luigi's signal, everyone was loaded aboard three large vehicles and we sped off down a twisting road that wound its way down from the heights to a secluded harbour on the south side of the island. Three large and expensive-looking motorboats were waiting at a jetty for us, their engines already turning over. Luigi led the way onto the jetty and oversaw the distribution of the men among the three boats. Then he indicated to me to join him in the lead vessel. We had hardly clambered aboard and taken our seats when the engines were gunned and we set off at speed into the moonless night. As ever with anything that belongs to Luigi Vanni, I was impressed by the quality of the vessel I found myself on. It gleamed with polished wood and brass as we roared through the night sea, carving a huge white wake in the black water.

The three boats headed roughly south-east in formation. Luigi was clearly enjoying himself, standing beside Bruno, who was manning the wheel, and letting the warm wind ruffle his thinning hair. He still hadn't told me where we were going and I felt increasingly uneasy as the lights of Capri dwindled behind us. It was a black, overcast night. They could throw me overboard out here and no one would ever be any the wiser. I'd just become a crossed-off name in Barry Cullis's book of clients, a missing name in next month's Radio Times. Somehow, though, I didn't truly believe they were going to all this bother just to bump me off and feed me to the fishes in traditional mafia style. They wouldn't need three boats for that for a start.

I'm not good in boats, incidentally. The constant motion always makes me feel queasy and smaller boats are the worst, what with the way they bucket about between waves. I hoped the journey would not prove a long one.

After about five minutes at top speed Luigi left his post beside Bruno and sat down next to me. I wondered if he was ready to tell me what we were doing out here in the middle of the night.

He stared at me ruminatively, his eyes small and not entirely friendly.

'I saw how you looked at Teresa tonight,' he said at last, speaking up against the muffled roar of the engine.

The bluntness of it took me by surprise. Oh, my God, I thought, they really are going to turn me into fish food after all! He must have witnessed that reckless hand-holding moment at the opera and reached the obvious conclusion – what a fool I had been!

But then Luigi leaned forward and slapped me heartily on my knee. 'Don't look so worried, my friend. No man with blood in his veins could fail to be attracted to my wife. She is a very beautiful woman. I know it better than anyone. And it pleases me that other men find her lovely to look at, as I do. I take it as a compliment. Though of course,' he added roguishly, 'if anyone tried to do something about it that would be a different matter entirely, eh?'

He smiled fondly at me. My stomach was squirming like I had swallowed a live octopus and I was sure he would register my alarm.

'I am not concerned that Teresa would ever betray me, you understand,' he added. 'You have to remember how much she owes to me. It may surprise you to know she was not always rich and elegant. In fact, just between you and me, she comes from very humble origins – a village in the hills, would you believe! She was nothing before I spotted her by accident one day when I was passing through. Really, you would not believe the place she came from – and as for her family! They were hopeless peasants, with no appreciation of the finer things in life. I expect they still are, though we haven't had any contact with them for years.'

He paused to steady himself against the movement of the boat before going on.

'So you see it does not worry me if you find Teresa attractive. She likes you, too, and I am glad about that. It is good for her to have a friend in the house. But I say only this to you. She belongs to my family. She is part of it. And you must remember that families are important here, probably much more so than in England, and it is the custom for the head of the family to have complete control over all its members. That is all I wish to tell you.'

I didn't think he was threatening me exactly, but I sensed I was being warned off somehow. Perhaps that was why I was being taken on this mystery trip with him and his men.

Further thoughts on the subject were cut short by a sudden attack of queasiness, which in a moment had me leaning my head over the side of the boat and retching.

The spasm passed and I slumped back in my seat.

Luigi laughed. 'Poor Tremayne! I thought you English were a seafaring nation!'

'We are,' I mumbled weakly. 'But even Nelson suffered from seasickness.'

'He did?' Luigi shook his head in a bemused fashion. 'You English are full of surprises.'

We continued to speed south-westwards for some time. The night was inky black and the few tiny stars visible far above us through the clouds shed little light upon the ocean around us. I felt hideously small and insignificant, huddled on my seat in the middle of the immense darkness. At times like that you look for comfort among your fellows, but this bunch were no source of comfort to me. Luigi, I suspected, would probably kill me if he knew what I'd really been up to with Teresa, and his men would toss me over the side without a second's hesitation like so much unnecessary ballast if they had reason to. My old familiar life back in London seemed incredibly far away. I would have given anything right then to be in some good old London boozer, enjoying some lively banter about the telly biz with darling Bettina and good old Barry Cullis, bless them. Not for the first time I regretted bitterly throwing my mobile into the canal in Venice. It would have done me good to hear their voices. I would buy myself a new mobile at the first opportunity, assuming I ever got one.

We had been going for about half an hour and I was still feeling utterly miserable, mentally and physically, when the engine slowed. I looked up and saw that the other two boats had throttled back as well. Ahead of us I spotted a large rusty fishing boat, motionless in the water. It appeared to be loaded with people.

Bruno shouted something and got an answering shout back. A few seconds later the three smaller boats were arranging themselves alongside the larger vessel.

My mouth dropped open as my gaze fell upon the scores of people who were standing packed on the fishing boat's deck. There were men, women and children of all ages staring back at us. They looked like a pathetic bunch, too, bedraggled and scared.

So this was what the mysterious shipment was! I was witnessing the illegal smuggling by Luigi and his men of migrants across the Mediterranean. My God, what the hell had I got myself mixed up in?

As soon as the boats were secured alongside the fishing vessel the migrants began to pour over the side. Luigi's men directed them from one boat to the next, gesturing at them to pack themselves in as tightly as they could wherever there was space to sit down.

There must have been a couple of hundred people in

all, and by the time they were all disembarked from the fishing vessel there was barely room to turn round. It was a chaotic process, too, much complicated by the difficulty elderly or sick passengers had in obeying the instructions that were barked at them and by small children crying and calling for their parents.

Pressed into a corner of our boat by the crush, I glimpsed Luigi talking to what I took to be the captain of the fishing vessel. Money was clearly changing hands, then the pair made a brief farewell and Luigi clambered back on board his own craft. A moment later all three boats started up and we were under way once more, heading back northwest in the direction from which we had come.

I looked around me at the people we had picked up. There appeared to be a rich mixture of races, with a variety of faces and clothing. A terrible smell of unwashed bodies and vomit filled the air. Some of them looked back at me, but most quickly looked away again when they saw me staring at them. No doubt they thought I was one of Luigi's gang.

After consulting with Bruno and presumably checking our course, Luigi joined me in my corner.

'Well, Tremayne,' he greeted me. 'What do you make of our operation? Was it what you thought it was?'

I shook my head, bewildered. 'I never thought for a moment... who are these people? Where are they from?'

Luigi gave the disorganised mob in front of us a cursory glance. 'Palestinians, Sudanese, Somalis, Syrians... they come from all over the place. The routes to Europe across the eastern and central Mediterranean are too heavily patrolled by the authorities these days. It's very bad for business, so we decided to open a new route from Tunisia, going north of Sicily to Naples. It is proving very popular, as you can see.'

'Isn't that a very long way round? For them, I mean?'

Luigi shrugged. 'They are so desperate to get here they will try anything. Anyway, it makes no difference to us how they get to Tunisia, as long as they get there and have money left to pay for the sea crossing.'

'Look at them...' I breathed, staring at the poor benighted mass huddled around us.

'Yes, I know,' Luigi agreed. 'Filthy, aren't they? But do not be deceived by appearances, my friend. Most of these migrants are people of means. We don't get the really poor people coming over. Most of these are educated people with skills they can use to make a living in Europe. Each one of them has paid more than two thousand dollars for their place on our boats. Even the children. So you can see it's a good business for us.'

I swallowed, stunned by his insouciance. 'What will happen to them when we get to Naples?'

'That is up to our friends the Albanians. We shall hand these people over to them and it will become their responsibility to take them further through Europe. I would prefer it was other Italians, of course, but our own operation was uncovered by the police so that is why the Albanians have moved in. They have a place in eastern Naples, a warehouse.' He tapped the side of his nose meaningfully. 'They think I don't know about it, but I know more than they think. That is one of the reasons I thought you should come along tonight, so you will understand what is at stake when we meet them tomorrow. Our part of the job is to get these people as far as the coast, but if no one takes over from us there and they end up being picked up by the authorities then they will stop coming, and what use is that to us?'

'I see,' I muttered. 'And you trust the Albanians to look after them?'

'I don't trust the Albanians to do anything. But what happens to these people after they leave our boats is no concern of ours.' He paused and looked at me again.

'You may be wondering what other reasons I had for bringing you out here tonight.'

I hesitated. 'Yes, I was.'

'I am putting a great deal of trust in you, my English friend. I want you to have no illusions about the seriousness of the business you are now involved in. You have witnessed a number of things that must have impressed you regarding the scale and range of my operations. The rewards I can offer you are great, but it is important for all of us, and especially for you, to do your part well.'

'Suppose...' I licked my lips, which suddenly felt very dry. 'Suppose I'd rather not be part of all this...'

Luigi chuckled. 'I don't think you have much choice, my dear Tremayne. It is too late now. After all, have you not lived in my house, carried messages for me, and now come along on an actual operation? I don't think the authorities would consider you a neutral observer, do you?'

I had to confess I didn't. It occurred to me, not for the first time, that the inspector who had interviewed me might yet need some convincing that I was an innocent party.

At this point Bruno called down to Luigi for advice on something and the latter turned away to answer.

I felt a tug on my trouser leg and looked down. A small boy in a tattered tee-shirt was looking up at me with pleading eyes.

'English?' he asked in a small voice.

I guessed he had heard Luigi speaking to me in English and nodded.

'Yes. Hello. What's your name?'

'I am Hashem. Who are you, please?'

'My name is Tremayne.'

The boy tried to say it but couldn't get his tongue round the unfamiliar name and smiled shyly instead.

'You have food, please?' he asked.

'Food? I'm sorry, no. Are your parents here?'

'My mother and sister. My father is in Europe. He waits for us.'

'I'm sorry I have no food for you. Don't you have any?'

The boy thrust a hand into his pocket and pulled out a small lump of flatbread.

'This is all. Yesterday they give us this bread. But there is no more. I keep this bit.' He shot me a doubtful look. 'You... you want some of it?'

I could see he was torn between the obligation to share what he had and the anxiety that it might be taken from him.

I shook my head. 'You keep it. How long have you been at sea?'

He didn't seem sure. 'Two – three days.'

'And all you've been given is this bread?'

He nodded. 'Have you water, please? We are thirsty.'

I frowned. I couldn't believe what these people were being expected to go through. I waited until I could attract Luigi's attention.

'They're asking for water,' I told him. 'Do we have any we can give them?'

For a moment I thought he was going to refuse the request, but then he grunted in a way that expressed impatience with my concern and disappeared into the cabin. He reappeared a few moments later with three small bottles of branded water. He handed them over to me and I passed them to Hashem. He looked absurdly grateful as he gathered them up.

'Thank you very much. Very very much, Ter... Termai.'

I watched as he turned round to a woman who was slumped behind him on a hatch. Hashem opened the bottle and handed it to her. She drank automatically, without speaking, then looked down at the bundle in her arms. I realised it was a tiny infant. It lay very still in her arms. I hoped, without much conviction, that it was just asleep. The woman saw me staring and lifted the edge of her shawl so the baby was hidden from sight.

I sagged against a bulkhead, too sick in both heart and stomach to think or speak to anyone. Everyone remained huddled in misery and exhaustion as the three vessels churned steadily towards the distant lights of the Italian shoreline. Hashem stayed close to his mother and sister, occasionally glancing at me with wondering eyes. The rest of the passengers stared without expression at the deck, from time to time lifting their heads to gaze at the slowly approaching mainland.

Sorrento

When we were about two miles offshore, somewhere beyond Sorrento I think, I sensed movement among Luigi's crew and roused myself out of my depressed reverie to see what was happening. Coming fast towards us from the dark shore were about a dozen large rubber dinghies. As they came closer I recognised the men in them as the Albanians I had seen before. Vaz Jakupi himself was in the lead boat, standing legs akimbo, and hands on hips, a gun in a holster under his left armpit, the very image of armed arrogance. In fact there were a lot of guns about all of a sudden. All the men in the dinghies were carrying one, and Luigi's men in the larger vessels had produced automatic rifles and had them trained on the Albanians. Some of the Albanians had their guns trained on us in reply.

After a brief and noticeably cool and formal greeting between the two bosses the business of transferring the migrants to the dinghies began. Fortunately the sea was calm, but it was still a hair-raising job getting some of the younger and more infirm passengers safely onto the smaller craft. As soon as each boat was full it sheered away and sped quickly back into the darkness towards the shore. First to go was the Vaz Jakupi's lead boat, which took its leave without any gesture of farewell of any kind.

The crew of the last dinghy to depart had trouble getting the engine restarted. The two men manning the crowded vessel swore at each other as they wrestled with the motor until it finally roared into stuttering life. Then they too began the two-mile trek to the distant mainland.

Luigi muttered something to Bruno and our own engines fired up and the three larger boats, now carrying only Luigi's men, began to wheel round to head back out to sea.

At the same moment the captain of the boat nearest to us called over urgently and pointed towards the shore. Luigi and Bruno stared in the direction he was pointing. We could just make out a black object coming out from the direction of Naples and following a course to intercept the last of the dinghies heading for the safety of dry land.

Luigi raised a pair of binoculars to his eyes. 'Polizia,' I heard him mutter.

In response Bruno increased our speed into the

concealing darkness of the night.

I squinted hard at the dinghy, which was still struggling across the yawning space between it and the other boats, which had by now reached the shallows of the coastline. There was movement on board the dinghy that I could not make sense of.

'What's happening?' I asked Luigi, who was watching through his binoculars.

'They are making them jump from the boat,' he replied calmly.

'What?'

'They are making the migrants jump into the sea.'

'But they are still a mile from the shore.'

'Yes. They know the police will have to stop to pick them up and they will be able to escape.'

'But they could drown!'

'Some of them probably will. But the Albanians will get away safely.'

I watched, appalled, as the little tragedy receded into the distant blackness and we roared into the blackness alongside the other two vessels. Luigi's callousness took my breath away. I prayed little Hashem and his mother were not among those who must swim to save their lives.

The three boats continued to accelerate into the darkness for another ten minutes until Luigi was sure no one was following, then he ordered a change of course back to Capri.

It was three in the morning by the time we approached the jetty from which we had set sail. I saw Luigi clap Bruno on the shoulder and smile at him.

'Bravo,' I heard him say in Italian. 'That all went very well.'

All the way in the car back up to the villa I could not get the image of little Hashem and his pathetic crust of Tunisian flatbread out of my mind. I was still thinking of him and building myself up to say something about it when my host bid me a curt good night and headed off to his bedroom at the far end of the building, depriving me of the opportunity to accost him about the events of the night. Dazed and alone, I wandered automatically to where I always feel safest, the kitchen. I was still thinking of little Hashem and his bit of flatbread as I picked up the bowl containing the main course for the big meal tomorrow and threw it at the wall with all my strength.

The Dish of the Day

I'm not sure I slept at all that night. It was late in the morning, however, before I felt strong enough to face anyone after the trauma of our night excursion. The villa was bustling with people making preparations for the big meeting to be held that evening. I glimpsed Luigi talking rapidly into his mobile phone, but decided I wasn't up to confronting him. In the cold light of day I doubted that any action on my part would do much good anyway.

The Filipinos had tidied up the mess I had made in the kitchen, presumably before anyone else saw it. What remained of the food I had got ready they packed into plastic containers to be transported to Naples. They looked questioningly at me when they saw there was no main course, but I ignored them. Instead I fired up the oven and set about preparing a replacement main dish.

I avoided the company of the Vanni family and any of Luigi's hoodlums all that afternoon. Once I had finished in the kitchen I retreated to my bedroom and left it to my team of Filipinos to provide food for those who wanted it. There I tried to catch up with my sleep in preparation for the ordeal to come, but my inner turmoil was such that my sleep was fitful and less than restoring. I gave it up in the end and pulled on the new set of chef's whites before returning to the kitchen to make sure my trusty old wok was included in the equipment we were taking with us.

The time duly arrived for us all to make our way to the venue in Naples. The mood in the villa had become noticeably quieter and everyone seemed tense and uncommunicative as we waited our turn to be ferried by helicopter to the mainland.

Luigi and some of his men went in the first flight,

after which it was the turn of more of his underlings. I was told to clamber aboard with Bruno, Teresa, Mariana and one or two others when the aircraft returned for the third time. As the helicopter lifted off the ground I looked down at the villa and, beautiful though it was, wished to God I'd never even seen the place.

'Once we arrive,' Bruno instructed us, 'we will be driven to the castle to join the others.'

'The castle?' I echoed. 'Where are we going?'

For those who don't know it, the medieval Castle Nuovo in Naples is a forbidding, brutish, sandstone structure with massive round towers and immense, impregnable walls. Situated in front of the Piazza Municipio and the city hall and separated from the water's edge by a dual carriageway but little else, it is a focal point of the old town with views over the bay towards Vesuvius. It has been the scene of much murky, blood-stained history and even with the floodlighting illuminating the castellated battlements in the evening it is a grim and ominous presence on the Neapolitan shoreline.

Castel Nuovo

As a former royal residence and home of the city museum the castle is normally thronged with tourists and other visitors. The city now owns the place and the fact that Luigi had been able to secure its use for his meeting was further testament to his influence. I suspected that a good deal of money had changed hands behind the scenes. I was also struck by the suspicious absence of police or other security, apart from Luigi's men, in the vicinity of the castle and speculated that they may have been paid to keep away.

After leaving the car that had transported us from the helipad, we crossed the wooden bridge spanning the castle's wide, dry moat and arrived at the main entrance, set into a triumphal arch of white marble between two substantial round towers. I glanced up and made out the statues of knights and saints high above our heads. We passed through a pair of ancient bronze doors depicting medieval battle scenes and into a paved courtyard hemmed in by high walls. Cannonballs stacked in neat pyramids were further evidence of the castle's violent past.

Bruno steered us up a balustraded stone staircase in a corner of the courtyard and through the doors into the Barons' Hall. This is a large, square room with a high vaulted ceiling, formerly used as a court house and still furnished with dark wooden benches and seats for judges and jury around three sides. The space in the middle had been set out with three long tables and chairs and places already laid out for the meal. There were no paintings or tapestries on the walls and little else to relieve the feeling of oppression that dominated the senses. I glanced up and saw how the arches of the stone vaulting met overhead like some gigantic spider's web.

Luigi was directing operations personally, casting an alert eye over everything. When he spotted us he came over immediately. After kissing Teresa and Mariana he eyed me speculatively.

'I hope you have everything under control, my friend.

Don't forget how much depends upon this occasion.'

I nodded.

'One of my men will show you where we have set out the food so that you can check everything is as you wish it. We have less than an hour before our guests will arrive. I will want everyone in here to welcome them.'

'You have a lot of men here tonight,' I observed drily.

'All of them. We must be cautious with these Albanians. They are a hot-headed people. If they start any trouble we shall be ready for them. But if they see how strong we are they may think twice about it.'

My Filipinos were waiting for me in a large room that had been converted into a temporary kitchen. I set about moving everything to the most convenient location, then checked that the portable fridge was doing its job and oversaw the firing up of the stainless steel ovens in which the hot food was to be heated. I went through the motions automatically, though my heart wasn't really in it. I felt numb and unable to think of anything beyond the immediate.

At length Bruno appeared to summon me to rejoin the royal party who were assembled in the Barons' Hall. When one of the other men came in with an automatic pistol slung openly over his shoulder Luigi rounded on him, cuffing him about the shoulders and insisting that all guns be kept tactfully out of sight, to reassure our visitors of our good intentions.

The last few minutes before the arrival of the Albanians were especially tense. Even Teresa, who was usually so calm and collected, looked nervous. Mariana, I noted, was being uncharacteristically obedient to her father's instructions. A sense of dread anticipation crept over me. The distracted feeling that had overpowered me all day long seeped away and was replaced by a clarity that finally brought home to me the peril I was in. All my fears came rushing back in a tidal wave of terror. I was surrounded by thugs with guns, none of whom would give tuppence for my welfare, and I couldn't rely upon anyone coming to help me from outside, even if I could persuade them of my innocence, which seemed highly unlikely. If what I served up did not pass muster I would give nothing for my chances of surviving the night.

Then the signal reached us that the Albanians were entering the castle. Luigi gestured to everyone to take their allotted places. I wiped my moist hands dry on my whites and gave a silent prayer that no one would lose their nerve and start shooting the moment our guests appeared in the hall.

We heard steps coming up the long stone staircase outside and voices speaking in Albanian. Luigi Vanni's men shifted about restlessly. Then figures appeared in the doorway.

First to come in were Vaz Jakupi and his girlfriend Luljeta. The scarred thug cast quick glances around the room, registering where everyone was and looking for signs of a double-cross. I noticed that he kept his girlfriend half a pace in front of him so that she would act as a shield if anyone started firing. Lule looked a lot less cheerful than when I had last seen her, as though the dangers of the situation were clear even to her. The rest of the Albanians, maybe twenty of them altogether, filtered into the room behind their leader and fanned out, keeping wary eyes upon their Italian counterparts. Nobody made any attempt to frisk them, but it was obvious that everyone was armed.

Luigi Vanni coughed and stepped forward. 'Welcome,' he said in English. 'I am so pleased you have agreed to meet us here tonight. We are all working in the same business and it is time we got to know each other. We should be friends, not enemies.'

Vaz Jakupi nodded coolly back at him. 'I thank you,

Signore Vanni. If you have anything to say that is worth hearing, we shall listen.'

Luigi's expression tightened, but then he made a visible effort to appear relaxed. 'There is good Italian wine waiting to be poured for you and your men. And my friend, Signore Truelove, will shortly be providing excellent food for us all to enjoy while we get to know each other.'

Jakupi looked at me. 'Ah, the famous international chef, Signore Truelove. I hope you have something good for us tonight. Something our bellies will not object to. We don't want to end up like Signore Pasquale, you know.'

A couple of the Albanians sniggered. Bruno scowled and took a step forwards, but Luigi motioned him back. 'Let us put that sad accident behind us. Tonight we must consider the future.' His gaze transferred to the young blonde at Jakupi's side. 'Is this charming young lady your wife?'

The Albanian snorted with derision. 'No, she is my whore.' He jerked his head at Teresa and Mariana. 'Who are they?'

'This is my wife Teresa and this is my daughter Mariana.'

Neither of the two women said anything or made any gesture of welcome, but Lule gave them both a nervous smile anyway. Jakupi looked each of the Vanni women slowly up and down, a lascivious grin creasing his lips.

'We share a love of beautiful women at least,' he observed briefly.

Luigi Vanni looked less than pleased with the way his opposite number was eyeing up his wife and daughter but gestured his guests towards the long tables that had been set out in the hall behind him.

'Let us all sit down. We might as well talk in comfort.'

Jakupi signalled to his men to take their places at the tables then he and his girlfriend took seats at the same table as the Vannis. I assumed that I would not be expected to sit with them as I had to supervise the serving of the food, which was a relief to me in one way but made my job of eavesdropping on any discussion they might have about their mutual business interests rather more difficult. I hovered nearby, hoping to overhear something, but Luigi became aware of my presence and motioned me back to the kitchen.

The Filipinos were waiting for me to give them instructions to take the first course in but I told them to go up and serve drinks first. They looked scared so I gave them what I hoped was an encouraging smile. Once they had all gone I inspected the plates of food and found everything ready. How my dishes would be received was something I had worried about at considerable length a couple of days before, but now it hardly seemed so important and I felt curiously detached from whatever was about to happen.

I considered slipping out of the castle while everyone was busy in the hall, but then I became aware of someone entering the kitchen behind me. I turned to see who it was and found Lule standing there, bold as brass, gazing straight at me.

She beamed me a smile. It was a big, generous, unfeigned smile too.

'I was looking for the lavatories. I hope you have cooked something nice for us,' she said guilelessly. 'Are we going to have Italian food?'

She was such a sweetheart that in any other circumstances I would have taken this as my cue to start the business of seducing her, but I was far too distracted for that. And the thought of what Vaz Jakupi might do to me if he found me with his girlfriend like this did nothing to persuade me to linger over her.

'There will be some Italian food, yes,' I replied briskly. 'And some Albanian food as well. We'll be bringing it through in just a few minutes. You will have to ask someone else where the lavatories are.'

The girl looked a bit startled at my peremptory tone. I was rather startled myself. I wasn't used to hearing myself giving attractive young blondes like her the heave-ho in such abrupt fashion.

She began to back out through the doorway, muttering apologies, but then it occurred to me that just possibly this girl could provide the information the police required of me if I was to escape judicial wrath.

'Wait,' I muttered hastily, 'that was rude of me – and I don't want you to think I'm like that. Please, come on in.'

She looked pleased at the change of tone and, as appeared her wont, seemed immediately reassured, her mood instantly returning to its characteristic bright and breezy norm.

'Can I see under the lids?' she asked, looking at the silver salvers under which the plates were concealed.

'Ah, but then there would be no surprise for you when it is all brought out,' I replied. 'And it would give me great pleasure to give a charming young woman like you a nice surprise. It's what makes my job worthwhile.'

I was cutting straight to the chase as there wasn't time to beat about the bush in the circumstances. She flushed at my forwardness.

'Oh, all right then. I think it will be delicious.'

'I hope your boyfriend will find it delicious too. Does he like surprises?'

She screwed up her pretty little nose. 'I don't think so. No, he likes to be the one giving the surprise.'

'I gather he has a lot to talk about with Signore Vanni. If they enjoy the meal perhaps their business will go more smoothly.'

'I don't think Vaz is so interested in making a deal with Signore Vanni. In fact, I don't know why he made us all come here tonight at all.'

I sensed a revelation and decided it was worth taking the risk of pumping her for more information. I was conscious that the Filipinos would be back soon having served the drinks so I took the girl by the elbow and steered her quickly out of the room by another door into a deserted corridor beyond. I noticed that she didn't resist.

'Listen,' I murmured in a low voice, glancing back into the kitchen to check there was no one there. 'You're clearly nice girl, a very nice girl, but I think you're too good for your boyfriend – if you don't mind me saying so – and I don't want you to be in danger.'

Her guileless blue eyes widened. 'Oh! You think I am in danger from him?'

'I think we both might be if things go wrong tonight.'

I tried to judge how she was taking it. I was acting on instinct to get her to tell me what she knew, but she could equally go straight to Jakupi to tell him what the strange English chef had been saying to her, in which case my sorry goose would be well and truly flambéed.

'He has done bad things,' the girl struggled out slowly, 'but I don't think he would harm me...'

I lifted a hand and softly touched her cheek in a way most women seem to like. Bettina does anyway.

'Maybe he wouldn't, but I don't think you should take that chance. Of course, I may be wrong. If only we knew what his intentions were, well, maybe we'd know if there's any real danger or not.'

She frowned. 'I don't know. He never tells me anything. But he told the others to bring their guns with them and he told them to start shooting if anything went wrong. He said he wanted to hear what the Italians wanted to give him, but that he would agree to nothing except them letting him take over their business.'

'The people-smuggling, you mean?'

'The what?'

It was clear she didn't know what line her boyfriend was in. But I did, and now I also knew what stance the Albanians would take on any deal that was about to be discussed. That should satisfy that blasted policeman. All I had to do now was get word to him so that he and his men (wherever they had got to) could swoop and arrest everyone, throw them in the clink, and, after filling out a statement or whatever, let me go on my merry way. I felt a surge of relief flood through me, and suddenly felt absurdly grateful to the fluffy little darling leaning against the wall in front of me.

'Thank you,' I breathed, smiling at last, 'thanks to you I think we shall be able to call a halt to this evening's charade before things get too ugly.'

I leaned forward and kissed her. It was only meant to be a thank-you-for-helping-out sort of peck, but somehow – well, she was absurdly pretty and apparently more than a trifle taken with me – it turned into a passionate snog.

I've noticed of myself more than once that when things start to spiral out of control, as they certainly had been these past few days, I find myself seeking refuge in any available woman to hand. I remember once being bawled out by a senior BBC executive about some bad press I'd attracted in the society columns after a drunken cavort with a married celeb, and going straight out of his office and locking myself in a steamy embrace with his secretary, whom I knew had the hots for me. With some people it's alcohol or drugs – with me, it's the fairer sex.

But that's by the by. The important thing was that I was now getting myself unintentionally involved with yet another gangster's moll. If I'd have stopped and thought about what I was risking, I dare say I wouldn't have done it – but stopping and thinking has never been my strong point. Anyway, it was a damned enjoyable kiss, even if at a most inopportune moment.

'You must go back before anyone notices,' I advised Lule earnestly once we had separated to take a breath. 'And you haven't been to the ladies' yet.'

'Oh, I didn't need to, anyway,' she confessed with startling frankness. 'I just wanted to see where you were.'

'Well, go back now – and maybe later…'

I didn't specify exactly what might happen later as I couldn't think that far ahead, what with all the dire dangers that had to be braved first. I had to send this girl back to her dreadful paramour before he came looking, and then I had to find some way to contact the police and persuade them to get me out of here. Oh, if only I hadn't thrown my phone into that canal!

I led Lule back through the kitchen area and shoved her out in the direction of the Barons' Hall. I can't remember if I gave her a helpful pat on her pert behind as I did so – it's the sort of thing I'd normally do, but such was my agitation that I may well have omitted to do so. I can only hope she forgave my negligence.

The girl had hardly made her way out before the Filipinos started filing back in, having finished serving the drinks. They looked subdued and frightened.

'How are things going out there?' I asked the only one of them who, as far as I could tell, had any English.

The man shook his head. The atmosphere in the Barons' Hall was clearly not reassuring, then.

I drew back into the kitchen and gestured to the Filipinos to sort themselves out in preparation for taking in the first course. While doing so I felt someone tap me on my shoulder. I gave a little start as I saw that it was Luigi.

'The Albanians are proving very unwilling partners,'

he murmured. 'I fear our hoped-for deal may not work out for us as I planned. I have extended the hand of friendship but it is clear to me that they have no intention of dealing fairly with us. I think they only seek to humiliate us. Or worse.'

'What do you mean, worse?'

'Much worse. It's possible that they only await a signal to kill us all.'

I stared at him in horror. My God, if that was true I may be caught up in a full-scale massacre before I got the chance to summon help from the police or anyone.

Before I could say anything, however, Luigi dug in an inside pocket and produced a small spice jar from it. 'I had hoped this wouldn't be necessary, but now I think there may be no choice. If things do not improve during the first course I want you to do something for me. If I decide that it really is impossible to work with these people then we shall have to take action. It is clear to me, in any case, that someone must have told the police about the operation last night, which is why they were able to intercept the dinghies. I think we can guess from whose ranks this treachery came. We were lucky last night, but I cannot risk such a thing happening again. I do not believe anyone on our side could have known the arrangements and passed them to the police so it must be a leak on the Albanian side, though they deny it and blame us for it.'

He paused and listened to the sound of the Albanians making a racket in the adjoining hall. It sounded like they were making the most of the free drinks they had been given.

'So,' Luigi continued in a rapid undertone, 'if things remain the same after the first course, to prevent any bloodshed, I want you to slip the contents of this jar into the food you serve our guests for the main course. Just our guests of course.'

He said it with such reasonableness that it took me a second or two to register what he had just said.

'What? What is it?'

'A powerful sedative. I am told it will work within a few minutes. If Vaz Jakupi is incapable of issuing orders his men are much less likely to kill us all, don't you agree? You could call it a safety measure, to ensure there is no unpleasantness.'

'I can't go spiking people's food! What about my international reputation?'

He fixed me with a hard stare. 'Yes, your international reputation. That rather depends upon me lending you my help to get that established, does it not?'

I stared back at him, my mind racing. 'You say that this is just a sedative?'

'Yes, my friend. Quite harmless. It will have no lasting effect.'

I fingered the jar, which had nothing written on it, no list of ingredients or anything. I unscrewed the top.

Luigi held out his hand in warning. 'I do not advise you to come into physical contact with it. To be on the safe side.'

I closed the lid carefully. I had a strong suspicion, nay certainty, that what I held in my hand was no sedative. My God, he wanted me to poison his rival for him!

I transferred my regard to my patron. 'I don't think I can do this…'

Luigi's expression changed. His eyes narrowed to slits and a slight flush of anger appeared high on his cheeks.

'Do this for me and you will be well rewarded. It is in my power to guarantee you a golden future. Believe me. But if you fail me…'

Without warning he slammed his fist on the table, making the crockery on it rattle. A knife fell to the floor with a clatter. My gang of Filipinos stood stock still, uncomprehending.

We stood in silence for a long moment, regarding one another.

Then Luigi's expression softened and he patted me on the upper arm. 'Bring the first course in. We will see how things go.'

I watched as he left the room, my mind spinning. I felt as if I was trapped in some nightmare in which horror piled up on horror. How the hell did I get into this?

The Filipinos were waiting for my signal, so I gathered my wits and gestured to them to follow me into the hall with the salvers containing the first course. My heart was pounding as I led our little cavalcade in. I was introducing an entirely new way of cooking to the world, but this was not the audience I would have chosen for my first foray. In fact, it was hard to think of a worse one.

I could feel Luigi's eyes on me. A salver was placed before each diner, the contents still concealed by the lid. The diners looked expectantly at what was put in front of them. I squeezed my eyes shut in silent prayer. Then, at my signal, the lids were lifted and the first course was revealed.

There was a bemused silence as everyone inspected the food before them. They obviously didn't get it. It was no surprise to me that they don't know at first what to make of the great culinary experiment in which they were to participate.

Jakupi picked up a spoon and prodded tentatively at what he had been given. 'What is this? Some kind of insult? You tell us you will treat us like honoured guests, then you spit in our faces with this – this – garbage! How dare you give us this!'

Luigi transferred his gaze from his plate to me. 'I don't understand... what is it? Explain.'

I cleared my throat and stepped forward where they could all see me.

'To honour this coming together of your two nations, I have selected some of the most famous national foods of each culture and brought them together in a way never before attempted. Thus, you see before you a combination of the best of two ancient culinary traditions. You will see that tonight I have prepared for you two old Albanian favourites, fried meatballs and nettle cakes and brought them together with the very best Italian chocolate ice cream, perhaps the finest in the entire world, and marinated eel. The sauce on top follows the same principle, combining the finest Italian wine vinegar with Albanian red wine, yoghurt and curds and just a hint of chilli pepper.'

'You cannot eat meatballs with ice cream,' Vaz Jakupi muttered, stunned. 'This is madness!'

I hastened to clarify things for him. 'But that is only half the story. For some time now I have been questioning the basic conventions upon which all our cooking around the world is based. Tonight is a very special occasion, for it sees the beginning of a whole new style in world cuisine, a revolution even.'

I had their attention now.

'You see, until now, all our cookery has been based upon ingredients that in some way complement each other, even if they come from different parts of the world – the style sometimes called fusion. But now I introduce to you a whole new way of thinking about cookery – fission, a cookery that is based upon colourful collisions of taste and texture in which the very fact that ingredients clash, and violently so, makes them come alive and become a celebration of all that is unique and marvellous about them. The presence of opposing ingredients in the same dish will cast new light upon the character and qualities of each ingredient.'

Luigi Vanni looked confused. 'But these things just don't go together.'

I rounded on him, becoming passionate in my own cause. 'Exactly! But think about it – why don't you think they go together? It is just the received wisdom of centuries of custom and habit that we have accepted wholesale. I am now challenging the world to question these hide-bound conventions that only serve to limit our approach to food. Opposites attract, in science and elsewhere. Why not food? We already have sweet and sour. We must learn to appreciate extremes in the variety of foodstuffs we eat, not force them to merge together in the bland and insipid way we have been for so long. Through fission I hope to surprise, no, shock your tastebuds into an entirely different mode of sensation. Please, try it – but keep your mind open to the richness of the tastes in your mouth.'

No one seemed too keen to be the first to give it a go. Even Mariana was looking at her plate with reluctance. But then one person summoned up the courage to taste it. Lule picked up her spoon and, smiling, lifted a bit of meat to her mouth.

'I like the meatballs,' she announced after a quick chew.

She tasted a spoonful of ice cream to her lips. 'The ice cream is nice, too. Can I eat one, then the other?'

'No, that's the whole point,' I told her. 'You have to eat them together so you get the full force of the contrast. And you need some of the sauce too, to experience the full explosion of taste.'

Some of the others began to lift their spoons, but before they got any further Jakupi hurled his spoon down in evident disgust, swearing, and then knocked Lule's spoon out of her hand too.

'No one is to eat this!' He glared at me. 'You have taken the national foods of Albania and turned them into food for animals! You insult our whole nation!'

As one his men laid their spoons down and stared at

me. Even Lule, who had been about to pick her spoon up, withdrew her hand sheepishly, looking nervously at her boyfriend.

Luigi signalled to his own men to lower their spoons as well. 'I think maybe the world is not yet ready for Signore Truelove's culinary revolution.'

He was trying to defuse the situation but I could tell from his expression that he was seething with fury at me.

'Let us forget the first course and refill our glasses in the spirit of our new friendship. Come!' he barked at the Filipinos. 'Take these dishes away and pour fresh drinks for all who need them.'

The Filipinos crowded round the table to obey his orders. I began to drift back to the temporary kitchen, stung by the response to my creation. Jakupi spotted me trying to slink off.

'Hey, you! Signore Truelove – the so-called celebrity chef with the international reputation. I have been asking around about you.'

I froze, then turned slowly.

'Yes, I have been doing my research about you, Mr Tremayne Truelove,' he continued, with a jeering note in his voice. 'You are not such a very big star, I think. I hear the BBC threw you out.'

'No one threw me out!' I protested. 'I walked away.'

I wasn't expecting that. I never thought for a moment your average Albanian would be so privy to my domestic ups and downs.

'Signore Truelove is a respected international chef,' Luigi Vanni broke in. 'That is why we asked him to cook for us tonight.'

Jakupi ignored the interruption. 'And now no one will employ you, Signore Truelove. They say you are finished. How do you say it? All washed away.'

I glared back at the man, but there was nothing I dared do. I would just have to stand there and take it.

'We have better chefs back in Albania,' Jakupi went on, smirking at his companions. 'I bet even Lule here can cook better than him! Even she wouldn't serve chocolate ice cream with fried meatballs and eel!'

The blonde blushed and his men guffawed, clearly enjoying my discomfiture.

Luigi Vanni's face was purple with anger as he rounded on me. 'I suggest you go away and bring in the main course, Signore Truelove. Before we all lose our appetite completely.'

He glared meaningfully at me and I knew exactly what he was meaning to convey.

Somehow I staggered out of the hall, reeling with indignation and disappointment. Why didn't they understand? How could they be so stupid that they did not appreciate what I was trying to do? How dare they insult me to my face? How dare they!

I pulled the little spice jar out of my apron pocket and stared at it. For several seconds I was strongly tempted to empty the contents into the food to be given to the sneering Vaz Jakupi, but then I relented. To administer poison would not only make me irredeemably and permanently one of Luigi's hirelings, but, more important than that even, it would make me just as bad as they were – a murderer who would end another person's life for no better reason than personal animosity or ambition. I have my faults, God knows, but that was something I was not prepared to do.

I replaced the jar and addressed myself to the job in hand. The Filipinos, who had no idea what I was going to give them to serve for the main course, waited patiently for instructions. I stepped over to the oven, which had been gently warming the food I had prepared on a very low heat for some time now. I opened the door and transferred the contents to my old wok, which happened to be handy. The Filipinos looked thunderstruck when they saw what I was doing, but remained silent as I gestured to them to pass me a tea towel with which to cover the pan and its contents.

There was nothing I could say to them to calm their nerves, even if they could have understood me. And there was no way back now. Besides, what was to have been the main course had ended up splattered on the walls of the kitchen on Capri and it was far, far too late to think of reconstituting it here and now.

I took a deep breath and signalled to the Filipinos to stand aside so I could take the second course in. They hesitated, as well they might, but I ignored their questioning expressions and walked towards the doorway into the Barons' Hall.

It took about three hundred years for me to cross the hall with my wok and its concealed contents. I didn't know what had been said between the two sides while I had been gone but the atmosphere was cold as ice. The three women, I noticed, looked decidedly scared. Luigi was watching me closely and his expression was not encouraging.

But it was too late to change tack now. Wok and contents in hand, I took up position immediately in front of the high table at which Luigi and Vaz Jakupi and their womenfolk sat. Then I cleared my throat nervously.

'I'm sorry the first course was not to your liking. I had hoped you would understand what I was trying to do, but I see now I should have stuck with spaghetti bolognaise or something boring like that.' I hurried on as several of the Italians swivelled in their chairs to cast unfriendly looks in my direction. 'For the main course I was going to make you a uniquely original dish that would bring together more of the best of Albanian and Italian cuisine, highlighting the contrasting flavours and textures. Albanian lamb with couscous and fresh Italian pasta made with white truffle and lobster were to feature prominently in it, together with a fabulous range of utterly opposed vegetables, sauces, herbs and spices. I fancied that it was a dish that would be written about and celebrated for decades to come.' I held up my free hand and shook my head with regret. 'However, a deep breath of sea air changed my mind about all that.' I shot Luigi Vanni a meaningful look. 'So this is what I give you instead.'

With a flourish I whipped the cloth off the wok to reveal – plain, ungarnished and unaccompanied – a single slice of freshly baked Tunisian flatbread.

Even now I wonder where on earth I found the courage to do it. Perhaps it was just my natural belligerence breaking through, or perhaps the events of the last few days had finally proved just a bit too much for my sensitive creative temperament and I had snapped under the strain. Whatever it was, I doubt anyone could have been more surprised by my actions than I was myself. It was like I was having an out-of-body experience, watching myself carrying out this ludicrous, suicidal, action from high up in the vaulted ceiling somewhere.

The Albanians stared at the contents of the wok in bewilderment. The Italians looked equally confused.

Luigi fixed me with a cold glare. 'What is this?' he hissed.

'It's quite simple really. It's Tunisian flatbread, made with oil and flour.'

'Tunisian – flatbread?' He spoke in a dull tone, almost a whisper, clearly still hoping there was some secret to it that he had yet to appreciate, something that would yet save the day. But I had nothing more to give him.

'I'm sorry, Luigi. But this is what you and your Albanian friends see fit to give the migrants you smuggle across the Mediterranean, even the old people and the children, so now this is what I give you,' I announced in a voice shaking with emotion and fear. 'Enjoy.'

Luigi's eyes blazed, but it was the Albanians who were first to react. They rose to their feet almost as one, sending chairs toppling over backwards and items of cutlery clattering to the floor. Luigi's associates were also getting to their feet, hands sliding into their jackets in sudden alarm.

But the Albanians had the drop on them. One of the men standing behind the table had produced an AK-47 automatic rifle from seemingly nowhere and fired a burst into the ceiling. Fragments of stone fell all around us and clouds of dust filled the air. Now all the Albanians had their guns out and were training them on the gaping Italians.

'Nobody is to move!' Jakupi yelled. He had seized Lule and was holding her in front of him, his arm round her throat.

Luigi Vanni was standing across the table from him, unmoving. Bruno, who had been sitting next to him, had a hand half in his pocket but he slowly removed it, empty, as the man opposite him jerked the barrel of his gun at him.

'Everybody take out your guns and place them on the table!' Jakupi ordered sharply.

The Italians looked at Luigi for guidance. After a tense couple of seconds, he nodded and the guns of the Italians were slowly removed and placed on the tables. The Albanians quickly scooped them up, while keeping their own weapons trained on their enemies.

Vaz Jakupi offered Luigi the thinnest of smiles.

'I knew it was a waste of time coming here tonight. But I thought I would listen to what you had to say. But you had nothing to tell me. Your time in Naples is done, Signore Vanni. You have become soft with your villas and your flashy boats. We will close down your operation here and do everything ourselves. Your men will leave the city tonight and if they ever return they will have cause to regret it. Naples belongs to Albania now.'

Luigi, whose expression had been growing increasingly thunderous, gave a deep growl. I sensed what was coming. He was going to tell these foreign interlopers all the things he had been bottling up all this time. He would tell them how they were nothing more than a bunch of amateurish thugs, with no culture, no tradition, no history, no refinement, no imagination, no intelligence even. He would dismiss them for street hoodlums, no better than pickpockets or muggers. No better than thieves who robbed their neighbours. No better than any Albanian should be.

I'm sure that was what he was about to say. But Jakupi didn't give him the chance. Instead he shot him three times, once in his left arm and twice in his chest.

The sound of the gun going off was deafening in the vaulted chamber and I ducked with my hands clapped over my ears. The other Italians cowered too, presumably fearing that any moment they too would be gunned down. Luigi himself collapsed in a crumpled heap, falling between his chair and the table. The back of his chair, I saw, was soaked in blood.

Lule squealed with terror. Neither of the Vanni women moved. I guessed they were too shocked and terrified to move a muscle, even as Luigi lay on the floor, the pool of blood under him quickly expanding.

Satisfied that none of the other Italians presented any threat, Jakupi motioned to his men to leave their places at the table and to follow him to the door. At once they began to fall into place behind him, still keeping their guns pointed at the unmoving Italians.

Just as he reached the doorway Jakupi stopped and pointed at me. 'You!'

I flinched and wondered if he meant me. He obviously did.

'Y-yes?'

'You will come with us.'

Before I could utter a word in response, two of his men had seized me by the arms and were propelling me forcefully out of the hall, still with my wok in my hand. I cast a despairing glance over my shoulder. All the Italian gangsters remained at their places at the tables, glowering after us. Luigi lay unmoving on the floor, while the two Vanni women stared after me with expressions on their white faces that I found impossible to read. No one was making any move whatsoever to help me out.

The next thing I knew I was being hustled down the stone staircase outside then across the inner courtyard, through the gatehouse, and across the bridge over the deep, dry moat. Jakupi led the way, hurrying Lule along by the elbow. She tried her best to keep up with him, though she was struggling in her high heels and protested weakly when he almost jerked her off her feet altogether.

Once over the moat we turned to one side and hurried round the side of the looming castle towards the water's edge. The men at the back of our group kept turning back, guns ready, in case the Italians came after us, but there was no sign of pursuit.

When we reached the dual carriageway, the Albanians waved their guns in the air at approaching cars, which duly screeched to a halt and let us cross the road. Still with no pursuers in sight, we dashed onto one of the piers and then climbed down into some large black rubber dinghies that were moored alongside each other. As soon as we were all aboard the boats their engines started up and we cast off. Within seconds we were surging away from the shore, hanging on to the seats for dear life as we buffeted over the water and into the darkness.

I still couldn't see anyone coming after us, so I looked ahead to see where we were going. Our course seemed to be set directly across the Bay of Naples towards the thousands of tiny, flickering streetlights that lined the eastern shore, under the huge shadow cast by Vesuvius herself. Then I shrank down out of the spray thrown up by our bows and cowered miserably under the muzzles of my captors' guns, wondering if I would ever see England again.

Cooking to Order

It took some time to cross the bay and I glanced up now and then from the bucketing craft to see if Luigi Vanni's helicopter was coming after us, but there was nothing to be seen in the night sky above us. I felt black despair creep over me, though God knew I would hardly be better off with the Italians after the evening's fiasco than I was with my present captors. I hugged my wok and felt too abandoned and wretched even to feel seasick as I usually did.

Eventually we reached the far shore and I was bundled out of the dinghy and blindfolded before being forced up a stony stretch of sand and rocks and into the back of a waiting truck. I sat on an uncomfortable slatted seat as the other Albanians crowded in behind me. They spoke few words and what little was said was completely unintelligible to me. I guessed that Jakupi and his girlfriend, whom I heard getting into the cab, were the only ones with any English so it would be futile trying to argue the case with anyone.

The truck lurched over an uneven road surface for some distance before transferring to a smoother road that, judging by the speed and frequency of the cars going past, might be the multi-laned highway that skirts round the foot of Vesuvius itself. It was not long, however, before I sensed the truck turning off the highway and negotiating slower and more twisting roads until it came to a complete stop and the engine was turned off.

I was manhandled out of the vehicle and through a doorway into a building of some kind. Judging by the echo, I was in a warehouse or similar enclosed open space. I heard Jakupi giving more orders to his men and presumed they related to me when I was seized once more and half-dragged up a flight of metal stairs and through a series of upper rooms, before being sat down forcibly on a plastic chair. The men who had escorted me left the room and I heard their footsteps clanging on the metal staircase as they returned to the floor below. I waited patiently, wok in my lap and blindfold still securely in place, terrified that somewhere the decision was being made to have me executed or beaten up or something.

After an eternity of suspense, I heard the footsteps of half a dozen or more people coming back up the stairs and to the room where I was sitting. A moment later and the owners of the footsteps were all around me. I held my breath and tried to fight down my terror. God, this was worse than being on Masterchef!

The blindfold was untied and I found myself blinking up at the faces of Vaz Jakupi and his confederates. There wasn't much sign of friendly feeling towards me in any of them. Jakupi eyed me for a long moment then pulled up another plastic chair and sat opposite me. I looked around and noted that we were in a dingy-looking room with bare floorboards and very little else by way of furniture and fittings.

'So, Signore Truelove,' the Albanian began, 'what was that all about tonight, eh? You thought you would play a little joke on us, was that it?'

'No, no, nothing like that–'

'Do you see me laughing?'

I shook my head. No, I didn't see him laughing.

'If I was laughing you would know,' he explained helpfully. 'But I do not find you funny at all, Mister Englishman. Mister comedian. Do you, Zog?' He turned to the bearded gorilla standing next to him. Zog shook his huge head. 'Or you, Dardan? Konstantin? Skender? No, none of us find you funny. So, tell me, what was it about, eh? Tell us. Explain your joke to us, mister funny Englishman.'

I stared blankly at him, struggling desperately to think of anything I could say to pacify him.

'Perhaps you were just trying to cause trouble between us and your Italian friends. Was that it?' He nodded slowly to himself, thinking it through. 'Yes, that seems more likely. Why would you want to do that?'

'I–I'm not their friend. I only work for them.'

He nodded again. 'As their cook, yes, you said that before. But why should you want to cause us so much trouble?' Then he shook his head. 'It does not really matter so much, the reason why – what I want is for you to tell us everything you know about the Italian operation. Will you do that?'

I grasped at the straw that was apparently on offer. As far as I was concerned I had no objection to telling them anything they wanted. 'Yes, of course. I'll tell you anything you want to know. Only…'

'Only what?'

'Only I don't know very much about it really. I wasn't invited to any of the meetings they held at the villa.'

'You were present when we put those people ashore two nights ago.'

'I think they took me along to frighten me. And to make it impossible for me to go to the police afterwards because it would look like I was involved.'

The Albanian frowned. 'That is a pity. So you don't know anything useful about their operations.' He shook his head slowly again and sighed. 'It seems to me that you are of no use to anyone.'

'I–I'm sorry about that.'

Jakupi leant back in his chair. 'Is there any point torturing you to find out what you know?'

I gawped at him. 'Torturing me? No. No! I can't tell you anything.'

He sighed again, then looked up at the huge bearded man called Zog. 'What do you think, Zog? Would there be any point?' He repeated the question in Albanian for Zog's benefit.

Zog stared impassively at me, then shook his head.

Jakupi turned back to me. 'Zog thinks not. So what are we to do with you, mister not-so-useful Englishman?'

'Let me go?' I asked in a tiny voice.

Jakupi laughed and the others all laughed with him.

'Why not let him go if he's no use to you?' a female voice piped up.

I hadn't noticed her before, but now I saw that Lule was standing behind the others, listening to what was taking place.

'Shut up,' Jakupi snapped, rounding angrily on her. 'No one asked you.'

The girl fell silent, looking hurt. Jakupi glared at her furiously, then grunted and resumed his contemplation of me.

'I must decide what to do with you, Englishman. And you must decide if there is anything you can offer us, even if, as you say, you know nothing.' He rose from his chair. 'We'll leave you to think about it tonight, Englishman. Make the most of your time. Your life might depend upon what you tell us in the morning.'

At Jakupi's signal, my captors all trooped out of the room, leaving me alone with my terror and my wok. One of the men returned a moment later with a blanket and a bucket, which he deposited on the floor before withdrawing and locking the door behind him.

I tried to think rationally about my options. As far as I could see my prospects were highly unpromising. What could I possibly offer these people? I knew nothing in detail about what Luigi and his pals got up to, and if my captors realised I had recently been in communication with the Italian police they'd probably bump me off there and then.

The room I was in presented no opportunity of escape that I could see. Apart from the two plastic chairs, the only item of furniture was an old couch with its springs gone. There was a small window, but when I finally got to my feet and tried to look out of it I discovered that it was rusted into place and that the dirty glass was reinforced by substantial metal bars. I subsided onto the couch, quite without hope of rescue, and there I remained all night, sometimes falling into an exhausted, fitful sleep before jerking awake in renewed terror at my situation. Rarely have I known such complete hopelessness and despair.

Morning eventually came, though I dreaded its arrival almost as much as I dreaded the thought of the night never coming to an end. Once more I heard heavy feet on the metal staircase outside my room and then the door was opened and Vaz Jakupi and his thugs crowded menacingly around me as before. I got a glimpse of Lule standing by the door.

When Jakupi demanded to know if I had remembered anything about the Italian operation that might be of interest to them I could only shake my head miserably.

Jakupi sat in the chair opposite me. 'So what are we to do with you, Signore Truelove? Perhaps we should kill you straightaway and drop your body in the Bay of Naples as a warning to others that we are to be taken seriously.' He paused and his brow furrowed. 'But look, I am not an unreasonable man. You say you are a great chef, a man of great talent with an international reputation, a television celebrity. Very well. I have been thinking. Perhaps we will ransom you to your friends back home, in nice British sterling, or dollars. You have plenty of rich friends who will pay money for you?'

I thought fleetingly of Barry's face as it would appear

when a ransom demand landed on his desk. He'd have a heart attack. I very much doubted he'd cough up the necessary, even if he could. And who else was there? Bettina might reluctantly put her hand in her pocket but it was unlikely she'd be able to produce the kind of money this crook was thinking of. And the same applied to my mother, too, who had dedicated most of her adult life to reducing the family fortune to so much pocket money. Apart from them, I couldn't think of anyone else I could call on in a fix like this. The BBC was hardly likely to stump up the cash out of the licence fee. But it wouldn't do to tell this thug that.

'Yes, of course,' I assured him. 'Plenty of friends. Good, rich friends.'

'Excellent.'

'Er, how much were you thinking of, incidentally?'

Jakupi rubbed his scar thoughtfully. 'How much do you think you are worth?'

I wasn't sure what to say to that.

Jakupi considered me. 'A million? Two million? Let's say half a million. That's more realistic, I think.'

'Right…'

'But first,' he added, tapping the side of his nose and winking, 'you have to prove to us you are what you say you are, that you can cook. Because of you none of us ate last night. We want breakfast. And we don't want that rubbish you prepared before, remember.' He got up from his chair. 'Cook something good for us and show us that you are worth keeping alive.'

I swallowed. 'Do–do you have a kitchen? Any ingredients to work with?'

'There is a kitchen in the basement downstairs. We have some things in the cupboards – not much, but that will be a challenge to your skill as a cook, I think. Zog will take you down there and he will stay with you, too, to make sure you don't try to give us meatballs with ice cream again. Here, you will need this.'

He handed me my old wok, then said something in Albanian to Zog and the big man hoisted me out of my chair and propelled me by the scruff of the neck towards the door. As I passed Lule she cast me a sympathetic look, only to earn herself a growl and a swift slap on the cheek from her beloved. As I was shoved out of the room I heard her being slapped again, once, twice, three times.

Zog directed me back down the metal staircase. As I wasn't blindfolded this time, I saw that we were descending into a large warehouse that was piled up with packing cases of varying shapes and sizes. One of them near the foot of the staircase had been opened and I glimpsed crates of bottles stacked inside. This, I surmised, was the heart of their operations.

We crossed the warehouse to a door in the opposite wall, then descended a rickety wooden staircase below ground. At the bottom of it I found myself standing in a very basic, grimy-looking cellar-kitchen with ancient cupboards, a stained metal sink and a very old oven. The scene was dimly lit by a single light bulb that dangled from the ceiling and by a faint ray of daylight that seeped in past the grime of decades on a narrow window high in the wall above the sink. Zog gestured to me to get to work. I laid my wok on the stove and tried to take stock. A door led into a small pantry with a very modest selection of tins and packets arranged untidily on its shelves. How the hell I was expected to knock up a meal worthy of an international chef and television celebrity such as myself in these circumstances I had no idea.

Zog watched me as I opened the cupboards to assess what else I might find. There wasn't much to choose from, I quickly discovered, though in a coolbox under the small wooden table I did find a packet of raw burgers and some supermarket noodles. The gang had clearly been living on uninspiring supermarket fare and there wasn't a fresh fruit or vegetable to be found anywhere. When I found the tiny store of dried herbs and spices the little pots and jars were so old I couldn't read the labels and it was impossible to tell from the smell what they were. They were also identical in colour – powdery and more or less grey.

The pots and pans and other utensils were nothing to get excited about either, though at least I had my sturdy old wok. When my eye lingered over an array of rusty carving knives and long-tined forks set in a wooden block beside the oven I got a tut-tutting noise out of Zog. I turned to look at him and saw that he was leering at me, revealing several missing teeth, and patting the gun inadequately concealed from sight in a capacious pocket, as though daring me to try anything. I decided against it.

I told you before that my favourite place in the world is a kitchen. But not this time. Not this kitchen. While the massive, fully bearded Zog leant against the wall and lit a cigarette, filling the tiny room with acrid fumes, my spirits dropped to rock bottom. I couldn't remember a time when I had felt so low in any kitchen, anywhere. All my dreams of a glittering life as an international chef with a trans-European reputation had been shot down with Luigi Vanni. Now here I was in the hands of bloodthirsty barbarians who would think nothing of slitting my throat and with no one in the world who would lift a finger to help me out of my predicament. Not during the course of my three tempestuous marriages, or of my on-off liaison with Bettina or my countless other emotional crises of one kind or another had I ever felt as distraught and hopeless as this.

I grouped all the foodstuffs I could find on the table and then sat down in the only chair to contemplate what I could possibly concoct from them. But it was hopeless. I literally had to cook to save my life but I could do nothing creative with these ingredients. No one could, not Jamie, not Bettina, not Gordo, not Rick, not Ainsley – no one. I was a dead man wokking.

Zog grunted and pointed meaningfully at the oven. Then he lit another cigarette. Clearly he was expecting me to start work.

I rose unwillingly and sifted through the packages in front of me. I had the meat, a bag of nuts, some tinned tomatoes and sweetcorn, the noodles, a few other unpromising odds and ends, and I had the unlabelled herbs and spices. All I could do was stick it all in the wok and cross my fingers.

I found some oil to heat up in the wok and then broke the burgers up into it. Then I dropped the other ingredients in one by one, feeling like I had really drawn the short straw this time. Even cooks in fast food places had more to work with than I had. I sampled the mixture. As I had expected it was utterly bland. I stuffed my hands in my apron pocket, as I tend to do when thinking in the kitchen and was surprised to come into contact with something. I was about to pull it out to see what it was when I suddenly remembered what it must be – the spice jar Luigi had slipped me at the Castel Nuovo. My mind raced. Could I? Dare I?

No, it would still be unforgivable. I was a chef, for heaven's sake. As a matter of principle, I couldn't deliberately go round poisoning people with the food I prepared. It was a matter of a chef's honour. I slipped the jar out of my apron pocket and deposited it on the table, resolving heroically not to think about it again.

I tried the mixture in the wok once more. It was almost completely without taste. I tried to remain calm. I had to do something to jazz it up somehow. My life was at stake here! Zog watched with a disinterested air as I started adding generous spoonfuls of herbs and spices to the sizzling contents of the wok. I tasted the mixture again. It was a slight improvement, but the herbs and spices were so old they were struggling to have much impact. Oh well, I told myself, in for a penny, in for a pound. I upended each jar in turn, dumping their entire contents into the wok until every single one of them was empty.

Well, it was too late to undo what I had done now.

I was about to taste the mixture again when I heard someone coming down the stairs from the floor above. It was Luljeta. She smiled uncertainly at me but I couldn't help noticing how red her cheeks were from the slaps she had received minutes before from her ghastly boyfriend.

'Vaz wants to know if the food is ready,' she told me in an unsteady voice.

'Just a couple more minutes,' I replied, stirring the mixture vigorously. I pulled a face and indicated her reddened cheeks. 'Are you all right?'

'I'm okay. It is not the first time,' she answered quickly. 'I shall get the plates.'

She took a stack of plates out of a cupboard and heaped some knives and forks on top of them. Then she directed a smile at Zog and asked him something in Albanian. Zog flushed and muttered something in reply, but she responded with a bright, somewhat forced, laugh and then handed the plates to him. She was evidently asking him to carry them upstairs for her. Zog's initial reluctance was no defence, it seemed, to her dazzling smile and I suspected he had more than a bit of a soft spot for her.

Zog placed a foot on the first step, but Lule stopped him and walked to the pantry, from which she produced a large plastic tomato ketchup bottle. She placed it on the pile of plates in Zog's hands and he continued up the stairs. Clearly ketchup was deemed essential in the diet of Vaz Jakupi and his men.

The moment Zog had disappeared at the top of the stairs the girl turned to me, looking anxious.

'You have to get out of here. They mean to kill you.'

'What?' I reeled at her words. 'But they haven't even tasted it yet.'

'I heard Vaz telling the others to take you away and kill you after they have eaten.'

'But what about their plan to ransom me?'

'They talked about it, but they think it is too dangerous. You are a famous person and the police will be embarrassed if they do not rescue you. So it is easier for them to kill you.'

My God, so there it was. My fame, the one thing I cherished above all else, was to be my undoing – the very thing that led to my demise.

'You have to get out of here,' she urged. 'What about that window?'

I looked up at the narrow window high up the wall above the sink. It looked a narrow squeeze, but I supposed it might be possible. But what would happen then?

'Where would I go?' I asked her. 'I have no idea where we are.'

'This is a bad area, full of bad men,' she informed me, not reassuringly. 'But if you turn left and keep going you will get to the main highway. You could stop a car there and it will take you to safety.'

Before we could discuss the details of this hare-brained scheme, Zog's heavy footsteps sounded on the stairs behind us. We parted hurriedly and I busied myself in transferring the food from the heavy wok to a bowl that Lule held out for me. Zog waited while we completed the task, his eyes focused more on Lule than on me, then he took the bowl from the girl and started back up the stairs with it.

The sooner I got out of that kitchen the better, I felt – but could I really trust this fluffy little article with my life?

'Why are you helping me like this?' I demanded to know.

Lule looked up at me and I could see tears springing into her eyes. 'These are bad people. I want to get away from them too. Perhaps we can escape together. You are a nice man, I think – you might help me get to England.'

'Why haven't you just run away and taken a plane to London, if that's where you want to go?'

'I can't. I don't have a passport. Vaz told me he would make one for me, but now he says he won't give me one.'

I saw her dilemma. I nodded quickly. 'All right then, Lule,' I reassured her, 'I'll help you if I can, if we get out of here. We must be quick, though.'

I motioned to her to help me clamber up on the old sink, which, fortunately for me, seemed to be securely fixed to the wall. I started grappling with the latch of the narrow window, but soon found that it was rusted shut. I tried forcing it with my hands, but it just wouldn't budge.

'I need something I can use to lever it up,' I told Lule in desperation. 'Find me something!'

The poor girl clearly didn't understand what I was

asking for. First she offered me a dish cloth, then she offered me a wooden spatula.

'No, no!' I hissed. 'That! That!'

I pointed at the metal spoon I had used to serve the food. She grabbed it and passed it up to me. It took several heaves, but eventually the catch gave and the window flapped open. I was about to try scrabbling through it when Luljeta tugged in warning on my trouser leg.

We had spent too long over freeing the window. Zog was coming back down the stairs again, so I jumped down quickly off the sink and dropped the spoon in the sink.

As soon as Zog reached the bottom he mumbled something rapid in Albanian to Luljeta, then glanced at me.

'He says they like the food,' Lule told me, forcing a smile. 'Very much.'

'Oh. Good.' I spoke without much enthusiasm now I knew that they intended to kill me anyway.

Zog was gesturing to Lule to go back upstairs. It seemed her presence was missed at dinner. Then he motioned at me to come too.

That was it, then. My one chance of escape had been scuppered by a rusty window catch and a fully bearded Albanian. I might as well go quietly, I told myself ruefully. It really wouldn't make any difference to the outcome if I resisted or not.

But Lule, I quickly realised, had her own ideas about how to evade the inevitable. Instead of trotting dutifully up the stairs as instructed she gave Zog a long, pouting look and murmured something in an undertone that sounded to me distinctly amorous. I don't know what it was but suddenly Zog was giving her his full attention. The little minx! She knew the big gorilla fancied her and now she was using her feminine wiles to distract him –

though how the hell we were supposed to escape through the tiny window while he was in the room was beyond me.

Lule giggled and fluttered her eyelids at the hairy lunk. Zog looked as surprised as I was, but he was obviously up for it. She murmured something else to him, soft and low, and now I was sure she was soft-soaping him into thinking she wanted some quality time with him.

Now, any sane person wouldn't have believed it for a moment. Lule, bless her, was no actress and anyone but a lovestruck moron would have seen through her act at once. But, fortunately for us both, a lovestruck moron was exactly what Zog was.

She moved closer to him and I must say that when Lule turned on the charm it was easy to fall under her spell, with her pretty little upturned nose and air of honeyed innocence. Despite the desperation of my situation, I found time to envy Zog what might just be in store for him.

The huge thug glanced apprehensively up the stairs, but Lule took his hirsute head in both her hands and forced him to look at her as she continued to murmur endearments. I couldn't understand what she was telling him, but I got the gist. She'd always fancied the socks off him, didn't he know that? She'd been waiting for a chance like this to be with him, without Vaz cramping her style. Didn't he know how he was driving her crazy with his muscles and big hairy face? Why didn't they do it here, right now? No one would know. Never mind the Englishman – he'll be dead soon anyway. They could do it on this table, this table that I'm leaning back on right now...

Zog didn't need more persuading. I dare say most Albanians usually observe the niceties of courtship like the rest of us, but I must admit I was taken aback by the rapidity with which things progressed with these two representatives of the country. With a low, lustful growl Zog bent over Lule and started to wrench frenziedly at her clothing. A moment later, with her apparent encouragement, he was going about the business of lowering his trousers with clumsy haste and climbing on top of her.

I wasn't quite sure what I should do while this was happening. It wasn't a situation I was familiar with, standing not two feet away while other people set about getting amorously involved with each other without being invited to join in the fun myself. Normally, I suppose, I would have made my excuses and left, but the only places I could go to were up the stairs to where my presumptive killers were or out through the window, which even Zog in the throes of passion might notice and have something to say about. I could step into the pantry, I supposed, but that would hardly remove me very effectively from the scene of action.

Then, while trying to ignore Zog's animal grunting as he got down to serious work, I noticed that Lule was signalling frantically at me with one of her hands. As her face was hidden I couldn't make out at first what she was trying to communicate to me. She seemed to be directing my attention to the oven, but I couldn't for the life of me think why. She didn't want me to cook her something to eat, did she? Surely she had enough on her plate already?

Then I realised. She was trying to draw my attention to what was on the oven. The wok. The immensely heavy, iron wok.

I'm no fool, you know, when I know what's expected of me. As swiftly and surreptitiously as I could I skirted round the table, avoiding contact with hairy buttocks, dangling feet and athletically splayed legs as far as possible, and reached for the wok's handle. After quickly checking that no one else was about to come down the stairs I lifted the thing high in the air and then brought it down on the back of Zog's head with every ounce of my strength.

The impact made a loud, metallic thud that I was sure would be heard on the other side of the Bay of Naples, but it did the trick all right. Zog abruptly lost all interest in what he was doing, or in anything else for that matter, and sagged unconscious onto Lule. I helped her roll him off the table and onto the floor, then lent a hand to pull her up.

'Quick,' she panted, as she rearranged her clothing. 'Before anyone comes!'

I put the wok aside and climbed back onto the sink. It was a struggle, but somehow I managed to get first my head and shoulders, then my torso, and finally my legs through the narrow window. A quick glance around revealed I had emerged into a dusty alley running along the side of the warehouse. The good news was that there didn't appear to be any of Jakupi's thugs around to inquire what I was doing.

I squirmed round so I could help Lule out after me. She reached her hands up for mine and I quickly got her head and shoulders through, but then her magnificent bust became wedged in the narrow opening. No matter how hard I pulled and Lule wriggled I couldn't get her any further through it. Then we both froze. Someone upstairs must have heard the almighty blow I had dealt Zog for now we heard his name being called. We both recognised the voice immediately as that of Vaz Jakupi himself.

'Come on!' I urged. 'Hurry!'

But Lule, the gallant little idiot, shook her head and started going back through the window. Footsteps were already sounding on the stairs behind her.

'Come on!' I repeated. 'I can't leave you like this!'

She withdrew her hands. 'You must. They will kill you.'

She was right, of course. She might get away with a beating, but they'd kill me for sure. And there wasn't time to argue. I could see the shoes of Vaz Jakupi coming down the stairs. I reached out and grabbed Lule's hand and gave it a kiss.

'Don't forget me!' I heard her whisper earnestly as I released her hand and scrambled to my feet outside, letting the window fall down behind me.

I didn't linger to listen to what Vaz Jakupi had to say when he found Lule alone in the cellar-kitchen with an unconscious and half-dressed Zog and me gone. I was off up the alley beside the warehouse like a rabbit out of a jug. I'd probably only got a matter of seconds before Jakupi raised the alarm and ordered his men in hot pursuit.

In fact, I'd hardly got to the narrow street adjoining the alley when I heard his voice raised in high dudgeon from the building behind me. I sprinted up the street in the direction that Lule had told me I would find the highway. If only I could find a policeman! But there was no one about anywhere.

I appeared to be in a very run-down suburb of the eastern Neapolitan urban sprawl, a neighbourhood of featureless industrial buildings and high wire-topped walls. I was going uphill too, and it was a straight stretch of several hundred yards ahead of me. Jesus! If I didn't get off this street soon the Albanians would spot me the instant they left the warehouse.

As if in answer to my worst fears, I heard angry shouts behind me. I half-turned and saw Jakupi's men emerging from the warehouse and gesticulating wildly in my direction. I thought they'd start running after me, in which case I would have a lead of about ten seconds, but then I saw to my horror that some bright spark had thought of following me in the truck parked across the street from the warehouse and was already climbing into it. Hell, I wouldn't get far if they were motorised.

I redoubled my efforts and sprinted towards the top end of the road, and then round the corner. All at once I found myself running past a short stretch of dilapidated local shops. There was still no one in sight and I was despairing of any refuge when I spotted a battered-looking bus about to pull away from a bus stop not twenty yards ahead of me.

I sprinted like I haven't done since leaving school and, somehow, just as the Albanians' truck hurtled round the corner behind me, managed to make the open door of the bus and throw myself inside. The driver looked startled but I suppose he had seen dishevelled Englishmen in chef's whites on the run from gangsters in this neck of town many times before because he just gave me a casual nod and concentrated on pulling out into the traffic.

Thanking my lucky stars, and the public bus operators of Naples for their immaculate timing, I pulled some money out of my pocket of my whites, which weren't quite as pristine as they had once been, and popped it in the driver's top pocket. I knew you're supposed to get a ticket in advance, but he'd just have to make an exception in my case. I then staggered towards the back of the bus to see what had become of my pursuers. They must have seen me leaping aboard the bus, of course, and sure enough there they were in their truck right behind us, Vaz Jakupi sitting beside the driver and giving me a venomous glare.

I found an empty seat in the crowded bus and sat down. As I endeavoured to get my breath back I tried to assess my chances. Jakupi and his gang might have a lot of pull in the area but they clearly didn't want to be seen snatching me from a crowded bus in broad daylight, so I was reasonably safe while I stayed on the bus, but once it stopped that might be a different matter. What was to prevent one of them slipping aboard and, for instance, quietly knifing me between stops? I needed to know where this bus was going.

I turned to the large, grey-haired woman I was sitting next to and shot her a disarming smile. Not disarming enough, maybe, as her eyes widened and she shrank a couple of inches from me.

'Sorry to be a nuisance,' I apologised, 'but do you speak English?'

The woman shook her head. Just my luck.

'Where is this bus going?' I asked, speaking very slowly in the time-honoured fashion of British tourists when confronted by foreigners who haven't been blessed with the opportunity to pick up a few words of our language. 'Where – bus – go?'

The woman still looked alarmed so I embarked on an elaborate mime to try to get my meaning across. It took at least twenty seconds of frantic gesturing before she got my drift.

'Ah!' she exclaimed with sudden enthusiasm, 'Si, si!'

I was glad she understood at last, but she still wasn't telling me.

'Where – bus – go?'

She rolled her eyes with amusement at my ignorance. 'Pompeii! Si! Pompeii!'

'Pompeii?'

'Pompeii!'

It seemed the bus was going to Pompeii. 'No stop?' I asked.

She shook her head.

I could have kissed her.

I paused to think for a moment. Pompeii. Police headquarters would have been better, but it could have been worse. The place was always thronged with visitors and that might give me the opportunity to give Vaz Jakupi and his men the slip. Then I'd just have to find a telephone somewhere and summon the authorities.

Then it occurred to me that someone on the bus might have a phone I could use to contact the police. I turned to my new bosom pal.

'Excuse me, do you have a phone I could borrow to make a call?' I mimed making a phone call. 'You – have – phone?

The grey-haired woman shook her head but from the way her hands closed over her handbag she was obviously lying. Perhaps she hadn't understood me properly.

'You – have – phone?' I repeated.

She shook her head but kept her hands clamped on her bag. For heaven's sake, I realised, the stupid woman thought I wanted to steal the thing!

I gave her a smile to reassure her and then pointed at the bag. 'I just want to borrow it to make a call,' I explained. 'I don't want to steal it. I'm not some sort of street bandit.'

Bandit wasn't, on reflection, the best word I could have chosen. It's an Italian word and it has the same meaning in both languages. When you're worried that someone is trying to steal your phone it's a word you really don't want to hear them saying. At the word bandit, the woman gave a squeak of alarm and started looking wildly about for assistance.

I saw that the bus driver was watching me with a suspicious expression on his face and I backed away from my neighbour immediately, with profuse apologies. The last thing I wanted was him stopping the bus to order me off and leave me to the mercy of my pursuers. So borrowing a phone was out.

The bus had pulled onto the A3, the six-lane highway built for residents of the area to make a quick getaway as and when Vesuvius next erupts. The Albanians' truck continued to follow us, keeping just a few yards behind. After a few minutes the bus driver signalled to turn off the motorway, following the tourist signs for the ruins of Pompeii. The approach road to the attraction was busy with vehicles, but as soon as the bus slowed for the stop I was up on my feet and first through the door, hoping to gain a little time over my pursuers, who had a truck to park somewhere. I looked all round for a policeman, but before I could locate one I spotted the Albanians pouring out of their truck, which they had parked at a crazy angle over the kerb. Where do traffic wardens disappear to when you really need one? In any case, I saw there would be no time for me to make complicated explanations to secure police protection before they were on me so I hurried for the main entrance to the ruins, where a large crowd of tourists had amassed. I huddled low and joined the teeming throng shuffling its way towards the gates.

It took a couple of minutes for me to get to the front of the queue, but as far as I could tell Jakupi's men hadn't yet spotted me, though they must be close behind me somewhere. When it was my turn I handed over the admission fee and slipped through the entrance and up the path beyond, trying to stay concealed amongst the tour groups and families making their way up the slope towards the spectacular ruins.

They spotted me just as I was about to reach the relative safety of the first ruined houses. I heard a shout from the entrance gates. I glanced back and saw Jakupi and his men trying to force their way through the barriers. Members of staff tried to stop them, but when Jakupi pulled out a gun they shrank away and the whole party of Albanians poured through unhindered. I gulped with fear as I counted them. There were eight of them in all, and they were all armed. I wondered fleetingly what had happened to the rest of the gang. Perhaps there hadn't been room for them in the truck.

I pushed my way past an elderly couple and made a break for the buildings. I had to get as deep into the massive site as possible. If I could find a good place to hide perhaps I could let them go by me and slip out again to make my way to the nearest police station. Alternatively, if I could keep out of the gang's clutches for long enough, perhaps some of the officials back at the gate would think to phone for back-up to tackle the armed intruders who had forced their way past them.

I had last been to Pompeii some years before and knew roughly where the main points of interest in the ruins of the ancient Roman town were located. The problem was that it was such a big site that, even with thousands turning up for a day sightseeing, the visitors quickly thinned out as they headed in different directions. I'd do best, I felt, to stick to the most popular sights, where the crowds would be densest.

Having turned the first corner and out of sight of my pursuers for the moment, I hurried to the forum, a wide open space at the lower end of the gently sloping site and the centre of the old city's network of roads. It was past mid-morning and the sun was high in the sky. I was already sweating and I felt very visible in my chef's whites, though fortunately many of the other visitors were also in white or pale summer clothing, so that helped a bit.

Once in the forum, where I was surrounded by the remains of the basilica, market and temple buildings, I had to make a decision quickly about which way to go. I had entered the site by the south-western entrance and could either head for the maze of streets to the east, where highlights included, in the extreme south-eastern corner, the gladiatorial amphitheatre, or go straight on up the wide street that opened up at the far end of the forum between the Temple of Jupiter and the fish market and head due north towards the looming mass of that sullen old mass murderess Vesuvius. Most of the tourists were heading east, so that, I reckoned, was the direction for me.

I hurried across the foot of the grassy public square and squirrelled my way into the midst of a large group of Chinese visitors, ducking a bit so I didn't stick out as unusually large among their diminutive figures. A shout behind me told me that the Albanians had spotted what I was doing, however. The Chinese were padding down the Via dell' Abbondanza rather more slowly than I would have preferred, so I worked my way towards the front of the party and then broke on ahead up the street.

Another party a little way ahead of me was filing into the Stabian Baths, a public bath complex that ranks among the best-preserved of all the buildings on the site, with complete roofs sheltering some of the remaining structures. I elected to join them. As I headed for the entrance I looked back, just in time to see Vaz Jakupi bursting through the Chinese party at the head of his men. Whether or not he had seen me I couldn't be sure, but he was alarmingly close on my heels. Should I hide somewhere in the baths? Or should I get through them as quickly as I could and exit by another entrance onto another street? I wasn't sure what was the best policy.

I hastened into the complex, and found myself among a crowd of people standing under a pillared portico that ran down two sides of a grassy inner courtyard. I tried to decide where best to lose myself in the warren of structures surrounding it. I opted to go left and careered through the tourists gathered round the empty pool in which countless Romans had once no doubt cavorted and amused themselves. This was no time for standing and taking my turn. Then I heard squeals from the tourists at the entrance as my pursuers arrived in my wake. I dashed for a doorway at the far end of the courtyard and careered through the small room it led to and into a passageway, where I turned right, then right again – and found myself back in the courtyard I'd just left, but now on the far side to that through which the Albanians were lumbering after me, seven of them now.

I fled down the portico on the east side of the courtyard then veered to my left into a larger enclosed space under an impressively decorated arched roof of honey-coloured stone. In the centre of the room were two glass cases, each of which contained one of the famous Pompeii casts of dead Romans, formed by pouring plaster into the impressions of the dead bodies left in the layers of ash after the great eruption that interrupted life hereabouts back in AD 79. One was the cast of a man lying with his head on his arm, as though asleep. The other was of a man apparently writhing in agony with one arm raised in the air as if to defend himself. I crouched behind the first of the cases as I heard running feet in the portico outside. I held my breath, hoping they would not come in after me, but suddenly the doorway through which I had just come was filled with the unmistakable shape of Vaz Jakupi.

He spotted me straightaway, of course.

Glass display cases are, I suppose I should have realised, far from ideal cover for the simple reason that of course you can see straight through them. Jakupi gave a cry of triumph and levelled his gun in my direction. As I darted behind the second glass case he fired and the air was immediately full of flying glass and fragments of shattered plaster. The noise of the gun inside the confined space was deafening. The second case met with a similar fate a moment later, but by then I had already moved on, leaping for another doorway out of the room. I wasn't going to stay to lament the damage my attacker was doing to irreplaceable ancient artefacts. Instead I hurtled on through the complex, with nary a glance for decorated walls, hypocaust heating systems or indeed the baths themselves. I could hear the feet of the pursuing Albanians pounding close behind me as well as more squeals from other tourists and was more than relieved when I came to an exit that led out onto another street. I was through it in a moment and sprinting for all I was worth up the alley outside.

There was an angry shout behind me as the Albanians tumbled out of the baths and spotted me tearing up the street like a startled deer. I immediately swerved into a narrow paved lane that had opened up to my left and then turned left again into a similar lane running between substantially complete buildings. A few yards into this alley a group of tourists were gathered round a doorway, crowding to get inside. Without bothering to ask people to make way I cannoned through them and into the gloomy interior, hoping to God that the Albanians would not this time have seen where I went. I heard shouts and six sets of running feet go by and, trying to catch my breath, began to dare to hope that I had managed to lose them.

There were tourists all around me, crammed into a

series of small rooms. I wondered why the place was attracting such interest. My eye settled on a faded wall painting above my head. It depicted a couple of ancient Romans on a bed and it left no doubt whatsoever what they were up to. There were more wall paintings nearby, all of them depicting different varieties of the same act. I realised belatedly where I must be. I was in the Lupanar, Pompeii's notorious brothel, with its licentious works of art, its frank graffiti left by the women and their clients, and its tale-telling stone beds. I frowned, but not because of any finer feelings about the location I found myself in. As far as I could remember there was no other way out of the building. Accordingly, not wanting my mother to read that I had died in a house of ill repute even two thousand years after its last client was entertained there, I waited a moment or two more until I thought the coast might be clear then cautiously emerged through the front door.

Unfortunately, the coast was not clear. I had hardly taken two steps along the high pavement, when a yell from further down the lane made my heart miss a beat and I was off again, pelting in a roughly north-easterly direction with no aim in my mind other than to put as much distance as possible between me and the men who seemed so set on doing me to death.

I ran blindly through street after street, quickly losing all sense of direction. I vaulted over the stepping stones to get from one side of a carriageway to another, took short cuts through houses where there was nothing left but the remains of four ancient walls, and changed direction whenever the opportunity presented itself. I even hid once or twice and tried to double-back after the Albanians had gone past me, but every time they spotted me just when I thought I had got away with it, and the chase was on once more. After so nearly getting myself trapped in the brothel I avoided the temptation to seek a hiding place deep in one of the more complete buildings as many only had one entrance and could easily bring the hunt to a premature end.

Every time I reached a corner I paused for a split second to check on the progress of my pursuers. Usually, to my dismay, I saw that they were no further away, or even that they had gained a few steps on me. That gave me new will to go faster yet. The third time I paused to check on them, I counted only five of them still coming after me, and that gave me a tiny boost, though God knew it only needed one of them with a gun and an accurate aim to spoil my day entirely.

I ran past towering colonnades, under brickwork arches, through roofless halls with massive pillars supporting nothing, past street fountains, domestic shrines, shattered statues, all the archaeological detritus of a lost civilisation. Here and there, within the buildings, I glimpsed more glass cases storing examples of the famous plaster casts.

As I passed some scaffolding where the work of restoration was continuing on one of the buildings I flinched as a helicopter swooped low overhead with a noisy roar. I looked up, only to be dazzled by the noonday sun. It wheeled sharply in the sky and flew directly over me again, but I couldn't make out any details. Was it the police? Had someone made the phone call I had hoped they would? Had talk of men with guns and a desperate man in chef's whites fleeing for his life through the site finally galvanised someone into action? It was possible, but unless they got on with things it was all too likely that they would arrive in time only to tidy up my dead body and notify the next of kin.

Even as I watched, the helicopter sheered off to somewhere outside the ancient city and began to descend a good mile off, disappearing behind a row of trees. If it really was the police they would have a fair amount of ground to cover before they could come to my aid.

The Albanians came into view again, about fifty yards behind me. One of them, I noted, as I leant on the scaffolding and tried to haul some fresh air into my straining lungs, was tottering in the rear and even as I watched he keeled over completely, apparently exhausted. That left just four. However, as I started off once more, still looking over my shoulder, another of them fell to the ground, making it three. It was a fiercely hot day now, and I wasn't surprised that all this racing about was starting to take its toll, but their lack of stamina surprised me. I was labouring, certainly, but I wasn't quite done yet. Perhaps my motivation, being the continuation of my life, was greater than theirs. Either that or I must be fitter than I realised. It was probably the lack of fresh fruit and vegetables in their diet, I told myself sourly. Still, three was better than the eight who had started out after me.

I staggered rather than ran another hundred yards or so to the next intersection and waited, panting, to see who came round the far corner I had just vacated. Vaz Jakupi was the first to appear beside the scaffolding, looking weary but still pointing his gun in my general direction, then another figure rounded the corner, but only one. So another of them had given up the chase.

I tried to work out where I was. I could see Vesuvius to the right, and gathered dimly that I must be somewhere in the northern sector of the site. I ought to turn left somewhere, I told myself, and lead the pursuing pair back through the maze of narrow alleys in which the broiling heat seemed to be working in my favour. If I could just keep going long enough maybe I'd leave them both safely behind.

But it was getting very hard to keep going. My lungs were rasping and my legs felt like lead. What would happen if I couldn't keep going I didn't like to contemplate, but I had to try. There was no other option if I didn't want a bullet in the head in about thirty seconds' time.

Sobbing with fear and exhaustion, I lurched off in what I felt was the right direction, all the time cringing at the thought that Vaz Jakupi might take his chance of a long shot and get lucky with a bullet striking home in the middle of my back.

I shambled past the House of the Vetti on my right, then the House of the Faun on my left, but I knew from the violent trembling that had started up in my calves and knees that it was nearly all up with me. I'd never make it back as far as the forum where it was just possible I could find shelter among the massed tourists once more – though quite what I thought they could do to thwart a couple of armed thugs bent on my destruction I couldn't say.

I sagged against a wall at the next corner and looked back. Only one figure was still coming after me. Vaz Jakupi, staggering almost as much as I was, but still coming on.

I let out a gasp of utter despair. I knew it was all up with me if I couldn't outrun him, and I couldn't do it. I just couldn't do it.

I rounded the corner of the House of Pansa and forced my legs to carry me a few yards further before I finally conceded that it was useless to go on. I reeled into the entrance of a roofless two-storied facade to my left in order to get off the street before Jakupi got the chance of a shot at me at close range. I don't know what I was hoping. I was really only trying to delay the last fateful, awful moment of reckoning, I suppose, however pointless that might be in the long run.

I took in my surroundings in a dazed fashion, hoping against hope that there might be a good place to hide. I realised I was standing in one of Pompeii's bakeries, with brick ovens complete with hearths and circular flour mills in more or less pristine condition. I stumbled to the back of the building till I could go no further, trapped in the corner between a stone wall and a big brick oven. There was nowhere to run, even if I could. It was all over.

Vaz Jakupi lurched into the doorway, breathing heavily. He looked white-faced and ill and his face was beaded with sweat. I also saw, as he stumbled towards me, gun levelled, that he was dribbling precocious amounts of foaming saliva down his black shirt front.

'So, Signore Truelove,' he gasped as he wiped a trail of spittle from his chin with the back of his hand. 'Have you stopped running?'

I nodded, too weak even to speak.

'Good. I think the time has come to finish this. Do you know what I think of you, mister ridiculous Englishman?'

I shook my head.

'I think you are a joke!' he wheezed. 'I think you are a fool to think you can match up to a man like me! You have seen what I did to Signore Vanni.' He paused for breath. 'If he couldn't beat me, why do you think you can do it? Hey?'

I assumed his question was rhetorical and didn't attempt a reply.

'As for that girl!' He spat saliva from his mouth and wobbled a bit as he wiped his mouth again. 'That girl. She was a fool to think, to think...'

His voice trailed off as though he couldn't remember what he was saying. Then he rubbed his eyes irritably, as though forcing himself to concentrate. He took a deep breath.

'Well, mister Englishman. We shall speak no more. We shall end it here, you and me.'

He gripped the gun in his hand more steadily and half

closed one eye to aim. I straightened myself up against the brick oven, last used over two thousand years ago.

So this was where it was all going to an end, in a kitchen. How appropriate. Despite my misery, I couldn't help but smile at the neatness of it all as I stared back at my assassin.

Vaz Jakupi squinted down the short barrel of his gun. I noticed that his hand was trembling and he frowned, then clapped his other hand over the hilt to steady it. He exhaled slowly then squinted again over the barrel at me.

I braced myself for the impact of the shot.

There was an infinitely long pause. Jakupi's eyes widened and he gave a little burp. Then a look of intense pain flashed across his face and his eyes opened wider yet. His chest gave a great heave. He gulped then heaved again and then, to my complete astonishment, staggered to the wall at his side and was violently and horribly sick.

I watched, stunned, as he sank to his knees, retching powerfully and noisily. The gun skittered across the hard ground towards me. I hesitated, then bent down painfully and picked it up, marvelling. What on earth had just happened?

As the Albanian continued to groan, feebly and clearly in great distress, someone else I recognised appeared in the doorway to the bakery. His appearance was as unexpected as it was welcome.

It was the police inspector. He gazed at me, then down at Jakupi, then back up at me, suspicious this time.

'What did you do to him?'

All Gravy

It was the Italian police sergeant who saw me off at Naples airport the following day. He explained to me that the inspector couldn't come himself as he was busy on another case. I was tempted to comment upon the senior officer's apparent ingratitude, but to be honest I was too tired and too relieved to kick up a fuss. I was only glad to be at the airport, about to board a private jet that would take me back to London, with their formal thanks. I'd given them a detailed statement of all that had happened and that, it seemed, was that as far as I was concerned. The rest, they assured me, could be left to them.

I bid the sergeant a cheery farewell and climbed the steps to the plane. My legs were appallingly stiff after the exertions of the day before but at least I was still in one piece and here to tell the tale, which must have been a considerable surprise to a number of people. The police had provided me with some fresh clothes to replace the thoroughly worn-out chef's whites and after a decent night's sleep in a hotel close to the central police station, at state expense, I felt ready to go home and pick up the threads of a more normal life. I wouldn't say that I was physically back in top form, but I was already starting to put the whole sorry affair firmly in the past.

The inspector had filled me in on some background information during my lengthy interview. It seemed the police had come (rather laggardly, in my opinion) to my rescue at Pompeii after receiving an anonymous tip-off identifying the whereabouts of the Albanian gang's headquarters. They had arrived at the warehouse in time to arrest several men and secure a vast amount of smuggled goods, as well as several firearms, quantities of drugs, forged passports and substantial amounts of money. Amongst those detained was a large thug with a fractured skull, who had still to come round. When I asked about Lule, however, I got the reply that no one of that description had been found at the address. It was a piece of news that dented my mood somewhat, and I feared the worst for her.

Unfortunately, the inspector explained, by the time the police arrived at the warehouse I had already decamped with Vaz Jakupi and the rest of the gang in hot pursuit. They were at a loss to know where I might have got to, until they started getting garbled messages from Pompeii that some lunatic in chef's whites was scampering all over their precious ruins being chased by mobsters with guns who, furthermore, had foregone the usual requirement of forking out the entrance fee. They had promptly put due and due together and come to quattro and arrived by helicopter just in time to find me standing in triumph over my mortal enemy, as previously described.

When I asked after the health of Vaz Jakupi and his associates I got a surprising response. It appeared that they had keeled over, one by one, as a result of having ingested a potentially lethal poison, probably taken (according to their experts) no more than an hour or so before succumbing to the effects. Several of them were still on the danger list.

The inspector was mystified as to how that had happened, and I couldn't help him. I was about to tell him how, as a matter of interest, Luigi Vanni had offered me poison to slip in the food I prepared for Vaz Jakupi and his boys but how I had decided not to as it just wouldn't be cricket when a horrible thought struck me. What had I done with the spice jar Luigi had given me? Then I remembered how I had put it down on the table in the kitchen, next to the other jars of herbs and spices. Good grief – had I inadvertently got it mixed up with the other herbs and spices and added its contents along with the others, with inevitable results? I suppose I must have done. It made me shudder to think that if I hadn't been so careless I would now probably be lying in an Italian mortuary with a hole in my forehead – or else left to lie for eternity among the plaster casts of the dead Romans of Pompeii. That Vaz Jakupi and his confederates were still, just, in the land of the living was due to the fact that they had been prevented from finishing what was on their plates by the hullabaloo I had raised in bashing Zog over the head with my wok and making my escape. I'd have liked the wok back but when I asked about it the inspector gave me such a look of derision I decided not to mention it again.

When, and if, the Albanians recovered from their current indisposition they would go on trial and could look forward to becoming long-term residents in a high-security Italian prison. Which was no better than they deserved, in my humble opinion.

After I had told him about events connected with the Albanians as far as I could, or was prepared to, the inspector expressed a keen desire to hear about the dinner I had alluded to at the Castel Nuovo, about which he was pretty much in the dark. Again, I told him what I could, but I don't think much of the information I gave him about Luigi Vanni's criminal activities was news to him.

'How did you know about the people-smuggling going on that night?' I asked.

'Another anonymous phone call. But we were too late to catch the Albanians. By the time we had picked up the migrants from the water the traffickers had escaped.'

It seemed to me the police had been benefitting from quite a few anonymous phone calls lately, all at the expense of the Albanians, but that was fine by me. Particularly when the person I suspected of making them was now apparently out of the picture, permanently.

'What about Luigi Vanni?' I asked. 'Did you find his body?'

The inspector pursed his lips. 'Nothing has been reported to us from the Castel Nuovo, where you say the shooting took place. As soon as we picked you up we sent a squad to his villa on Capri but it was deserted. Everyone had gone. Everything packed up. All we found was your bag and your passport. Perhaps they panicked after the shooting. We don't know where they are now.'

I mused thoughtfully. 'So that's the end of your investigation then?'

'There would be little point continuing when the man responsible for everything is dead.'

Well, I conceded privately to myself, that was good news for Teresa and Mariana at least. They would be free to start fresh lives somewhere without the dread shadow of Luigi Vanni blighting their existence. I wished them well. And I wouldn't press the inspector for any more information about the Vannis in case it caused them trouble in the future.

I sighed deeply. 'It's been quite a frightening experience, one way or another,' I told him. 'You'll never know how close I came to shuffling off this mortal coil in that bakery. Just like all those dead ancient Romans.'

'A dangerous place, Pompeii.'

'Yes,' I agreed, smiling and feeling my old cocky self for the first time in I don't know how long, 'I've read that there is a greater than fifty per cent chance of a major eruption each year.'

The inspector stared at me, distinctly unamused by my attempt at humour, which I considered rather unkind of him. After all, I reckoned it was positively heroic of me to be so debonair and off-hand after what I'd been through in his blessed country.

I settled into my seat in the leather-lined luxury interior of the private jet as it soared into the air at the end of the runway and climbed high above the clouds over Naples. Yes, I congratulated myself, I'd acquitted myself pretty well considering. And things had turned out satisfactorily on most fronts. The Albanians were behind bars. Teresa and Mariana were no doubt blessing me for the beneficial effect I had had on their lives by proving the means whereby they had got rid of Luigi. And through my efforts there would be a temporary halt at least on people-trafficking into that part of Italy.

It was only poor Lule I felt bad about. I wished I could have had time in that kitchen to thank her properly for what she did for my sake. It shook me more than a little, the realisation that she might be dead because of me. There really had been one person who had been prepared to sacrifice herself wholly for me throughout the whole business. And before I even realised her worth, she was lost to me.

I began to grow despondent, so I tried not to think about poor Lule and instead to speculate upon what Barry Cullis would make of the publicity opportunities surrounding my role in smashing not one but two international crime syndicates. I'd sent him a long text giving him the basic details using a phone I borrowed from one of the policemen. By now he would be busy arranging photographers and journalists to greet me at the airport. There would probably be a mob of well-wishers who had picked up the news through the website he ran for me. It may even have been on the radio and television news, come to that.

There should be no difficulty picking up the series with the BBC now, surely. I would probably get a good deal on a new one, too, capitalising on all the publicity.

Not to mention the book that would result from all this – what a sensation that would cause! I would relate my adventure in colourful detail for all the world to share and maybe add a final chapter of classic Italian recipes with a characteristic Truelove twist for good measure. I smiled contentedly as I envisaged the negotiations the big papers and magazines would engage in with Barry over the serialisation rights. I might even get to the top of the bestsellers lists. I couldn't wait to see the look on Jamie's face!

I snuggled happily into the seat and closed my eyes to dream of what was to come, while the headphones played Vivaldi.

I must have fallen asleep, for the next thing I knew I was being woken up by someone shaking me roughly. I opened my eyes and, to my utter confusion, found I was looking up at Bruno.

'Wake up! Wake up, Englishman!'

Was I dreaming? The plane had landed, but what was Bruno doing in London? What on earth was going on?

'Wake up!' Bruno repeated.

I glanced out of the window and was bewildered to see, instead of a drizzly Heathrow, a view of mountains on one side and a vast expanse of bright blue water on the other.

'Is this London?' I asked stupidly.

Bruno shook his head and gave me a grin.

The penny dropped. Bloody airline staff! They'd done it again!

'I–I think there's been some mistake,' I stammered. 'I was supposed to be taken to London. Where am I?'

By way of an answer Bruno hauled me out of my chair and started hustling me down the aisle to the door, which was open.

I blinked in the bright sunshine outside. It was terribly

hot. I didn't recognise the place at all.

Bruno prodded me and I stumbled down the steps, wincing at the ache in my legs. He then propelled me across the dusty tarmac to a waiting car with a youth at the steering wheel. Bruno opened the door and pushed me into the back, then got in beside me and motioned to the youth to get moving. Then he turned to me and gave me another ominous grin.

'Welcome to Palermo,' he said.

Now, I know that at this point you will be expecting, and probably looking forward to, one of my wonderfully evocative flights of purple prose about the exotic holiday island of Sicily. You'll be expecting descriptions of charming sun-bleached hill villages, historic town centres, breathtaking vistas of glittering seas and lush green valleys – but no, not this time. You ask too much of me after all I have suffered. All I can tell you is that once my confusion had ebbed on the long, bumpy ride away from the airport and up into the bleak and jagged mountains inland it was replaced only by a mute, bewildered fear.

I was in Sicily. I didn't know very much about Sicily. I knew it had a volcano, Mount Etna. I knew it was fought over during the war. And I knew it is home to the mafia. It was that last bit of knowledge that weighed most heavily on me as we rocked and swayed over the increasingly dodgy road that twisted and turned further and further away from all other signs of civilisation. That fact made the island a very unhealthy place to be for anyone who only that morning had been enjoying a lengthy conversation with the authorities about everything he had happened to learn recently about the activities of various international crime organisations. I shrank into my seat and tried to work out how this unhappy turn of events could possibly have come about. But it was completely beyond me. One minute I had been safely en route for home, with only the brightest of prospects ahead of me, now – well, who knew what was in store for me?

We were so high up now in the desolate, deserted landscape that it felt like we were climbing to the top of the world. Our road, though it seemed over-generous to call it that, seemed to be heading up via a terrifying series of hairpin bends towards the top of a particularly brutal-looking craggy height. As we grew closer I saw that there was a building standing in splendid isolation just below the highest point of this promontory and this was evidently our destination. The structure had the appearance of a large, traditional Sicilian farmhouse, though previous owners seemed to have had pretensions to make it more than that, embellishing its roof with turrets and other ornamental flourishes. The front of the house was enclosed by a rough wall and it was through the gates set in this wall that the youth steered our vehicle and finally brought it to a halt by the front door. Bruno disembarked and gestured at me to follow.

I got out warily and Bruno escorted me over the threshold, while the youth waited outside. Once inside the house I took rapid stock of my surroundings, seeking some clue as to what I was doing there. It had an air of faded grandeur about it. The carpets were richly embroidered but tatty, the portraits on the walls old but black with dirt, the furniture antique but lacking polish. A general air of benign neglect pervaded the building, as though it was a long time since anyone had given it much attention.

Bruno pointed to a door on my left and I understood that he expected me to go through it. I took a deep breath and stepped into the room indicated. It was a formal reception room I had been shown into and there were three people waiting for me in there, grouped at the far end before a colossal stone fireplace.

My mouth dropped open when I recognised them. Standing to the left was Teresa Vanni, looking as elegant as ever but also very startled to see me. Standing to the right was Mariana Vanni, looking equally trim and just as surprised. And in between them, sitting slumped in a wheelchair, and not looking surprised at all, was none other than Luigi Vanni himself.

I stared at my former patron, shocked to the core. He had changed a lot in the past forty-eight hours or so. He looked grey and haggard and clutched his chest, which I could see was heavily bandaged. I also saw that he had his left arm in a sling. He didn't look well at all, but there again considering I had supposed him to be dead he looked rather better than I would have expected.

'L-Luigi,' I stuttered. 'You're alive!'

'So it seems,' he croaked drily.

'Tremayne?' Teresa said in a small voice. 'What are you doing here?'

'I might very well ask you the same question,' I responded. 'Though I might add that I have only the vaguest notion where "here" is.'

'This is my family home,' Luigi Vanni answered for her, struggling to get the words out. 'The Vannis have lived here for centuries. Did you not know that we are an ancient Sicilian family?'

I shook my head. 'No. I had no idea at all.'

'Of course,' he went on, 'I left here many years ago. I wanted to expand the family business and this place was hardly suitable to serve as my headquarters. But now...' His voice trailed away and he gave me a pained look. 'Now this is all I have left. Everything else is lost now the police have issued a warrant for my arrest. I daren't set foot on the mainland. I may never leave Sicily again.'

I don't know why, but from his look I got the distinct impression he was looking for someone to blame for the present downturn in his fortunes.

'I'm sorry things didn't turn out so well for you, Luigi,' I endeavoured to explain, faintly hoping we could all be friends again and let bygones be bygones, 'but you have to admit you were mixed up in some pretty shady business. You're probably better out of it, though I understand if you are a little upset right now.'

'Upset?'

His eyebrows rose but then he was struck by a fit of wracking coughs that had him doubled up in his wheelchair and awkwardly fishing a handkerchief out of his pocket. I noticed that neither Teresa nor Mariana made any move to help him. They were too busy staring at me, it seemed, to notice his discomfiture.

'Well,' I continued, trying to clear the air once the coughs had subsided, 'it's lovely to see you all again, but I was rather hoping to get back to London–'

Luigi waved his handkerchief in the air. I noticed that it was spotted with blood. 'Nonsense,' he wheezed. 'After you have done so much for us I could not let you leave without some lunch.'

'Lunch?'

Did he really mean to tell me he had got me all this way just to give me lunch? The nerve of the man!

'Yes, just you and me,' he responded. 'So we can talk privately. I am sure my wife and daughter would not want to be bored by talk of business. I thought we would have a picnic at the viewpoint–'

The word "picnic" had an extraordinary effect on both women. They both looked aghast and immediately began to protest. Now, I know that some people love their picnics, with all the rigmarole of preparing hampers and making sandwiches, but the women's reaction at missing out on one did seem a bit extreme. Personally I can't bear them. I hate the shortcuts you have to take for the sake of practicality and the likelihood of local wildlife expressing too close an interest in your food as you eat it. I supposed the girls, appreciating my elevated status in the world of food, must have guessed this, bless them.

'You can't!' Teresa insisted. 'Please don't! Tremayne is our guest and a friend–'

'You can't do it, father–'

But Luigi shut them up with a raised hand and an icy glare that brooked no argument. Teresa shot a despairing look at me and then, tears welling up (which I took as a huge compliment), hurried from the room to hide her distress.

Mariana made to follow her but at the last moment veered to one side and held me by both arms as she whispered hastily in my ear.

'Don't go, I beg of you! Get out now while you can. Take me with you!'

That left me feeling rather bemused, I can tell you. Luigi couldn't hear what she was whispering, of course, but he was looking daggers at her and started to say something, but was then afflicted by another series of hacking coughs.

Mariana took advantage of the moment to repeat her admonitions.

I looked down at her. She looked so pretty, so sweet, so damned sexy. It was terribly tempting to whisk her away and I've always been one for giving in to temptation. But she was revealing a taste for melodrama that made me uneasy and I knew in my heart that it would never work in the long run. I would only make her miserable, and then I'd be miserable, and everything would turn sour. I couldn't do it to her, however much I'd enjoy it in the short term. And it was obvious what Luigi would think about it and I didn't want to make things any worse with him either, incapacitated though he appeared to be. So, while Luigi coughed loudly into his handkerchief, I took a deep breath and steeled myself to do, for once, the right thing.

'I'm terribly grateful to you, Mariana,' I murmured. 'You're a lovely girl and I think the world of you. But you were right, what you said back there in Venice – I really am too old for you.'

It was courageous and self-sacrificing of me to admit it, in my opinion, but it seemed the easiest way to help her to accept the cruel disappointment of not leaving with me.

She stared at me, looking very tragic, then she backed away from me towards the door.

'Goodbye, Tremayne,' she whispered.

'Bye then,' I returned, giving her a consolatory smile.

She disappeared. It had gone better than I'd thought it would, so all I had to do now was make my peace with Luigi and get him to order Bruno to drive me back to the airport at Palermo and this whole unexpected and unasked-for episode could be consigned to history.

Luigi had got over his coughing fit and was calling for Bruno, who dutifully came in from the hall. There followed a swift exchange in Italian and Bruno left.

'Bruno will fetch us our picnic,' Luigi explained. 'We will take it to the viewpoint behind the house. It is a wonderful place from which you can see much of central Sicily.'

'Sounds lovely.'

'I am sure you will never forget it.'

Bruno returned carrying a small metal tin. I had been hoping for a hamper and a bottle of bubbly, but I guessed we were only getting sandwiches. Luigi was obviously short on staff after all his recent setbacks. It seemed that apart from the two women he only had Bruno and the callow youth outside to fetch and carry for him.

Luigi placed the tin on his lap and then motioned to me to precede him out of the room. Bruno took up position at the back of the wheelchair and began to push him towards the door.

There was no sign of the two women in the hallway, so the three of us carried on through the front door and turned to our left, where a narrow pebble path led upwards towards the highest point of the mountainous crag. It was certainly a lovely day for a picnic and I could see why Luigi was so keen for me to stay long enough to get a glimpse of his place in the country.

Perhaps, it occurred to me, he was hoping that by showing me round a bit he might be able to retain my services as family cook a little longer. Well, if he tried that he would have another think coming. I hadn't forgotten the scrapes I had got into lately as a result of getting mixed up in his so-called business and I hadn't forgiven him either, not only for my sufferings but for those of the poor benighted migrants he had sought to make a profit from. No, he could look elsewhere to complete his domestic arrangements. This was one chef who was going home just as soon as suitable transport could be found.

The views opening up on every side as we ascended the path were truly stupendous. The land dropped away very steeply and we could see for miles across the island. Beyond the deep ravines and valleys closer at hand there were distant mountains that shimmered in the heat haze. No wonder the Vannis had chosen this mountain fastness all those years ago.

I paused and looked back the way we had come. The house was below us now and I saw two figures looking back up at us. One of them, Teresa, was standing at the back door, twisting her handkerchief in her hands. The other, Mariana, was at an upstairs window and had her hands to her mouth.

I gave the pair of them a cheery wave, but got no response. Instead, Teresa turned and went back inside, while Mariana withdrew from her window and drew the curtains. Charming, I thought to myself – and so typical of a teenager to go into a huff when she doesn't get her way. I had been right to resist her girlish appeal, I told myself.

Bruno and Luigi had apparently reached the viewpoint that had been described to me as they had come to a stop on a level bit of turf growing on an outcrop of rock jutting over a dizzying drop. Bruno bent and applied the brake on the wheelchair, while Luigi waved to me to have a better look.

'Go to the edge,' he encouraged me. 'There is no view like it in the whole of Sicily.'

I took a few steps beyond them, where the top of the outcrop sloped gently downwards before ending in thin air. I halted a few feet short of the edge as I'm not very good with heights and the drop below was terrifying – a sheer fall of many hundreds of feet down to rocky, wooded slopes and boulders.

'Isn't is a marvellous view?' Luigi asked behind me.

'Wonderful,' I answered.

It was too. In the far distance, several miles away I supposed, I could just make out a mountain village high up on the opposite mountain range. Far, far, below I could also make out rivers, lakes, an isolated hamlet or two, but otherwise nothing more than scrubby slopes and stony pastures, all baking under a sky that was so intensely blue it hurt the eyes to look at it.

I turned to smile at my hosts and saw that Luigi was grappling with the lid of the tin he had in his lap. It had been a long time since breakfast at the police station and I was about ready for a bite to eat.

Luigi delved in the tin and took out a revolver, which he then pointed at my belly. I stared at the thing in horror.

'What–what's going on?'

'I'm afraid there is no picnic, Signore Truelove,' Luigi grated, wincing. 'But I do want to have a talk with you. Do you realise the trouble you have caused?'

'I–I'm not sure what you mean…'

'In the past week I have lost all my businesses, all my men, all my influence. I have become a fugitive from the law. I have also nearly died after being shot. I may never recover properly. I have had to flee in secret back here because it is the only place where I am safe from arrest. Bruno proved the only man loyal enough to stay with me.'

'What about the lad with the car?'

'He is just a local boy, the son of a friend who owes me a favour. No more than that.'

'Well, I'm sorry about that, Luigi, really I am, but I don't see why–'

'It is thanks to you all this has happened!' he snapped angrily. 'If you had done what you were supposed to do at the Castel Nuovo and provided a decent meal for my guests I might have been able to make a deal with the Albanians–'

'You're wrong to think they had any intention of doing a deal with you–'

'The fact is,' he pressed on, his voice taut and angry, 'that I put my trust in you and you betrayed me!'

'Now look here!' I objected. 'It's not just you who has lost out, you know. Look at me – I was planning a glorious new career on Italian television–'

Luigi barked a short, breathless, laugh. 'You thought I would really spend my money to make you a television star? How stupid you really are.'

'What? But…'

'Once you had cooked us a marvellous meal and I had successfully made my deal with the Albanians I was going to put you on a plane back to London and forget all about you. If things went wrong and I had to kill the Albanians then I was going to say you murdered them, if the police became involved. After all, it was you who was going to put the poison in their food. I would have blamed it all on the madness of my crazy celebrity chef.'

My head was spinning. 'I don't believe it. You promised me…'

Luigi shook his head at my confusion. 'Signore Truelove, you underestimated me. That makes me sad. You never realised that everything that happened was under my control. Who did you think told the police about the boat trip that night? Who told the police where to find the Albanians' warehouse?'

I looked dumbly at him.

'Ah, so you worked that out for yourself,' he continued, nodding. 'Perhaps you're not always quite as foolish as you appear.'

'I still don't understand why you sabotaged your own operation,' I admitted.

He shrugged. 'I made sure it was the Albanians who would be at risk, not me. And it would be worth it to get them out of the picture.'

I stared at him, trying to piece it all together in my mind.

Luigi eyed me speculatively. 'How do you think you ended up coming to Sicily not England this morning, eh?

I struggled to find my voice. 'It – it was a mistake by the airline, or– or–'

'Or I paid a certain police sergeant to put you on my private jet instead of on the plane to London,' he said, completing the sentence for me. I believe I warned you I had connections in the police.'

I swallowed hard. 'So that's it then. You're nothing more than a mafia mobster.'

He grunted. 'We do not use that word. It is the rest of the world that calls us that. And all the other words too – the Cosa Nostra, the Camorra of Naples, the 'Ndrangheta of Calabria, the Sacra Corona Unita of Apulia... But no one is the equal of the old Sicilian families, even today. Those Neapolitan amateurs and the others spend most of their time fighting each other. They have their uses, but we modern mafiosi are more intelligent. More cunning. More professional.' He paused and eyed me steadily. 'And anyone who gets in our way must be punished.

Now he was really beginning to frighten me. Standing on the edge of the vast drop behind me, I realised for the first time what a vulnerable position I was in.

Luigi nodded slowly to himself. 'I know I should thank you for your part in the downfall of my Albanian rivals. And I do. But the fact remains that I have been humiliated and my business concerns have suffered badly. In time I hope I can make good much of what has taken place, but there is still the question of you breaking what we Sicilians call omertà – the code of silence. You spoke to the police.'

I held up my hands in desperate self-defence. 'You don't need to worry about that. I've seen "The Godfather". I haven't told anyone any details about your business affairs. Never! You can rely on that.'

'You are a bad liar, Signore Truelove,' Luigi wheezed. 'I know that you told the police in Naples everything you know about me. You forget my friend the sergeant. No. I trusted you and you betrayed me. How could I ever trust you in the future? Like so many people today, you are shallow, Signore Truelove. You would do anything for fame, for celebrity. So I am afraid it must end here.'

'But–but I thought we were friends!'

'We were friends, you and I. Of course we were. Never doubt it. But we are not family. And this is Sicily, not London.'

'Now, look here–'

'When we were all in Rome, I asked you to take my wife out to eat, do you remember? You took her to a restaurant and when she cried you put your arm around her. True?'

I goggled at him. How the hell did he know about that? Unless, oh my God – Paolo. My old chum Paolo, the snivelling rat, had shopped me to Luigi after he saw us in his restaurant! Is there really no honour between fellow chefs? Well, no, obviously there isn't. Never has been.

'Later,' Luigi went on, 'you took her hand at the opera. I saw it myself.'

'Yes, but–'

'You have betrayed me!' he hissed. 'First I will punish you, then I will punish her.' He coughed a couple of times, then waved absently at our surroundings. 'Beautiful up here, isn't it? Such a view. That is one of the advantages of being so high up.' He smirked at me through his pain. 'And there are other advantages.'

I waited for him to go on, though I had a nasty feeling I wasn't going to like it.

'Did Teresa show you the Tarpeian Rock in Rome? This is our Tarpeian Rock. It is an old tradition in my family to bring our enemies up here and throw them from the top of this cliff. Other families favour the garrotte but we Vannis have always had our own way of doing these things.'

He said it like it was a cherished family heirloom, not a means of cold-blooded murder.

'You – you don't mean –'

'It is a punishment we reserve especially for traitors within the family. You are not a member of our family, true, but you lived among us as though you were, and you betrayed us, so now I must extend to you the privilege of dying in this manner.'

Something in his stare told me that even if I had been family he still wouldn't have hesitated to kill me. It was irrelevant now, I supposed, but it was just as well he didn't know I'd slept with both his wife and his daughter. That might really annoy him.

I licked my lips. 'Look, I don't deserve…'

Luigi smiled. 'But you do, you do.'

We stared at each other in taut silence for a few seconds. Then he shifted his aim slightly and fired a bullet into the earth between my feet. I leapt about three feet in the air in shock, then staggered on landing just a handful of inches from the petrifying drop behind me.

Luigi wasn't smiling any longer. 'Your choice,' he informed me coolly, 'is to jump or else to suffer the pain of me shooting you, first in the arm, then the other arm, then your feet and your legs and finally your chest and head – a painful death. Then your body will be thrown off the rock anyway. One cannot go against tradition.'

'Please…'

'Your body will never be found but the word will go round. People will see what happens to those who defy the Vannis. I will rebuild my businesses with your dead body in its foundations. I hope that is consolation to you for what must happen.'

He waited for me to indicate what my choice was to be. I gurgled incoherently, unable to say a single thing.

'It will be less painful if you jump,' he assured me.

Coming from a man who had recently been shot himself, I was inclined to believe him, but I couldn't budge an inch.

Luigi sighed. 'Very well then.'

He raised the gun and sighted slowly and deliberately along its barrel. I glanced in terror at the slablike Bruno standing behind the wheelchair. Bruno stared back at me, unblinking, apparently unmoved by my plight.

Then he did something entirely unexpected. As Luigi's trigger finger tightened on the trigger Bruno bent quietly and released the brake on the wheelchair, which immediately began to roll forwards down the short slope towards me.

It took Luigi a moment to realise what was happening. Then he registered that the wheelchair was moving and with a curse began to scrabble frantically for the brake lever. Unfortunately the lever was on the left side of the wheelchair and with his left arm in a sling it was impossible for him to reach it. He gave a short cry of alarm as the wheelchair gathered pace and headed inexorably towards the vast emptiness beyond the cliff edge.

At the last moment I stepped out of the way as the chair picked up speed and threatened to send me flying into oblivion. As he shot past me, his face contorted with fear as he continued to grapple for the brake, Luigi tried to get the gun trained on me once more, but it was too late. Already the wheelchair was lurching over the edge and pitching him out into the void below. He fired twice towards the sky, then the chair plummeted downwards towards the scrubby slopes far, far below.

I turned my face aside but we heard him scream all the way down.

Bruno shambled towards me as silence descended once more. His face gave nothing away.

I looked at him apprehensively as he peered cautiously over the edge of the drop. 'Why? Why did you help me?'

He straightened and then turned slowly to me, his expression deeply serious.

'You and me. We are – simpatico.'

And then he enclosed me in a huge embrace.

Afters

Though I tell people I'm in my early forties, and they almost always believe it, it says on my passport that I am well into my fifties. I've been in the telly business for upwards of twenty years; I have three ex-wives, a spacious London apartment to retreat to, and on the whole no complaints. I've been lucky, very lucky.

But I've never stretched my luck like I did during my stay in Italy. As the regular passenger flight crossed the Alps I found myself shuddering at the risks I had so recently survived and reminded myself of the reality that I could so easily have lost it all – all the things I, like so many others, tend to take for granted. I looked nervously around to check the plane I was on really was heading for London this time. Everything seemed okay so far as I could tell.

It had been quite an adventure, I had to admit, but it was all too vivid and horrifying to dwell on in any detail just yet. Even thoughts of the women brought with them unpleasant associations. Teresa and Mariana were both lovely in their different ways, there was no denying, but they'd come with a bag load of trouble and continuing with either of them would have been fraught with difficulties. They'd be all right now, of course, without Luigi blighting their lives. Teresa, I imagined, might pick up her rural idyll with Granny and her mother in the Italian countryside. Mariana – no doubt she'd make up her own mind about what she wanted to do. At least she had a free choice now. As for Bruno... admittedly, he had looked broken-hearted at my leaving, but he would get over it in time. I think he understood when I explained to him that anything he had in mind concerning me was quite impossible.

I found myself comparing them all with Bettina. The women, anyway, not Bruno. She too was impossible sometimes but equally lovely – and isn't love, like cooking, often ultimately the art of making the apparently impossible possible?

At least I still had my cookery to go back to. It had nearly proved my undoing back in Naples, mind. Fancy me imagining I could launch a whole new cuisine based on conflict and violence. Fission, indeed! What was I thinking? It couldn't possibly work. Or could it?

I don't know why, but next I started wondering how the migrants might be getting on... especially little Hashem and his tiny sister. My heart ached for them. I hoped fervently that they reached their destination safely.

Yes, prompted by all these things, I found myself reassessing my life at a most fundamental level as we soared over the verdant pastures and blooming vines of south-eastern France, with its sleepy whitewashed villages and moustachioed peasant farmers, its tinkling church bells and accordion bands, its pavement cafés and – but I was too exhausted for another flight of purple prose. That would just have to wait till I was safely back in London and had had a good rest.

A voice from further up the passenger cabin attracted my attention. It sounded distinctly familiar. I frowned and straightened up in my seat, trying to identify the source, and immediately recognised the back of a blonde head some four or five rows in front of me.

Good heavens! It was Lule, speaking to one of the cabin attendants.

Lule.

She obviously didn't know I was there, bless her. A huge smile creased my lips. I'd given the dear girl up for lost, no more than just another piece of flotsam adrift in the Bay of Naples, but somehow she'd managed to get out of there and here she was, on her way to England just like she wanted. I surmised that perhaps she had helped herself to one of the forged passports the inspector had mentioned finding at the warehouse in Naples.

I leant back in my seat, delighted and promising myself I would renew my acquaintance with Lule before we got to London. Apart from anything else, it was a good while since I'd last renewed my membership of the mile-high club.

But right now I was hungry.

The flight attendant arrived with my airline meal. I folded down the table and contemplated the rectangular box the attendant placed before me. Then I removed the cover and prodded at the contents with the plastic fork before lifting some to my mouth.

The chicken was tasteless, the cheese like rubber, and the rice lukewarm.

Perfect.

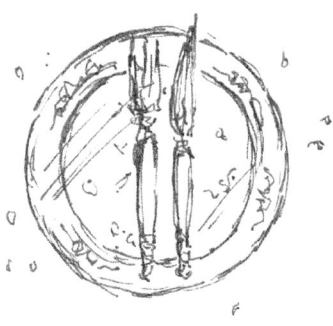

Epilogue

Tremayne Truelove's latest series for the BBC is scheduled to be screened next spring. He has also been invited to host a new cookery quiz show and to narrate a documentary on Mediterranean cuisine. A major Hollywood company is currently in discussions to buy the rights to film his life story; British actor Rupert Everett is rumoured to be among the favourites to play Tremayne himself.

Also available by David Pickering

Fiction
And Stones Shall Dance
Things Lost
Things Undreamt Of
The Devils of Mons

Anthologies
Classic Short Stories
Classic Love Stories
Classic Ghost Stories
Classic Ghost Stories 2
Classic Horror Stories
Classic Horror Stories 2

Reference
Lucky You!
Dictionary of Superstitions
Witchcraft: A Dictionary
Witch Hunt (with Andrew Pickering)
Chambers Dictionary of Great Quotations
Buttering Parsnips, Twocking Chavs (with Martin Manser)
Penguin Dictionary of First Names
Penguin Pocket Jokes
Collins Gem Pirates
Collins Gem Ancient Rome
Cassell Dictionary of Folklore
Cassell Dictionary of Proverbs
Random House Perfect Family Quiz
Gale Research Encyclopedia of Pantomime
Facts on File Dictionary of Theatre
Brewer's 20th Century Phrase and Fable
and many more…